ERROR
IN DIAGNOSIS

MASON LUCAS, M.D.

BERKLEY BOOKS, NEW YORK

BERKLEY

An imprint of Penguin Random House LLC
375 Hudson Street, New York, New York 10014

ERROR IN DIAGNOSIS

A Berkley Book / published by arrangement with the author

ISBN: 978-0-425-27908-3

PRINTED IN THE UNITED STATES OF AMERICA

10 9 8 7 6 5 4 3 2 1

Cover design by Jason Gill.
Interior text design by Laura K. Corless.

Penguin
Random
House

EMERGENCY ACTION!

Brickell glanced to the side of the room. Urging her to wrap things up, Julian gave her his most subtle *cut* sign.

"I have time for one more question," she said.

Before she could recognize anybody, an uninvited voice asked, "Is there any possibility GNS is an act of biological terrorism?"

Her eyes found the young woman in the center of the room who had asked the question. She had no clue who she was, but she didn't feel she could use her refusal to follow proper protocol as a way of dismissing the extremely valid question.

"All possibilities will be carefully evaluated," she was careful to answer. "But at this time, we have no evidence that GNS is the result of a biological weapon." Brickell took two short steps backward. "I'm sorry. I'm going to have to stop here. I encourage all of you to refer to our website for the exact date and time of our next briefing."

She turned away from the lectern, and with Julian in tow, she quick-walked out of the briefing room.

"Excellent job," he told her. "Especially that last question."

"Excuse me?"

"Your responses were honest and on point. I'm sure they helped to diminish the anxiety of an impending crisis."

Brickell was well aware that part of Julian's job was to contain prickly situations and curry favor with her regardless of how difficult the situation seemed. But today, his fairy-tale optimism was over the top.

"Julian, we're dealing with a potentially devastating disease that's spreading out of control. To make matters worse, it's selectively attacking pregnant women, one of any society's most vulnerable groups." She looked at him as if he should know better. "What did you call it—'an impending crisis'? This crisis is hardly impending. It has a large gray fin, is finished circling, and just about ready to bite us all on the ass."

For Jax, Lucas, Charlee, Jacob, Maya,
Mason, and Madison,
who continue to keep me young and
provide me with inspiration.

1

Tess Ryan was lost.

Gradually maneuvering her SUV down one indistinct street after another, she bemoaned her spinning instructor, Cal's, decision to build his new gym in a warehouse district that was more confusing than an English hedgerow maze. But in spite of the fact that every building and street appeared identical, she still couldn't explain how she had gotten lost driving to a location she had easily found four times a week for the past eleven months.

Fearing she would miss the beginning of her class, she allowed a frustrated sigh to escape her lips. Had this morning's dilemma been an isolated event, she might not have been so dismayed, but of late, she had been plagued with repeated mental errors and memory lapses. Earlier, she had had to look up her sister's phone number, a call she had made a hundred times a year for as long as she could remember. A couple of days ago, she was stuck at an ATM machine struggling to remember her PIN number.

Heading west, she shaded her eyes from a sun that was settling above an endless row of flat gravel roofs. After a few more minutes of randomly creeping up and down the grid-like streets, she spotted a line of familiar cars parked in front of the gym. With an appreciative glance overhead to acknowledge the divine intervention, she pulled in behind the last car. Grabbing her gym bag, she pushed open the door. With her first step she was out of the car, and with the next she was standing in front of the gym. Curling her fingers around the knob, she took a cleansing breath, and then with a ginger push, she slipped inside.

Cal's gym was hardly a showroom for the modern workout facility. The collection of basketball jerseys that hung randomly from the rafters did little to divert one's eye from the grit and black smudges that tattooed the cinderblock walls. His artistic masterpiece was the wall outside of his office that he had wallpapered with dozens of collapsed Red Bull cartons. Over the relentless objections of his students, he insisted on keeping the gym oppressively hot. Normally, Tess didn't mind but today, she felt as if she were standing in front of a wood-burning oven. Making matters worse, the pungent smell of ammonia cleaner permeating the air sent her stomach into a series of backflips.

By the sound of Paul Simon's "Diamonds on the Soles of Her Shoes" blaring from Cal's boom box, Tess knew the class was still in its warm-up run. She chanced an apologetic smile his way. From his bike, which sat atop a three-foot wooden platform, the ex–Navy corpsman wagged a reprimanding finger in her direction, but then with a wink and an indulgent grin, he motioned her to join in. Tess mouthed, *Thank you*, made her way between the first two rows, and climbed on her bike.

Long-legged with elevated cheekbones and shadowy blue eyes, she was in excellent physical condition and never had any difficulty keeping up with the class. But today, after only five minutes, she was breathless. Assuming the heat and ammonia fumes were to blame, she decided to press on. To ease her breathing, she stood up and leaned forward over the handlebars. But her performance didn't improve, and she found herself grunting and gulping for air even more feverishly. While she struggled to figure out what was happening to her, she felt the room begin to spin. Setting her ego aside, she slowed her pace and sat back down. She waited a few seconds but the whirling sensation only got worse.

Wondering if Cal hadn't noticed her struggling, she raised her head and looked toward the front of the gym. Instead of seeing his usual determined face pushing the class on, all she could make out was an obscure silhouette. She craned her neck forward and squinted, trying to bring his blurred image into focus, but everything around her became a shapeless convergence of oscillating gray and white shadows.

Consumed with terror, she clutched the handlebars and closed her eyes. To her further dismay, the loss of visual cues only made her vertigo worse. She felt her body rolling and pitching as if she were in a fragile skiff on high seas. She could still hear the music and Cal's shouts of encouragement but they were garbled and soon became distant echoes—echoes that would be the last thing her brain would process.

Tess's head plunged forward and her body wilted. Toppling from the bike like a Raggedy Ann doll, she was moments away from her head hitting the cement floor when the woman next to her screamed. Fortunately, Cal had seen Tess falling several seconds earlier and was already racing toward her. His final stride was followed by a desperate lunge. With his arms fully extended, he snatched her up before she hit the ground. Then, with one powerful jerk, he had her safely cradled in front of him.

"Get me some water and a cold towel," he announced to the class.

Hurrying toward the other side of the gym, he carried her past his bargain-basement artificial Christmas tree before easing her down on a sprawling canvas mat used for a women's self-defense class. Well trained in CPR, Cal knelt down beside her and studied her breathing pattern. It was rapid but not labored. Her lips were pink—a reliable sign she wasn't suffering from oxygen starvation. Her pulse was strong and regular. Next, he checked her pupils. They were neither pinpoint nor dilated—another good sign.

"Can you hear me, Tess?" he asked, taking note of a small pool of foamy saliva gathering at the corner of her mouth. When she didn't answer, he repeated his question, "Tess, if you can hear me squeeze my fingers." Still no response. He looked up at the group and in a voice that now boomed to a fever pitch said, "Somebody call nine-one-one right now."

Just at that moment, the woman standing next to Cal gasped. With a quivering finger, she pointed at Tess's face. Cal's head snapped back. Seconds earlier Tess's eyes were motionless—now they ricocheted back and forth as if they were two Ping-Pong balls in a wind tunnel. Cal had spent six months of his enlistment at the Great Lakes Naval Hospital assigned to the neurology floor. He was quite familiar with the signs of a seizure. If Tess were having one, it was unlike any he'd ever seen. His eyes remained locked on her like a laser. He felt helpless knowing the only thing he could do until the EMTs arrived was to monitor Tess's pulse and breathing. If either faltered, he'd begin CPR immediately. He swept his clammy hand across his forehead, wiping away a few beads of sweat. And then, in a room overtaken with a deafening silence, he waited.

2

Eleven minutes after Cal's student had called Palm Beach Fire Rescue, two paramedics were at Tess's side. Squatting catcher-style, the first one, a slight woman whose name tag read R. PONTE, wrapped a blood pressure cuff around Tess's upper arm. Her partner, a stubby man packing an extra fifty pounds, unraveled several feet of oxygen tubing, connected it to a mask and then fitted it squarely over Tess's nose and mouth.

"What happened?" Ponte asked. "Was she hurt?"

"No," Cal answered. "She was fine until about ten minutes into the workout when she . . . she just passed out and fell from her bike."

"She didn't hit her head?"

"No, I caught her before she hit the ground."

"What's her name?"

"Tess Ryan."

"Tess, can you hear me?" Ponte asked.

Cal said, "Her eyes began darting back and forth like that a few minutes ago."

Ponte placed a tourniquet around Tess's biceps and waited for a suitable vein to pop up. Without looking up she asked, "Do you know if she has any serious medical conditions?"

"I don't think so. She's been working out with me for almost a year. She's never had a problem."

"When did that begin?" she asked, gesturing at Tess's legs.

Unsure of what he was being asked, Cal's eyes shifted to Tess's lower body. His breath caught. Under her black leggings, her calf muscles rippled erratically as if they were being shocked by repeated bursts of an intense electric current.

"I don't know. It . . . it must have just started," he answered, swallowing hard against a throat that had suddenly become as dry as cotton.

"The IV's in and her vital signs are okay. We can roll," Ponte told her partner. Together they transferred Tess onto the stretcher, locked it into position, and hurried toward the exit.

"I'll call her husband," Cal said. "What hospital are you taking her to?"

"Southeastern State University."

"Her husband's going to ask. Do you . . . have any idea what's wrong with her?"

"Well, if we were out in the Everglades, I'd say she'd been bitten by a rather large poisonous snake."

Cal walked across the room and sat down at a wooden desk that was beyond restoration. The three-foot, artificial and unornamented Christmas tree standing next to the desk did little to add to the spirit of the season. He didn't have to announce the class was over. In an awkward silence, the other students gathered their gym bags and moved toward the door. Lost in the moment, Cal rested his chin on his steepled fingers, half listening to the wail of the ambulance's siren fading into the morning.

He tried to reassure himself that Tess Ryan would be fine, but for all his efforts he couldn't shake the uneasy feeling that he might never see her again.

3

With a steady rain tapping against the ambulance's windshield, Ponte eased into the receiving dock of Southeastern State University Hospital's emergency department. Based on her en route instructions, she and her partner wheeled Tess into a critical care unit designed for the most seriously ill patients.

Much to Ponte's surprise, there were three grim-faced doctors, two nurses, a respiratory therapist and a hospital administrator waiting for them. She exchanged a guarded look with her potbellied partner as they transferred Tess to the hospital bed. In her ten-year career, she had brought dozens of desperately ill patients to emergency rooms all over the county. Some were accident victims who were traumatized beyond recognition. Others were scarcely holding on to life from a massive heart attack or stroke. The memory of those patients was vivid in her mind. What she didn't remember was ever being met by an entourage like the one now hovering over Tess Ryan.

The physician in charge, James Lione, stood with his arms tight against his side. As soon as the two paramedics finished and stepped back, Dr. Lione stepped forward and began his examination. Sliding his stethoscope from Tess's left chest to the right, he threw a momentary glance in Ponte's direction.

"Did she have a fever when you got her first set of vital signs?" he asked.

"No."

"Any drop in blood pressure?"

"We checked it three times. They were all normal."

Lione looked up. "Was anybody else in the class sick with similar symptoms?"

"We didn't specifically ask, but nobody mentioned feeling ill."

"Was she responsive at any time?"

"No."

"Do you know if she works?"

"One of the women at the gym mentioned she works in fund-raising."

"I don't imagine that would pose a great risk for a toxic exposure," Lione said.

"Have you spoken to any family members to get a more detailed history?"

Ponte shook her head at the strange question. "There were none at the scene and we wanted to transport her as quickly as possible."

With the other two physicians flanked closely at his

side, Lione completed his examination. Backing away from the bed, a restrained sigh slipped through his lips. He thumbed his ear a couple of times and then motioned the other two physicians to join him on the other side of the room. They spoke softly. Ponte tried to remain as unobtrusive as possible as she struggled to hear what they were saying.

It was at that moment that Dr. Helen Morales, the dean of the Southeastern State University School of Medicine, walked in and joined the group. Before any conversation amongst the physicians began, Lione looked over at Ponte and said, "Thanks for bringing her in. We'll take it from here." Becoming more perplexed with each passing moment, Ponte only nodded. Generally, paramedics were considered part of the team. Most physicians went out of their way to explain things to them regarding the patients they transported to the emergency room.

They quickly collected the rest of their equipment, left the room and walked down the hall to the staff lounge. Ponte had just grabbed a cup from the cupboard and was headed toward the coffeemaker when one of the nurses who had been present in Tess's room walked in. Ponte knew K. P. Burnham well. She had worked with her for years, and her husband was a fellow paramedic.

"Three doctors and two nurses to meet the patient, and then we practically get thrown out of the room. What the hell's going on . . . what's all the mystery about?"

K. P. walked over to the watercooler and shrugged. "I'm not the one to ask."

Ponte's stomach tensed. She raised her hands. "What's

that supposed to mean? I'm a licensed paramedic. I'd like to know what's going on with a patient I brought to this hospital. I don't feel like the request is out of line."

K. P. took a swig of the ice water. After a cautious glance around the room, she started for the door. "I've been instructed not to discuss these cases with anybody."

"These cases? Are there other patients with the same symptoms?"

K. P. crumpled the paper cup and tossed it into a wastebasket.

"Sorry, I'm really not supposed to say anything."

Looking around the room as if she were searching for answers on the walls, Ponte pressed her lips into a thin line. She had great faith in the physicians and nurses who worked at Southeastern State, but if there was a method to their madness regarding their care of Tess Ryan, it was a mystery to her.

4

John F. Kennedy Center for the Performing Arts
Washington, D.C.

Since first seeing *La Bohème* during her freshman year at
Georgetown University, Dr. Renatta Brickell, the surgeon
general of the United States, had been a die-hard opera
aficionado. Time had done nothing to erode her passion,
and there were few things in life she coveted more than
her season subscription to the opera.

With Christmas carols playing softly, she sat in her
aisle seat marveling at the lavish red-and-gold silk curtain. Lost in thought, she barely noticed the light tap on
her shoulder. When she looked up she saw her assistant,
Julian Christakis, standing over her. His mere presence
and the apologetic half smile on his baby face caused her

to groan inwardly. Five years ago, she had hand-selected Julian from hundreds of applicants. Diplomatic to a fault, he had become one of her key advisors and an invaluable member of her team.

He cleared his throat and spoke in just above a whisper. "I'm sorry for disturbing you, Dr. Brickell, but there's a . . . a situation."

With more than an inkling her evening was in peril, she turned to her husband.

"I'm sorry, Stan. I'll be right back."

With a dubious look, he tapped his watch crystal. "The curtain's about to go up, Renatta. You don't have much time."

She gave his hand a reassuring squeeze, came to her feet and accompanied Julian to the lobby. After scanning the area, she motioned toward a relatively secluded area in front of the donor recognition wall.

"This better be good," she told him.

"Once you hear what's been going on, I suspect you'll agree it is." He exhaled a lungful of air, scanned the lobby and then continued in a guarded voice, "I've been on the phone with the Centers for Disease Control for the past two hours. It seems they've been receiving calls all day from dozens of hospitals from Florida to California that have been treating hundreds of women with a bizarre illness that none of their doctors has ever seen before."

"What are their symptoms?"

"Mostly neurologic: memory loss, confusion and severe muscle twitching of the legs. What's particularly disturbing is that many of the women have developed a dancing eye syndrome."

"I thought that only occurs in infants and children."

"Except in rare circumstances, that's usually the case."

"How seriously ill are these women?"

"Some of them are unresponsive and have been admitted to intensive care units."

"Any deaths?" she inquired, becoming more concerned with each passing second.

"None reported so far."

"Just exactly how many cases are we talking about here, Julian?"

"The CDC's not exactly sure. Their best guess is around four hundred, but there could be a lot more."

She folded her arms and stared at the ceiling for a few seconds. "Has anybody considered that this may just be the beginning of some new strain of flu?"

"None of these women has a fever, sore throat or any other flu symptoms. And, none of their immediate family members is sick. Besides, why would a flu only affect women?" He lightly shrugged his shoulders. "I've spoken to a lot of people today. None of them has the first idea of what the hell's going on."

"For God's sake, Julian, you have nine advanced degrees in health care and epidemiology." She paused briefly to gather her thoughts and then asked, "What's the first rule of diagnosis we all learned in medical school?"

"That's easy. The most common things occur most frequently."

"It's a little corny, but it's also very true, which leaves us with only two rational explanations: The first is this is a contagious disease. The second is we're dealing with some type of widespread toxic exposure."

Just at that moment, Julian's cell phone rang. He plucked it from the leather case and checked the display. "It's the CDC," he told her, raising the phone to his ear. "This is Julian Christakis," he answered, pacing in a tight circle while he listened. He suddenly stopped, and then with a solemn nod added, "You're absolutely sure. There's no chance of an error? I see. Thanks very much for calling, Dr. Emerson. No, that won't be necessary. I'm with the surgeon general now. I'll brief her immediately."

Julian slid his car keys from the inside pocket of his black blazer. He was generally unflappable but at the moment his expression was ominous. He leaned back against the wall.

"There's obviously something else," Renatta stated in a guarded tone.

"I'm afraid so. Not only are the hospitals reporting more new cases every hour but most of the women who were admitted earlier are getting worse. I don't have the exact numbers but quite a few are now in a near coma." He paused long enough to push his hand through his curly blond hair. Renatta was familiar with the habit, which was a sure sign of his uneasiness. "Emerson also confirmed something we suspected earlier."

"I'm listening."

"All of the affected women are pregnant."

With his words seemingly suspended in midair, Renatta could feel the color drain from her face.

The lobby lights flickered.

"Give me a minute," she told him. "I'll let Stan know I have to leave. You can drive us to the office."

Renatta made her way back into the opera hall. Clutching her rolled-up program, she descended the center aisle. With her stomach clenched and plagued by a rising sense of urgency, it occurred to her that perhaps the most sensible thing to do was skip the trip to her office and have Julian drive her directly to the White House.

5

NUMBER OF CASES: 823

Dr. Jack Wyatt's plan to spend a relaxing week at a plush Caribbean hideaway had fallen well short of his expectations. After a punishing two-hour tennis lesson with a fanatic pro, he limped back to his oceanfront casita. Dumping his gear on the floor, he resisted the temptation to collapse on the canopied four-poster bed in favor of watching another spectacular sunset.

With one brief stop to pluck a chilled imported beer from the refrigerator, he made his way out onto the veranda and flopped into a wicker love seat. With his angular legs outstretched and the fading warmth of the afternoon sun on his freckled arms and shoulders, he gazed out to sea. A couple hundred yards from the beach, two WaveRunners with their engines whining sliced across the water in tandem.

Since his divorce nine months earlier, Jack had done little to kick-start a new social life. It had been a process, but he finally admitted to himself that his wife had stopped loving him long before she'd asked him to move out. The ink had barely dried on their divorce decree when she packed up her belongings and their daughter and moved to France, where she had been born and raised. He never pined for her, but he missed Nicole terribly.

He had never given serious thought to vacationing alone, and it was only at the insistence of a few concerned friends that he needed some time off that he finally caved in and booked the trip. Unfortunately, the change of surroundings did little to improve his emotional indifference.

A few days after he arrived, he gave serious consideration to cutting his vacation short and returning to Columbus. But his grueling schedule of teaching and patient care as chief of neurology at the medical school left him precious little time off. In spite of the disappointment with his vacation, the meager two weeks he could manage each year were far too precious to give up.

It wasn't long before the rigors of his tennis lesson, the premium beer and the light tropical wind levied their full effect. With the droning of the WaveRunners disappearing to the north, Jack closed his eyes and yielded to the inevitable.

It wasn't more than a few minutes later, when the shrill alert of his phone snapped his eyes open, that his tranquil nap came to an abrupt end.

"Hello," he muttered, assuming it was the concierge confirming his dinner reservation.

"Jack. It's Mike. I'm sorry to bother you on vacation but something's happened to Tess." Jack pulled his legs in and shook the fuzz from his head. "She's pretty sick. The doctors put her in the intensive care unit at Southeastern State."

Jack was unaccustomed to the trepidation in his best friend's voice. Having grown up in Fort Lauderdale across the street from each other, Jack and Mike had been inseparable from their first day of kindergarten until high school graduation in spite of diametrically opposed personalities. Even though they had attended different colleges, time and distance had done nothing to erode their friendship. They spoke frequently and still shared an inviolate golf trip to Arizona every September.

"Was she in an accident?" he asked Mike with a mixture of alarm and uncertainty.

"No, nothing like that. I got a call yesterday that she had passed out during her spinning class. Her instructor called nine-one-one and the paramedics took her to Southeastern State."

"Is she still unconscious?"

"No . . . not exactly. I . . . I guess you'd call it more like a daze. Her eyes were going crazy, so they called in a specialist. As soon as he saw her, he had her admitted to the intensive care unit."

"Is the baby okay?"

"They told me she's okay . . . but I'm not sure any-body . . ." Mike paused for a few moments. "I need you to come up here, buddy. I'm scared shitless. I guess I didn't realize how bad things were until a few hours ago. The ICU doctor told me she's . . . she's not sure Tess is going to make it."

"I'll call the airlines as soon as we get off the phone," Jack said, pushing his sunglasses atop his head. "I'll be there tomorrow."

"Don't bother calling the airlines. I'll fly down tomor-row and get you. Just come to the general aviation center at the Saint Kitts airport at around ten."

"Has Tess had an MRI or CT scan of her head?"

"Both," he answered. "Look, I'm calling from Dr. Helen Morales's office. She's the dean of the medical school. She can fill you in a lot better than I can."

Although they had never met, Jack recognized the name immediately. Helen Morales was a trained radiologist but for the past fifteen years, she had been a nationally recog-nized innovator in medical education. Two years ago, she had left her position at Dartmouth to become dean of Southeastern State University's medical school.

It wasn't hard for Jack to connect the dots why Mike was calling from her office. In addition to Tess and Mike being alumni of Southeastern State, they both had an undying passion for philanthropy. Mike was a dorm-to-empire techno-genius. By the time he was thirty, he had made his fortune designing and producing video games. Last year he had been named to Southeastern State

University's board of trustees. Soon after the appointment, he pledged five million dollars toward construction of the new business school, an architectural marvel that would bear his name.

"Dr. Wyatt?" came a pleasant voice. "This is Helen Morales. Let me begin by adding my apology to Mike's for disturbing you on vacation, but we're all very concerned about Tess."

"Mike and Tess are family, Dr. Morales. You're not disturbing me."

"He obviously feels the same way about you. As Mike mentioned, Tess was brought to ER early yesterday morning with a major alteration in her mental status. We ran two complete urine and blood toxicology panels thinking she might have accidentally ingested something, but they were completely negative. She's had both an MRI and a CT scan of her brain, both of which were normal." Even as she spoke, Jack was racking his brain trying to recall any neurologic illness that fit Tess's symptoms. "So, as you can see, in spite of a rather extensive evaluation, we don't have a diagnosis."

Jack was well aware that Dr. Morales's call was a courtesy briefing only. Being a family friend and not a treating physician, he was mindful not to step across the line of professional ethics by making any suggestions regarding Tess's care.

"It certainly sounds like you've done everything by the book," he told her.

"Coming from a neurologist of your preeminence, I'll take that as a compliment. All of us here are quite familiar with your outstanding work on elusive neurologic diagnoses. Your book chapters and scientific publications are required reading for our neurology residents."

"That's kind of you to say."

"As I'm sure you're aware, we consider Tess and Mike extremely important members of the Southeastern State family. When Mike mentioned to me that you two were extremely close friends . . . well, I encouraged him to call you. I understand your main reason for coming here tomorrow is to support Mike, but I was hoping I might be able to persuade you to make your visit a little more formal. I'd like to extend you an invitation to serve as a visiting professor of neurology at Southeastern State. That way you'd be able to formally consult on Tess's case."

Jack was quite familiar with visiting professorships. It was a common practice amongst medical schools to invite faculty members of other schools to spend time with their residents and students in order to expose them to different medical insights and perspectives. Over the years, Jack had been invited to serve as a guest professor on many occasions. His schedule permitting, he always accepted. But Dr. Morales's invitation was a bit different. Serving as a guest professor at Southeastern State would directly involve him in the care of his closest friend's wife, which was a touchy situation at best and one fraught with a host of potential problems. But his concerns paled in comparison to his friendship with Mike, which meant that turning down Helen Morales's invitation was not an option.

"I would be happy to accept your invitation," he said.

"That's excellent, Jack. I'll make sure the staff's prepared to familiarize you with the details of Tess's hospitalization as well as with the other cases."

A little puzzled by Helen's comment, he inquired, "The other cases?"

"We've admitted several other women with the exact same symptoms as Tess. Our information's still pretty sketchy, but it seems there are numerous other hospitals in the country which are also treating women with the same illness."

Planting his bare feet firmly on the teak deck, Jack stopped the love seat from rocking. He stroked the three-day stubble that roofed his straight jaw and said, "You'll have to excuse me but I've been cut off from the world for the past few days."

"Specific details of the illness haven't been widely publicized as yet, but I'm sure it won't be long until the media gets wind of things."

"I suspect I'm repeating what the physicians at Southeastern State have already suggested, but if there are multiple patients with the same symptoms, wouldn't the diagnosis be more likely a contagious disease rather than a primarily neurologic one?"

"That's exactly what we thought at first, but that doesn't seem to be the case. Hopefully, you'll be able to help us figure this out," Helen responded.

"I'll be happy to help in any way I can," he said. "I should give Dean Hutchins at Ohio State a call just to let him know that—"

"I hope you won't consider it too presumptuous of

me, but I already called Hutch to make sure he'd have no objection. Fortunately, there have been no reported cases in Ohio or I'm sure he would have already summoned you back. He asked me to tell you to stay as long as we need you." Jack thought to himself that there weren't too many people in the country who called Eric Hutching, the venerable dean of the Ohio State University College of Medicine, Hutch. "Mike would like to speak with you again. I'll put him back on. I look forward to meeting you tomorrow."

Jack stood up and walked over to the railing where he spent the next ten minutes trying to calm his friend down. Mike had a litany of questions, very few of which Jack was able to answer with any authority or certainty. Nobody was more aware than he that patience was not one of Mike Ryan's virtues. Regrettably, at the moment his need for answers that simply weren't there stoked the fires of his frustration.

Watching as the last bit of daylight dissolved into the temperate night, Jack made the short walk to the beach. He strolled along the water's edge, staring at a massive freighter steaming to the south with its running lights flickering off the water. Taking a few steps back, he reached dry sand. He thought about Tess. Ever since Mike had started dating her in high school, she and Jack had been close friends. She was one of the most even-tempered, caring people he'd ever met. She was as devoted to Mike as he was to her. As innovative as he was, she founded a company that specialized in event planning for major children's charities. The corner of his mouth creased into a hint of a smile when he thought about how often he had kidded Mike that he was lucky he'd met Tess first.

Trying to make sense out of everything Helen Morales had said, he sat down and pulled his knees up to his chest. With a growing sense of trepidation regarding the days to come, he continued to watch the huge freighter until it dwindled to a speck on the horizon and then finally vanished into the darkness.

In spite of his efforts to force it from his mind, he was left with one chilling thought. Even if the cause of this strange new disease could be discovered, there were no guarantees it could be cured.

6

NUMBER OF CASES: 1,265

With a measure of reluctance, Dr. Renatta Brickell approached the lectern for her nine A.M. press briefing. Ill at ease in front of a microphone, the surgeon general tightened her fist around the gold butterfly charm her father had given her for luck the day she'd graduated from medical school. She had never held a press conference in the White House, nor to the best of her knowledge had any of her predecessors. It was at the suggestion of the president, Kellar, that the briefing take place there.

Renatta waited a few seconds for the last of the journalists and other media correspondents to find their seats.

"Ladies and gentleman, before I take your questions, I have a brief statement," she began with her signature smile conspicuously absent. "I'd like to summarize what we know to this point regarding the outbreak. Beginning approximately two days ago, a large group of otherwise healthy women began contracting a severe illness. The disease attacks the nervous system and, to the best of our knowledge, has never been seen before. What is particularly disturbing is that all of the women are at least twelve weeks pregnant. The disease has been identified in twenty-two states across the country." She paused briefly to pull the microphone a few inches closer to her lips. "We are calling this illness GNS, which is an acronym for Gestational Neuropathic Syndrome." She flipped her legal pad back to the first page and looked up. "That concludes my statement. I'll be happy to take your questions." The room was filled with a sudden flurry of hands. Brickell had a good idea which reporters had an argumentative, bulldog style. At least for the first few minutes, she would intentionally avoid recognizing them. Scanning the audience for a few seconds, she pointed at a wiry man wearing a sweat-stained white dress shirt seated in the front row. "I'll begin with Ben Halpern from the AP."

"Have there been any deaths to either the mothers or their babies?"

"None that have been officially reported."

"What about brain damage or other permanent injuries?"

"We have no way of knowing for sure, but considering the impaired mental status of these patients . . . well, frankly, it would be impossible to completely rule out the possibility." An instant murmur filled the room. Brickell raised her hand. "I would, however, like to point out that the consensus amongst our perinatologists is that the babies are stable."

"Have you been able to determine for certain if the fetuses are suffering from the disease—or is it only affecting the mothers?"

"Unfortunately, at this point, we have not been able to determine that."

Brickell next recognized Melinda Casey, a health care analyst for C-SPAN.

"In his remarks earlier today, the president said he considers this disease to be a significant threat to the public health of this country and that he would make every conceivable resource available to find the cause and a treatment. Can you provide us with some of the specifics?"

"Of course. The Centers for Disease Control in Atlanta has been working around the clock investigating this outbreak. Hundreds of physicians and medical researchers have been assembled from a wide variety of specialties to participate in the GNS project. A select group will be part of a presidential task force. The most up-to-date equipment and support services have been placed at their fingertips. With over a thousand women already affected, I expect this investigation will become as comprehensive and far-reaching as any medical inquiry the Centers for Disease Control has ever embarked upon."

"Has there been any progress at all with respect to finding the cause?" Casey asked.

"Not so far, but we are pursuing any and all plausible leads."

Not wanting to entertain any further follow-up questions from Casey, Brickell hastily shifted her eyes to the opposite side of the room. She gestured at John Versellie, from the *Boston Globe*.

In a high-pitched voice, he inquired, "Do you have any idea at all how the disease is being transmitted?"

"Not at this time."

"According to the information released by your office, many of these women are in their final trimester, yet none of them has gone into labor or delivered. Can you tell us why?"

"The simple answer to your question is, no, I can't. What we do know is that none of our patients is beyond thirty-two weeks, which means none has reached her expected delivery date. Another possibility is the disease itself may be delaying the onset of labor. We know that certain neurologic conditions such as multiple sclerosis and spinal cord injuries can do that." Versellie again raised his notepad, but instead of recognizing him, Brickell said, "In anticipation of your next question, John, we don't know why women in their final few weeks or those in their first trimester seem to be immune to GNS."

Brickell next called upon Maggie Fitzsimmons from MSNBC, a physician who had resigned from her internal medicine residency at the University of Miami five years earlier to pursue a career as a medical correspondent.

"Generally, a baby born at thirty-two weeks would have an excellent chance of survival. Has any consideration been given to either inducing labor or performing a cesarean section to see if ending the pregnancy will cure the illness?"

"Yes, we have considered that possibility. The problem is that delivering these babies could be extremely dangerous and perhaps even fatal to both mother and baby. The stress of labor and the administration of anesthetic drugs are all unknowns in patients with GNS. The other issue is that these infants might be highly contagious and even using the most sophisticated isolation techniques, they might represent an enormous risk to other infants and their caretakers."

"If it is determined that ending the pregnancy will halt the disease, will President Kellar address the possibility of recommending termination for those women whose babies are too premature to be delivered?"

"I don't speak for the president, but as a rule, the chief executive doesn't make medical recommendations."

"But wouldn't the president and his administration consider this more of a moral question than a medical one?"

Brickell raised her hand above the murmur.

"Ladies and gentlemen, we have a serious problem on our hands. For the moment, our goal is to quickly isolate the cause of GNS and to formulate an effective treatment plan that will lead to a cure. That's what we all need to stay focused on."

As Dr. Brickell expected, the reporters were relentless,

and for the next thirty minutes she continued to field one difficult question after another. Finally, she leaned forward and placed her hands on either side of the lectern. Her eyes found a persistent young man who had moved into the aisle. With a nod and a gesture, she recognized Tony Williamson, a new correspondent from Reuters whom she had met at her last press conference. It was immediately obvious to her then that whatever he lacked in experience he more than made up for with his instincts and talent.

"With an epidemic of this magnitude has the president given any consideration to—"

"Excuse me for interrupting, Tony, but GNS is not an epidemic. An epidemic, by definition, is a dramatic rise in the expected number of cases of an established disease with a known epidemiological history. Since GNS has never been seen before, this present situation can't technically be classified as an epidemic."

Regarding Brickell through unconvinced eyes, Williamson said nothing for the moment. It wasn't hard for her to read his thoughts. Her comment was evasive, making her look as if she were sidestepping a tough question by providing a piece of information that was true but at the same time totally irrelevant.

After a forced smile and a slow nod, Williamson renewed his question, "Irrespective of what we call this . . . this outbreak, the fact remains our nation's facing a disease that's spreading to the tune of roughly five hundred new cases a day. Can you give us some sense of what the CDC and our other key government health care agencies are recommending to thousands of pregnant women and their families who are becoming increasingly more terrified with each passing day?"

Brickell wasn't surprised by the question. Before she'd even walked up to the lectern, she'd expected someone would ask it. She took a few seconds to gather her thoughts before responding.

"We are working closely with local, state and national medical societies, public health organizations and physician groups to help us educate and inform all pregnant women and those who are considering becoming pregnant of the present situation. We've created a telephone hotline and an interactive website for doctors. I assure you, we are critically aware of the rising anxiety across the country. But until we have more specific information about this illness, it would be irresponsible of us to make any recommendations beyond general cautionary measures."

Brickell glanced to the side of the room. Urging her to wrap things up, Julian Christakis gave her his most subtle *cut* sign.

"I have time for one more question," she said. Before she could recognize anybody, an uninvited voice asked, "Is there any possibility GNS is an act of biological terrorism?"

Her eyes found the young woman in the center of the room who had asked the question. Brickell had no clue who she was, but she didn't feel she could use her refusal to follow proper protocol as a way of dismissing the extremely valid question.

"All possibilities will be carefully evaluated," she

answered cautiously. "But at this time, we have no evidence that GNS is the result of a biological weapon." Brickell took two short steps backward. "I'm sorry. I'm going to have to stop here. I encourage all of you to refer to our website for the exact date and time of our next briefing."

She turned away from the lectern, and with Julian in tow, she quick-walked out of the briefing room.

"Excellent job," he told her. "Especially that last question."

"Excuse me?"

"Your responses were honest and on point. I'm sure they helped to diminish the anxiety of an impending crisis."

Brickell was well aware that part of Julian's job was to contain prickly situations and curry favor with her regardless of how difficult the situation seemed. But today, his fairy-tale optimism was over the top.

"Julian, we're dealing with a potentially devastating disease that's spreading out of control. To make matters worse, it's selectively attacking pregnant women, one of any society's most vulnerable groups." She looked at him as if he should know better. "What did you call it—'an impending crisis'? This crisis is hardly impending. It has a large gray fin, is finished circling, and just about ready to bite us all on the ass."

"I understand, Dr. Brickell but we—"

She waved her hand, which prompted his immediate silence.

"This is an enormous problem, which isn't going to

go away by simply sprinkling a little pixie dust on it. It's probably only a matter of days, maybe hours until we start seeing fatalities. Americans are a resilient people, but I don't think they're ready to see helpless pregnant women and unborn babies die."

Just at that moment, a young man tapped on the door. Julian waved him forward.

"I have a message for Dr. Brickell."

Julian took the note and handed it to her.

"We haven't even begun to hear the outcry from the conservative and religious organizations," she said, unfolding the note. "Every government agency having anything remotely to do with health care is being barraged with thousands of frantic calls. Families are desperately looking for answers, and our only response is to tell them to remain calm and give us more time. And in case you didn't get the memo, Christmas is three weeks away, so the timing of this disaster couldn't be worse." She shook her head as she read the note. "Great," she muttered, crumpling it in hand. "C'mon, we have to get back to the office. We have a lot of prep work to do."

"What's going on?"

"The president's cutting his trip short. He arrives at Andrews at seven forty-five tonight. He wants to meet with us at soon as he gets to the White House."

Leading the way out of the room, Brickell wondered what new information she could gather in the next ten hours that might help her respond to the tough questions President Kellar was sure to pose. At the moment, the only thing she could tell him was that if the task force she'd assembled didn't figure out how to stop this outbreak pretty damn soon, they would have to brace for what would likely be the worst national health crisis since HIV.

7

Standing at the stern of the aging ferry, Jack watched a frenzied formation of seagulls swoop down to snatch bread chunks that had been tossed into the churning wake by a raucous group of tourists.

A product of modest means and an only child, Jack grew up in Fort Lauderdale less than two miles from the beach. As far back as he could remember, he had always loved spending time on the ocean. He preferred sailing catamarans but irrespective of the vessel, he liked being on the water. He enjoyed boating just about as much as he detested flying. Since the moment Mike had offered to send his plane, he had been unable to shake the lingering discomfort of traveling in a small corporate jet.

The ferry trip took just under an hour and, after a short but perilous ride in a taxi held together by daily prayers and superglue, the cab pulled up in front of the general aviation terminal at the Saint Kitts airport. With no assistance from the apathetic driver, Jack retrieved his luggage from the trunk.

Through a heavy cloud of dust kicked up by the fleeing taxi, he saw Mike walking toward him. With peach-fuzz for a beard and cropped brown hair, Mike had barely attained the height of five foot six. His small stature had left him five inches shorter than Jack; a fact Jack had teased him about with regularity since they were teenagers.

With a container of coffee in hand, he gave Jack a firm one-armed hug.

"How's Tess doing?"

"I checked on her right before we left," Mike answered with an uneasy half smile. "There's been no real change overnight."

Mike took a step toward the plane but Jack put his hand on his shoulder. "How are you doing?"

"Tess was born a Christmas fanatic. The house is decorated like Rockefeller Center and she's been consumed with planning our yearly holiday party for the past two months," he answered in a forced but even tone. "A few miles from here, the woman I cherish more than anything in this world is lying comatose in an ICU." With a darting gaze, he asked, "How do you think I feel?"

Jack nodded a few times, but said nothing.

"I'm sorry, buddy," Mike said.

Jack gave his best friend a reassuring smile. "No apology necessary."

Mike managed a quick grin in return and then pointed

at the red-and-white Hawker parked on the tarmac. "C'mon, we can talk on the plane."

Jack studied the eight-passenger aircraft. His slumped shoulders revealed his mounting angst.

"Where's the rest of it?" he asked.

"Don't tell me you're still afraid of flying."

"I love flying. It's the crashing part that bothers me."

Shaking his head, Mike now placed a hand on Jack's shoulder. "Relax. I have the two best pilots in the business." Feeling only slightly reassured, Jack reached for his bags. Mike took his arm. "Just leave them. I promise they'll be in West Palm when we get there." Mike tapped his lip and asked, "When did you shave the mustache off?"

"Last week."

"Part of the new image?"

Jack responded by rolling his eyes. They climbed the stairway and stepped aboard. Jack ducked his head as he trailed Mike toward the back of the cabin. "Take that one," he told him, gesturing at one of the cream-colored leather captain's chairs. Jack settled in and immediately yanked his seat belt across his lap. Mike looked at him askew, "You'll be more comfortable if you can still breathe."

Jack took a brief look around. He had to confess the upscale appointments were nicer than anything in his apartment. His eyes flashed forward when he heard the whoosh of the cabin door being secured by the pilot. Being more accustomed to the glacially slow world of commercial aviation, he was astonished at how quickly things were moving.

The plane taxied out to the active runway and after a brief pause started its takeoff roll. With added power, the low hum of the engines became an earsplitting whine. Sixty seconds later the jet was in a steep climb, leaving the island of Saint Kitts far below. It wasn't until they leveled off above the clouds that Jack's pulse slowed to a normal rate.

"Something to drink?" Mike asked.

"No, thanks. I'm good," he answered, noticing the small slit-like scar over Mike's eyebrow—an injury he had sustained in high school when Jack accidentally had caught him with an elbow in a heated one-on-one basketball game.

Jack had spent an hour online the previous evening learning as much as he could about the outbreak. From a medical standpoint the information was limited but there was enough to give him a sense of what questions to ask.

"Did you have any clue Tess was ill before you got the call?"

"Hell, Jack. I don't know. You're the last person I need to tell what Tess has gone through the last twelve years to get pregnant. Two second trimester miscarriages and traveling for weeks on end seeing every fertility expert in the country." He lowered his chin. "I . . . I had no idea anything was wrong."

Sensing his guilt, Jack said, "If it makes you feel any better, most of the doctors I know have a hard time deciphering between illness and a routine pregnancy. Assume for a minute that Tess wasn't pregnant, would you say her behavior and mental functions have been normal?"

"She seemed a little . . . a little confused maybe for the past couple of days, but I thought she was just pre-occupied."

"What was she confused about?"

"She mixed up some of her friends' names and messed up her daily schedule a few times. I mentioned it to her, but I think I embarrassed her. She kind of blew me off. You know Tess. She never complained about anything and I stupidly didn't press the issue."

"Have you guys done any traveling in the last few weeks?"

Mike shook his head and then laced his fingers behind his head.

"Has Tess had any recent flu symptoms, like a cough or a fever or trouble breathing?"

"The Everglades aren't too far from the house. When we found out she was pregnant, we began taking a walk every evening. We had to stop a week or so ago. She said there was an odor in the air that was making her sick to her stomach and a little short of breath."

"Did the symptoms go away when you stopped taking the walk?"

"Totally."

"Is she taking any new medications, homeopathic compounds, herbal remedies—things like that?"

"Christ, Jack," he said with a corded neck. "There are hundreds of women around the country with this thing.

I don't think this is about Tess's travel schedule or drinking herbal tea. None of this is fair. Tess is the kindest, gentlest human being in the . . ." With a pained expression, Mike turned his head and stared out the window.

"I've seen countless family members drive themselves crazy looking for justice when it comes to illness. It's never there." It crossed Jack's mind to continue to try and persuade Mike to stop beating himself up, but he knew he'd be shouting at the rain.

Jack's mind continued to fill with a host of unanswered questions, but he could see Mike needed a break. He knew he could talk himself blue in the face trying to convince him that Tess would recover. But even as kids, their relationship had always been an honest one free of pretense. To blow sunshine in his best friend's direction would be at the very least transparent and at worst insulting.

In smooth air, the Hawker jetted effortlessly toward South Florida. With a strengthening sense of confidence, Jack lifted the shade and peered out. Below him, a gathering of willowy gray clouds partially obscured the white caps.

Mike had reclined his seat and was still looking out of his window. If asked, Jack would be the first to say that Mike was an intelligent and pragmatic man who hadn't achieved his success by requiring others to connect the dots for him. Thinking about their conversation, Jack realized two things. The first was that Mike hadn't asked him if Tess might die. The second was that his failure to do so wasn't an oversight.

8

Working in the ICU was the only job Lori Case had had since graduating nursing school. After fifteen years, she was a battle-hardened veteran who was completely unflappable. For the past two days, she had been taking care of Lizette Bordene, Harbordale General's fourth patient admitted with GNS. Lizette was the assistant manager of a small clothing boutique and the mother of two. Until a few days ago, she had never been seriously ill in her life.

Lori returned from her break to find Lizette's mother exactly where she'd left her, sitting forward in a small plastic chair at the foot of the bed.

"Why don't you go home and get some rest?" Lori suggested. "I'll call you if there are any changes."

"I'm . . . I'm not sure. Maybe I should—"

Lori put her hand on Gail Bordene's shoulder. "Go ahead. She'll be fine. You need some rest."

Gail reluctantly came to her feet. With an empty stare, she looked at her daughter. After a few seconds, she removed her purse from the back of the chair.

"I'll be back in a few hours. You have my cell phone number."

"It's written on the board and it's in my phone book," Lori assured Gail as she walked her to the door with her arm around her shoulders.

For the next two hours, Lizette's condition was stable. Lori had resigned herself to another long but uneventful shift. But all of that abruptly changed when, without any warning, Lizette's blood pressure went into an uncontrolled free fall.

The room instantly reverberated with a cacophony of alarms and alerts. Lori's eyes flashed to the cardiac monitor. In addition to a dangerously low blood pressure, her pulse was erratic. As a reflex more than anything else, Lori smacked the Code Blue button on the wall summoning the rapid response team. She had barely gotten back to the bedside when Dr. Stephen Arrani and two nurses charged through the door. Lori held Arrani in higher regard than most of the other doctors she worked with because he was knowledgeable and decisive, which were skills that seemed to be lost on many of the newer physicians.

"What's going on?" he asked, snatching the stethoscope that lay draped across his shoulders.

"She's crashing," Lori told him, checking the IV tubing. "Her pressure suddenly took a dive for no reason. It's down to sixty, and her cardiac rhythm's all over the place."

"Looks ventricular. What was her last potassium level?" he asked, cranking up the oxygen to one hundred percent as he snugged the mask around Maggie's nose and mouth.

"I drew one a couple of hours ago. It was normal."

By this time, a respiratory therapist and a pharmacist had dashed into the room and had taken up their assigned positions for a Code Blue.

"Looks like she's in V-tach," Arrani said. "Give her a dose of lidocaine."

"I've already drawn it up," the pharmacist said, handing the syringe to Lori who immediately injected it into the IV port. Silence settled over the room as everyone's eyes locked on the monitor waiting to see if the medication would correct the irregular heart rhythm.

"She's still in V-tach," Arrani announced, his voice building in intensity.

"Her pressure's down to thirty," Lori said.

"Start chest compressions," Arrani ordered. "And get a ventilator set up. She's going to need it."

Lori was all too familiar with the razor-sharp pinch in the pit of her stomach she was now feeling. As a seasoned ICU nurse, she had taken care of countless patients who had taken an unexpected turn for the worse, but it was something she had never gotten used to.

"She's not breathing. We need to tube her right now," Arrani said, craning his neck in the direction of the door. "Who's here from anesthesia?" Carrie Sherman, the nurse anesthetist on call, moved to the head of the bed. "Are any of the obstetricians in house?" he asked.

"I saw Dr. Crossman up on labor and delivery about twenty minutes ago," Carrie answered. "He was just finishing up a delivery. He's probably still here."

"Tell the unit secretary to find him stat. If we can't get her heart rhythm back to normal and her blood pressure up in the next five minutes, she's going to need a crash C-section."

While Arrani continued to shout out orders, Lori carefully slid a metal scope in Lizette's mouth. The highly practiced maneuver brought her vocal cords into clear view. She reached for a curved plastic tube and eased it between the cords and down into her windpipe. As soon as she had it securely taped into place, she connected it to the ventilator. Lizette was now completely dependent on the machine for every breath of air that filled her lungs.

"Her pressure's still thirty," Arrani called out. "We're losing her. Where the hell's Crossman?" He turned back to Lori. "Give her an amp of epinephrine and keep going with the chest compressions."

Arrani's words were still suspended in air when Jim Crossman burst into the room with his chief resident in tow. Crossman was one of only three obstetricians on staff who agreed to cover the trauma center. After responding to dozens of critically injured pregnant women who were the victims of serious car accidents, gunshot wounds and stabbings, he was no stranger to performing a crash C-section to save the baby of a dying mother.

"Somebody talk to me," Crossman said, making his way to the bed.

"She's a thirty-year-old with GNS," Arrani answered between quick breaths.

"How far along is she?"

"Twenty-nine weeks."

"What happened?"

"She went into V-tach and her blood pressure dropped." He shook his head. "I'm trying, but I can't get it back up." His eyes shifted to the cardiac monitor. "She's going to arrest."

"How long has her blood pressure been that low?" Crossman asked.

"Four minutes."

"Any chance you can reverse all this in the next minute or so?"

"I doubt it."

"Keep up the chest compressions," he ordered. "If we don't keep Mom's heart pumping, the baby doesn't have a chance."

At that same moment, two nurses from the operating room with a huge metal box of sterile instruments came through the door.

"I think we should get her ready and move her to the operating room," Arrani said.

"The operating room is two floors away," Crossman reminded him. "From what I'm looking at, she wouldn't survive a change of socks at the moment, let alone a trip to the OR. We're doing the section right here." He stole a quick glance around the room. "I need everybody who doesn't absolutely need to be here to get the hell out right now. What do you say, Carrie? Can I start?"

"Go. She's not going to move."

By this time, his scrub nurse, Kate, had carved a path to the front of the room and had set up two sterile trays of instruments.

"We're ready," she told him.

"Somebody call the neonatal ICU," he said, slipping on his sterile gown and gloves. "Dr. Armbrister's on call. Tell her to get her butt down here right now."

The stalwart look on his face left no room for misinterpretation. His decision to proceed with the emergency C-section was not up for discussion. "Don't stop for me," he told Dr. Arrani. "The sooner you get her heart rhythm fixed, the better chance she and the baby have of surviving."

He then reached his hand behind him. Kate handed him a sterile metal basin filled to the top with iodine prep solution. There was no time for the usual neat application of a coat or two. Crossman tossed the entire contents of the basin across Lizette's abdomen. And then, except for the rhythmic snap of the backboard with each compression of her chest, the room again became silent.

9

Two minutes after he had made an incision, Crossman held Lizette's uterus cupped in his hands. Selecting an area between the engorged veins, he quickly made an incision just large enough for the baby to fit through. Working his way through the thick muscular wall, he entered the body cavity of the uterus. Carefully scooping the baby out of the organ, he clamped the umbilical cord and cut it.

"I'm right behind you," Armbrister said, with her arms outstretched and draped with a sterile towel.

Crossman set the baby into her waiting arms. She was profoundly blue and limp as a Raggedy Ann doll. She made no sounds, not even a whisper of a cry. With the help of her nurse practitioner, Armbrister positioned the baby on a warming bed and swiftly slid a breathing tube through her graying lips and down into her trachea to assist her breathing.

"Talk to me, somebody. How's the baby doing?" Crossman inquired without lifting his eyes from the operating field.

"She's alive," Armbrister answered, using a plastic bulb to suction out the baby's nostrils and mouth. The instant she was finished, she transferred the baby from the warming bed to an incubator. "We're out of here," she announced.

"Does she have a chance?" Crossman asked.

"Ask me in about twenty minutes. Right now things aren't looking so good."

During the entire time the C-section was in progress, two medical residents alternated performing CPR on Lizette. At the same moment Crossman finished stapling closed her incision, her heart suddenly stopped. Arrani and the others continued to work like madmen for the next twenty minutes to restore a heartbeat but with no success.

Finally, he looked away from the monitor. His eyes dropped and in a monotone drenched in defeat, he said, "We can stop the chest compressions. I'm calling it. Somebody note the time of death for the record please."

By this time, the floor was littered with empty medication boxes, paper heart tracing strips and an endless assortment of used medical supplies. Allowing a full breath to flow out from his lungs, he leaned over and picked up a box. As far as he knew, Lizette Bordene was the first death from GNS in the country.

After a minute or so, he crumpled the box in his hand and tossed it into the trash. As much as he dreaded doing it, he walked over to the phone to call Lizette's mother.

10

—/\ᴠ/—

The moment Jack stepped off the plane in West Palm Beach, he was struck by a squall of wind rich with the scent of ozone. Shading his eyes, he gazed to the east at the remnants of a rogue storm moving offshore.

"My car's right over there," Mike said, gesturing to a small gravel lot protected in part by a weather-beaten chain-link fence. "It's only about a thirty minute ride to the hospital."

When Mike turned his SUV into the Southeastern State University Medical Center, Jack was immediately taken back. The sprawling medical complex bore no resemblance to the small hospital he remembered. In addition to the new school of medicine, the medical center now boasted a six-hundred-bed teaching hospital, a seven-story research center, and a children's hospital. To the west, Jack noticed a modernist building nearing completion. A large banner in front of it indicated it was the future home of Southeastern State University's Women's Cancer Hospital.

As they approached the valet parking area, Jack's attention shifted to the dozens of media vehicles amassed in a parking lot alongside the hospital. Their antennae spiraled upward like the towering masts of a flotilla of great sailing ships. Around the vans and SUVs, dozens of broadcast personnel congregated in small groups. Some were dressed casually and stood with cameras hoisted on their shoulders. Those who were more formally attired gripped microphones in their hands. The largest group jockeyed for a preferred position directly in front of the main entrance to the hospital. The GNS outbreak was an enormous story. He wasn't surprised that the prediction Helen Morales had made on the phone regarding the inevitability of a media circus at Southeastern State had come true.

Mike and Jack made the short walk from the parking lot and entered the hospital through a revolving glass door. They hadn't taken more than a few steps when a slight woman wearing a teal-colored suit approached at a brisk pace.

"Jack, I'd like you to meet Dr. Helen Morales."

A peculiar habit of Jack's for as long as he could remember was conjuring up an image of a person's appearance based on his or her telephone voice. He smiled to himself. As usual, he was light-years off of the mark. Helen wasn't matronly, stout or on the fashion police's most wanted list. She was just the opposite.

Helen took Jack's extended hand and gave it a vigorous shake.

"Welcome back to South Florida. I can't thank you enough for accepting our invitation."

"It's nice to meet you."

With more than subtle apprehension in his voice, Mike asked, "How's Tess doing?"

"I just came down from the ICU. I'd say she's about the same."

Mike pushed out a quick breath but said nothing. As well as Jack knew him, he couldn't be sure if he was encouraged or dismayed by Helen's report.

"Would it be all right if I catch up with you two a little later?" Mike asked. "I have a couple of things to take care of." Mike took a few steps forward and gave Jack a brief hug. "I almost forgot," he said. "I had some clothes sent over to your hotel. I figured your vacation attire might not be appropriate for the hospital. They may not fit perfectly but I think they'll be close enough."

"Thanks. I'm sure they'll be fine," Jack said, wondering if Mike really had something to do or if, for the moment, he just couldn't bear seeing Tess.

"I'll take you up to the ICU. We can talk on the way," Helen said to Jack gesturing toward the elevators. "As of nine this morning, we've admitted thirty-five women with GNS. All indications are that we can expect more . . . a lot more. Our facilities are already stressed. From what I hear, the same scenario's being played out in hospitals from here to California." The elevator doors rolled open and they stepped aboard. "The frustration amongst our physicians is soaring. We really need a fresh pair of eyes. I can assure you, Jack, that everyone on staff is excited about collaborating with you."

Jack smiled politely. He hoped his expression didn't betray his anxiety. He wondered if Helen Morales's expectations of him were even remotely realistic. He was a well-trained and experienced neurologist; but he wasn't bestowed with divine diagnostic or healing powers. It wasn't that he lacked confidence, but his gut feeling was that figuring out the cause of GNS and how to treat it would be the greatest challenge of his career.

11

The entire sixth floor of Southeastern State University Hospital was a designated critical care area consisting of four separate intensive care units. After walking down a wide corridor, Helen and Jack arrived at ICU 3. She tapped on a metal plate and the two frosted glass doors swung open.

The unit was laid out in a circular configuration with the nursing station and all of its monitoring equipment in the middle. The patient rooms ran the entire circumference of the spacious unit like the spokes of a wheel. Similar to the lobby, it was obvious to Jack no money had been spared on its design and construction. It was always amazing to him that irrespective of what state he was in, all intensive care units had the same mineral scent.

"Tomorrow night we've arranged a dinner at your hotel," Helen said. "It will be mostly social but we'd like to spend some time discussing the GNS cases if you're amenable."

"Of course," Jack said. "I understand Dr. Sanchez recently stepped down as your chief of neurology. Have you named his successor?"

"Not yet, but our search committee has already interviewed a few promising candidates. In the meantime, Hollis Sinclair is serving as interim chief. He's an excellent clinician and teacher." She paused briefly. From her expression, Jack got the feeling she was collecting her thoughts and had something to add. "At times, Hollis can seem a little proud and single-minded, but I assure you he always has the best interests of his patients at heart. I'm sure you two will work well together."

Helen's comments struck an immediate cautionary note in Jack's mind. He assumed in the interest of diplomacy, they had been understated. He'd never met Sinclair, nor did he know of him by reputation, but when somebody was easy to work with, it generally wasn't necessary to point it out.

"I fully understand your close friendship with Mike may complicate matters," Helen mentioned. "If there's anything I can do to help, please don't hesitate to ask."

"Thank you," he said, thinking to himself it was nice to hear Helen acknowledge that she was keenly aware of his predicament.

Helen motioned to a young man working on a laptop. He returned the wave, stood up and walked over. Appearing sleep deprived and skeletal, his Brillo-y black hair and Ringo Starr mustache were both screaming for a grooming. An iPod was hitched to his frayed brown belt right next to a standard-issue hospital phone. The pockets of his white coat overflowed with an assortment of folded papers and medical manuals.

"I'd like you to meet Marc Jaylind," Helen said. "He's our senior fellow in perinatology. He's been working very closely with our division chief, Madison Shaw, on these cases. He'll get you acquainted and answer any questions you may have."

Marc extended his hand, "Welcome to Southeastern State, Dr. Wyatt."

"I appreciate the invitation. It's a pleasure to be here."

"I have a meeting so I'll let you two get started," she said above the shrill alarm of one of the cardiac monitors.

"Dr. Morales mentioned you'd probably want to begin by being briefed on Tess Ryan before we discussed the other patients." Marc pointed toward the nursing station. "There's a physician's conference room over there."

"How did you get interested in perinatology?" he asked Marc as they made their way past a portable X-ray machine.

"I saw a lot of high-risk pregnancies at Northwestern during my OB residency. Most of the other residents hated complicated obstetrics. I really liked it."

"Well, if Southeastern State's perinatology fellowship's anything like Ohio State's, I'm sure you've been working your tail off."

"It hasn't exactly been a pajama party, I'll give you that. I was an optometrist for five years before I decided to go to med school, so I'm a little older than most of the other residents and fellows." He grinned and held up a hand. "I know. It sounds kind of strange."

"Not really. I did a year of vet school before switching into medicine."

"Any regrets?" Marc inquired with a sidelong glance.

"From time to time, I guess," he answered. "Are you coming to dinner tomorrow night?"

"I'm afraid not. No bottom-feeders. Only the elite are invited."

Jack chuckled. "Well, at least you can take comfort in the fact that you're only a few months from the promised land. If it makes you feel any better, we all had to pay our dues."

The main part of the ICU was visible from the physician conference room through a large glass window. In the center of the room was a table with six chairs around it. Marc sat down, extending his legs and crossing them at the ankles. Jack took the seat directly across from him.

"I heard you've spent quite a bit of time with these patients. I guess that makes you the GNS expert."

"I'm afraid GNS expert would be a strong contender for the oxymoron of the month."

Jack smiled. "How are the babies doing?"

"They seem to be holding their own—at least to this point. Two quad screens have been done on each of them, which have all been normal. The other hospitals are reporting the same thing. We are planning on—"

Jack held up his hand. "Quad screen? My perinatology's a little rusty. You'll have to refresh my memory."

"Beginning at eighteen or nineteen weeks, we measure

four hormones levels in the mother's blood. If any of them is abnormal, it can be an indication of fetal distress or the development of a serious malformation. We've also done ultrasounds and amniocenteses on almost all of the patients, and they've all been normal."

Jack would be the first to admit he suffered from his fair share of professional shortcomings, but being completely clueless regarding a medical case had never been one of them. But at the moment, that's exactly how he felt. Just then, the door opened and the unit secretary poked her head in.

"Everybody's looking for you, Marc. They're ready to start rounds."

He stood up, removed his stethoscope from around his neck and shoved it into his back pocket.

"C'mon, I'll introduce you to Dr. Shaw. I'm sure she's looking forward to meeting you."

Jack followed Marc out of the room. He had always relied heavily on first impressions. Marc struck him as bright, personable and mature. Spending a great deal of time with the residents and fellows at Ohio State, he often wondered how a particular one would fare in the real world after his or her training was over. In the case of Marc Jaylind, he had little doubt a promising career awaited him.

12

Poised to begin rounds, an anxious group of residents and students congregated in front of the nursing station. As a frequent visiting professor, Jack had seen the same scene play out at a dozen different medical schools. While some of the aspiring doctors feverishly paged through pocket-size manuals, others shuffled index cards packed with medical information, preparing to present their assigned patients to the group.

Marc raised his hand, signaling to a petite-framed woman in a knee-length white coat who was talking on her cell phone. She gestured back and a few seconds later, she slipped her phone into her coat and walked over.

"Dr. Wyatt. This is Madison Shaw."

"Dr. Wyatt," she said.

"Please call me Jack." He smiled, extending his hand. Even though his social life was in the doldrums, it would have been difficult for him not to notice she was an attractive woman. She had willowy fingers, a thinly pointed nose and the neck of a ballet dancer. "It's nice to meet you. Dr. Morales had a lot of nice things to say about you."

"That was kind of her," she responded, stone-faced with a clipped handshake. "If you need anything, please let Marc know." She looked at the assembled group and then motioned to one of the residents who walked over. "Go ahead and get started with rounds. Have J. C. present the first case. I'll join you in a couple of minutes." Madison turned back to Jack. "As I said, if there's anything you need, just let Marc know. Please excuse me. I have to get back to rounds."

"Of . . . Of course," he answered.

With a stiffened posture, he watched Madison start to walk away. Just at that moment, Helen Morales approached. She motioned for Madison to return.

"I'm glad to see you two have had a chance to meet. I just got off the phone with the Office of the Surgeon General. There's an emergency meeting tomorrow in Atlanta at the CDC. I think it would be an excellent idea for the both of you to attend." Her gaze turned to Jack. "Do you think you can make the trip?"

"Of course."

"It's a three-hour meeting. It's scheduled to begin at eleven. I'll have my assistant make the travel arrangements and e-mail you the information. You should make it back in plenty of time for our dinner." She looked down at her watch. "Just once I'd like to be on time for a meeting. I'll speak with you both later."

"Will you be attending the dinner tomorrow evening?" Jack asked Madison.

"It's not voluntary, Dr. Wyatt. Dean Morales expects all of us to be there."

Madison returned to the group, leaving Jack's head nodding like the Woody Hayes bobblehead doll that sat on his desk in Columbus. After an awkward few seconds, he had the sudden urge to feel his checks to make sure the flesh hadn't completely melted from his face. *So much for the warm greeting and heartfelt expression of gratitude for agreeing to serve as a guest professor*, he thought to himself. He chanced a look in Marc's direction.

"Did I miss something here?" he inquired, scratching the back of his head, unable to remember the last time somebody had taken such an instant disliking to him.

"I'm not sure. Do you frequently have this effect on women?"

"From time to time, but it usually takes a little longer. Is she always like that?"

Marc couldn't contain a short laugh. "Actually, she's one of the most easygoing, pleasant people I've ever worked with."

"All evidence to the contrary," Jack said with a huff.

"You probably just caught her at a bad moment. Things have been pretty tense around here the past couple of days. I'm sure she'll be in a better mood the next time you meet."

"Well, you've certainly honed your diplomatic skills," Jack responded as if Marc were somebody trying to sell him enough life insurance for three people. Jack was still wondering what he'd done to deserve such an ungracious welcome when one of the interns rushed up.

Between clipped breaths, she said, "Marc, Dr. Shaw wants you stat. Tess Ryan's crashing."

13

Tess's room was generous in size but not designed to accommodate twelve crane-necked medical students and residents, all struggling to see what was going on.

Jack followed Marc as he cut a path through the group. When he reached the head of Tess's bed, his gaze instantly fixed on her face. Her eyes were hollow, glazed and frozen open. Her skin was the color of a clamshell, and at the corners of her mouth, filmy puddles of saliva lightly bubbled.

"What's going on?" Marc asked John Fuller, the ICU physician on duty.

"About half an hour ago, she developed sudden bursts of non-purposeful movement and arching of her back. Her pulse went crazy but it's slowing down now." He then gestured toward her upper body. "At about the same time, a facial rash appeared." Jack took a moment to study the brightly speckled crimson rash on Tess's cheeks.

"Does she have a fever?" Madison asked.

"No, which surprises me a little because this disease is starting to look more and more like a virus every hour."

"Do any of the other patients have similar findings?" she inquired.

"Not yet," he answered, unfastening the top button of his white coat. "But Tess was one of our first patients, and since they've all had identical symptoms to this point, I suspect the others will follow suit soon enough."

"Has she had a recurrence of dancing eye syndrome?" Jack asked.

Fuller gazed over at him. A curious look crossed his face.

"I'm sorry," Marc said. "This is Dr. Jack Wyatt. He's chief of neurology at Ohio State. Because of his special expertise in elusive diagnoses, he's serving as a guest professor and consultant on the GNS cases."

Fuller took a couple of steps forward and shook Jack's hand. "Welcome. I think we've got her dancing eye syndrome under control, but she's becoming less responsive with each passing hour. I've ordered another MRI but I'm not sending her up to radiology until I'm sure she's stable."

"Has Dr. Sinclair been informed?" Madison inquired.

"I spoke with him a little while ago. He's in a lengthy budget meeting, but he agreed with ordering an MRI. He also wanted to repeat an EEG to see if there's been any change in her brain wave pattern. He said he'd be down to see her as soon as the meeting was over." From the tone of his voice, Jack suspected Fuller was miffed that Sinclair didn't share his sense of urgency regarding the abrupt change in Tess's condition. Jack was in agreement: No budget meeting should take priority over a patient in trouble. Fuller continued, "Her blood pressure and pulse are okay for now. So, apart from an assessment of the baby's condition, which I'll leave to you and Marc, I can't think of anything else to do at the moment except keep a close eye on things."

"Have we notified her husband?" Madison asked.

"No, but I was just about to do that. I'll give him a call in the next few minutes."

Madison stepped up to Tess's bed and slowly began an examination of her abdomen. While she was still feeling her lower belly, she turned to Marc. "Find an ultrasound machine and get it in here stat. When you're ready to go, come and get me. I want to have another look at the baby." She pulled the covers back up and then led the group out of the room. Jack and Marc were a few steps behind them.

"As soon as we're done with the ultrasound, I'll give you a ride over to your hotel," Marc said.

"That won't be necessary. I'll be happy to take him," came a voice from behind them. Jack recognized it instantly. It was Mike Ryan.

14

"What's all the excitement about?" Mike asked, peering into Tess's room. The forced calmness in his tone did little to mask his anxiety.

"We were just about to call you," Marc said. "There's been a change in Tess's condition. She's developed some new neurologic symptoms and a facial rash."

Mike took a hard look at Jack before turning back to Marc. "What does all that mean?"

"We can't be completely sure. There are several possibilities we're looking into."

"It sounds like you're saying Tess is getting worse, and you don't know why."

"Dr. Shaw and I are looking after the baby, so it would probably be better if you spoke with Dr. Fuller directly."

With his eyebrows drawn together, Mike said, "If Tess had suddenly improved, I suspect you'd be more than happy to share the news with me." Mike was not one to become easily unhinged or forget his manners. Jack suspected the pure weight of the stress he was under was to blame.

"Take it easy, Mike," Jack said in a calming voice. "The new symptoms don't necessarily mean things are worse. It may just be the natural course of the disease. Marc and Dr. Shaw are going to do an ultrasound of the baby to make sure she's okay."

"I don't think you're as convinced as you're trying to sound."

Before Jack could respond, Mike turned and walked toward the nursing station. With his back to them, he shook his head slowly. Jack was tempted to join him but thought better of the idea and decided to give him a few moments alone to regain his composure.

As Jack suspected, after a minute or so, Mike walked back down the hall.

His words were measured. "Ever since Tess was admitted I've listened to one learned medical opinion after another. The only thing I know for sure is that none of the doctors has the first damn clue of what to do to help Tess or our baby. I'm not naïve and I don't believe in miracles, so I wasn't expecting you to breeze in here and instantly tell me what's wrong with her, but I was hoping you'd . . . you'd at least have some—"

"We're only a few days into this illness. The only thing I can tell you for certain is this will be an hour-to-hour process. Right now, nobody can say when the pieces will start coming together."

"Or if they ever will," Mike stated.

"I'm not going to paint a rosy picture for you. Figuring out what's wrong with Tess isn't going to be easy. I understand that right now you're a little frantic, but every disease leaves footprints. We need more time to find them, and then see where they take us."

For the moment, Mike guarded his silence, looking at Jack through a barely perceptible veil of tears. "Tess isn't going to die. It's not her time. There are thousands of people out there with sick kids she hasn't met yet who are going to desperately need her." Without waiting for Jack to answer, Mike turned around and walked into Tess's room.

Jack's instincts were telling him a cure was possible. But he suspected they didn't have a lot of time, and in the absence of swift treatment options, GNS would turn out to be a fatal disease. Jack felt his resolve strengthening. He thought to himself that irrespective of how discouraging things appeared at the moment, he was light-years away from taking a knee on saving Tess Ryan's life.

15

> NUMBER OF CASES: 1,606
> NUMBER OF DEATHS: 1

After a night plagued by restless sleep, Jack threw back the covers and got out of bed. Last evening, when he returned from dinner, there was a voice message from Madison informing him she would pick him up at seven fifteen to drive him to the airport. For obvious reasons, he assumed her offer was not the result of his charming personality but came at the behest of Helen Morales.

Jack telephoned the ICU and spoke with the nurse taking care of Tess. She reported she'd had a stable night but was still unresponsive. Her rash was still present, but her muscle spasms had improved with heavy sedation. She also mentioned that as Dr. Fuller had predicted, almost all of the other women with GNS were showing the same new symptoms that Tess had exhibited. Word of the first GNS death had reached him the night before. The news only served to heighten the urgency of a situation that was already a ticking time bomb.

While he finished getting dressed Jack flipped on the TV and did a quick lap. Every morning news program was featuring coverage of the outbreak with special attention to the first death. Feeling more and more discouraged with each story, he turned off the television and went downstairs. Having some time to spare, he walked through the lobby's expansive atrium and exited the back of the hotel onto a terrace that overlooked a private marina. He strolled past an endless line of yachts, one more spectacular than the next. Some were already adorned with lights and other elaborate Christmas decorations for the yearly holiday boat parade on the Intracoastal Waterway due to take place in a couple of days. A sudden frenetic squawking pierced the air. Although he hadn't lived in Florida for many years, he had no difficulty identifying the sound. Looking up, he watched a flock of wild parrots diving and climbing in synchronicity as if they were tethered together with a clear fishing line.

After a few minutes, Jack headed back to the terrace and found a seat at a wrought iron table. Gazing without purpose across the waterway, his thoughts turned to Tess. His pulse quickened while in his mind's eye he found himself intensely studying her disease, personifying it as if it were his sworn enemy, a phenomenon common amongst physicians. When an elderly couple engaged in a heated conversation strolled past, Jack was suddenly snapped back to the here and now. He glanced down at his watch. He stood up and headed back toward the front of the hotel to meet Madison.

Standing under the arched stone entranceway, Jack watched the piercing rays of the sun streaming through the palm trees. He wasn't paying particular attention when a black Mini Cooper convertible pulled up. It was only when he heard two quick taps of the horn that he bent over and looked in the passenger-side window.

"Good morning," he said.

"It's open," Madison told him.

The parking attendant, his lips pressed tightly together to stave off a smile, opened the door.

"You don't happen to have a shoehorn on you?" Jack whispered to him.

After a series of maneuvers that would have made even the most seasoned Cirque du Soleil contortionist stand up and applaud, Jack managed to work his way into the passenger seat.

"Great car," he said. Madison didn't smile or say anything. Undaunted, Jack went on, "I called the ICU when I got up. The nurse taking care of Tess told me she had a relatively stable night."

"I know. I called too."

"I assume you heard about the woman in Spokane who died."

"I did. Since then, two more have been reported. One

from New Jersey and the other from New Mexico. Both the babies were delivered by emergency C-section and are alive."

Jack's stomach rolled. "No, I hadn't heard. I guess we can assume the topic will come up at today's meeting."

During the ride to the airport, the conversation remained civil but strained. Waiting for their flight in the gate area, Madison continued to answer Jack's questions with chopped answers and rare eye contact. The flight was more of the same. By the time they landed in Atlanta, whatever hope he had had that Madison was just having a bad day when they had first met had long evaporated.

16

Centers for Disease Control and Prevention
Atlanta, Georgia

Jack had a pretty good idea that the spacious conference room he and Madison had just been ushered into had been the site of dozens of landmark medical conferences. On the walls, hanging in a semi-ordered fashion, were black-and-white photographs of some of the greatest names in the history of American medicine. Even for someone of Jack's accomplishments and national reputation, the experience was a humbling one.

Seated around a leather-topped conference table, eighteen of the brightest and most talented physicians in the country chatted while they awaited the arrival of the surgeon general. Jack and Madison found their name cards and took their seats.

Ten minutes later, with her usual entourage, Dr. Renatta Brickell entered the room. Before calling the meeting to order, she made her way around the table individually greeting and thanking each physician for attending. When she finished, she took her seat at the head of the table. She began by asking the attendees to briefly introduce themselves and give a synopsis of their backgrounds and special area of expertise. When the last of the group had complied, she interlocked her fingers and placed her hands on the table.

"I want to begin by wishing you all a happy holiday season. I met with President Kellar earlier today. He wants me to assure each and every one of you that there's nothing more important on his national agenda right now than the GNS outbreak. He extends his heartfelt thanks to all of you who have agreed to serve on this task force." Renatta paused long enough to glance down at her notes. "By now, each of you should have received an e-mail summarizing our most current information on the disease. Based on those facts, we will be concentrating our efforts in three main areas: the first is the possibility that GNS is a contagious disease—most likely a virus. The second possibility is an environmental toxic exposure of some type. Right now the two leading candidates would be a toxin from e-waste or nanotechnology." She paused for a few moments and then added, "I would like to leave a discussion of the third possibility until the end of the meeting." She looked up from her notes and glanced around the room. "So, if there are no pressing questions, I'd like to begin by asking

Dr. Maddox to give us a brief update on the CDC's efforts to this point."

Over the years, Jack had worked with Ezra Maddox, a virologist, on several occasions, mostly relating to outbreaks of meningitis. Jack found him to be plodding in his approach to problems, but not one to be sidetracked by minutiae. Bringing his own special brand of meticulous management to every project, he had long been recognized as a national authority on all types of epidemics, but especially viral ones.

"Thank you, Dr. Brickell," Maddox said, straightening his paisley bow tie. "As part of an initial evaluation, we have cultured and evaluated hundreds of fluid and tissue samples. We realize that we are only a few days into this investigation, but as of this morning, all of those tests have failed to reveal a specific virus, bacteria or fungal agent as the cause of GNS." He removed his bifocals and tucked them into the breast pocket of his sport coat. "It also bears mentioning that the symptoms we are seeing with GNS are only suggestive of a viral illness, certainly not diagnostic."

For the next fifteen minutes Maddox elaborated on the CDC's findings. He concluded his remarks by repeating that they didn't have a single iota of evidence that GNS was a contagious disease. Maddox then opened the floor to questions, none of which were eye-opening.

The problem was the same—a lack of any definitive medical information about GNS, a reality Jack suspected would surface over and over again as the meeting progressed. Maddox's disheartened manner and dampened voice betrayed the same frustration Jack suspected every-body in the room, including himself, was feeling. After answering the last question, Maddox turned the meeting back to the surgeon general.

"As I'm sure we're all aware, the outbreak of GNS in so many women over a wide geographic area raises the question of a possible toxic exposure. As I mentioned, there are two specific areas that should be discussed. I'd like to begin by asking Dr. Grandeson to give us an update on her work."

Plain-faced with a sparse patch of freckles over the bridge of her nose, Mary Grandeson had devoted her entire professional life to the study of environmental toxins. In spite of a career filled with major scientific accomplishments and professional accolades, she religiously avoided the aca-demic limelight. "Since the first cases of GNS were iden-tified, we've been looking at all environmental toxins as a possible cause, but with a particular focus on microscopic toxins produced by nanotechnology."

Jack's knowledge of nanotechnology was elementary at best. Essentially, the science was about twenty years old and dealt with consumer products, mostly cosmetic and electronic, that contained microscopic materials. Over the past several years, a rising concern had been raised by the scientific community that these microscopic components could possibly be toxic.

Dr. Grandeson's presentation was concise but compre-hensive, giving an extensive review of nanotoxins with special emphasis on those that theoretically could be linked to GNS. She concluded by saying that it was possible a nanotoxin could be responsible for GNS, but beyond that she had no evidence that pointed to a specific one.

"Which brings us to the second environmental toxin of concern," Brickell said. "Is there any possibility that we might be dealing with an e-waste toxin?"

Grandeson answered, "Disposal of massive amounts of electronic equipment such as computers has become a major problem not only in this country but worldwide. This is especially true when these items are disposed of illegally. There are millions of them being dumped without regard for public safety on a daily basis. Their breakdown by-products can be extremely toxic to people, animals and the environment."

"Any ideas regarding a specific source?" the physician sitting directly across from Jack asked Grandeson.

"Unfortunately, e-waste research is still in an embryonic stage. Much of what we think we know is guesswork at best. If GNS is being caused by an e-waste toxin, it would take us months, maybe years to discover its exact origin and how to eliminate it."

"Can you at least speculate as to a possible mechanism of exposure?" the same physician inquired.

"Direct contact with the skin or oral ingestion is possible. But my best guess would be by inhalation. For that reason, we're carefully looking at the weather conditions across the country during the past few weeks."

The notion that GNS could be caused by a virus or a potent toxin launched a long discussion. There was a host of theories advanced and concerns raised but no consensus was reached. Working through lunch, the presidential task force was able to formulate a plan moving forward to coordinate their investigative efforts.

"It's almost three o'clock and I think we've just about exhausted our time for today," Brickell announced to the group. "But prior to adjourning, I have two additional matters to share with you. The third possibility to explain GNS that I referred to at the beginning of the meeting is something I'm sure everyone in this room has thought about. The president called me early this morning and asked me to join him this evening at the Army War College to discuss the possibility that GNS is an act of bioterrorism. It is my understanding we'll be meeting with key personnel of the strategic studies unit on bioterrorism."

"Can you give us a better idea of just how serious the president believes this threat to be?" Madison inquired.

"I think he believes it to be unlikely, but he's firm that even if it's a faint possibility, it has to be completely ruled out. The other problem we're facing is that now that we're seeing our first deaths . . . well, we're really under the gun to figure out how to stop the spread of this thing."

From his basic knowledge of bioterrorism, Jack couldn't fathom how any individual or radical group could design a biological weapon that would specifically target pregnant women. But he was a scientist, and if he had learned one thing over the years, it was that anything was possible. The thought made his blood run cold. If GNS were the premeditated act of a terrorist group, the wholesale loss of human life could become staggering.

Brickell moved forward in her chair and tapped her fingertips together. "President Kellar has also asked me to share with you his concern regarding the sensitive ethical and moral challenges we will all be facing. Perhaps the most important is the prospect of early termination of these pregnancies. Therefore, in the next few days, you will be advised of a series of meetings and webinars we're arranging with nationally renowned ethicists and religious leaders. We will also be talking with right-to-life and pro-choice organizations." She forced a guarded smile to her face. "I again want to thank everybody for attending today. My office will advise you of the time and location of our next meeting. I understand that our progress has been somewhat discouraging to this point but it's imperative we remain positive and redouble our efforts to find the cause of GNS."

After a few moments, everybody slowly stood up. A few small groups formed to discuss the distressing news. Jack waited for Madison to gather her things. Together, they started for the door.

His mind fixed on Tess and Mike, Jack said, "We can't assume these deaths are isolated events. My guess is there'll be many more before we figure this thing out."

Although Brickell had already been descended upon by several other physicians, Jack was able to catch her eye and motion a quick good-bye. With a pained smile, she acknowledged Jack with a wave and returned to her conversation. The instant he stepped out into the hall, he reached for his cell phone and called the ICU at Southeastern State to check on Tess.

17

The boarding process of the flight back to Florida went smoothly and the departure was on time. It wasn't until they had been in the air for an hour and Madison had finished a glass of white wine that Jack decided the time was right to take another swipe at the piñata.

"How long have you been at Southeastern State?"

"Eight years. The last four as division chief."

"Do you like it?"

"It's a great job."

"That's pretty high praise. I'm not sure all of my colleagues at Ohio State would say the same about their positions."

With a dry half smile, she said, "Southeastern State may be different than what you're used to. Everybody I work with is a caring professional who you can really trust."

Although he wasn't going to ask her to elaborate, he

still couldn't figure out whether she was just congenitally unfriendly or if it was him who naturally made her skin crawl. Whatever her reason, it was clear the time to stop tap-dancing around her nasty attitude toward him had arrived.

Clearing his throat, he said, "I've never viewed myself as particularly paranoid, and this may sound a little strange to you, but ever since we met, I've gotten the feeling you—"

She turned and looked at him, her eyes boring into his. "We didn't meet yesterday, Jack. We met a long time ago."

"Uh . . . really?" he asked, flogging his memory for some clue. He lowered his glass of sparkling water from his lips. Hoping she'd toss a hint in his direction, he went into a four-corner stall. "It's funny, but now that you mention it, I do have a recollection of us meeting—"

"Save the crap for somebody else, Jack. You don't have any idea who I am."

She then laughed at him as if he were trying to pick her up by claiming he was a two-time winner of the Congressional Medal of Honor.

He grinned and then sighed in contrition. "Okay. You're right. I don't remember. Where did we meet?"

"At the University of Florida. I was a third year medical student rotating on neurology. You were the chief resident."

Jack studied Madison's face again. All at once, he did have a fuzzy recollection of her.

"I may be confusing you with somebody else," he began cautiously, "but weren't you using a different . . ."

"I was using my married name, Madison Casas."

He raised his finger and pointed hesitantly at her hair. "You looked different . . . I mean you wore your . . ."

"Let me save you the embarrassment. I was blond, twenty-five pounds heavier and couldn't afford contact lenses and posh hair care."

Jack was now certain he remembered her. But he recalled nothing of a problem between them, leaving him totally perplexed as to why she harbored such resentment for him. As the chief resident, he was much more involved in teaching than most of his fellow residents. Twice during his residency, he had won the Neurology Teaching Award, an accolade presented by the medical students to an outstanding resident teacher.

Seeing no way of putting it gently, he asked, "Did we have some kind of a problem?"

"You mean other than you being the reason I failed the rotation?"

"Wait a sec," Jack said holding up his hand. "I was only the chief resident. I didn't have the authority to fail anybody. I didn't even assign grades. I was asked my opinion of each student's performance but the chief of neurology was the one who assigned the grades."

"But you were the one who gave us our final practical oral examination."

"That's true, but so what?"

"Are you saying you didn't discuss the results with the attending physicians in charge?"

"Of course I did, but I never failed anybody on the test."

She looked at him with dubious eyes. "My written evaluation couldn't have been clearer. It said I had failed the final practical examination and therefore the entire rotation, which I would be required to repeat. Apart from being one of the most humiliating experiences of my life, I almost didn't graduate with my class. The failing grade also appeared in big bold letters on my transcript, which didn't help very much when I applied for OB-GYN residencies. I was so afraid I wouldn't get one, I wound up applying to thirty programs from Gainesville to San Diego. Needless to say, I didn't exactly get my first choice."

In spite of her impassioned speech, Jack was certain he hadn't been the reason Madison failed her neurology rotation.

"I don't remember any student having to repeat the clerkship," he informed her.

"Do you really think I would repeat it with you? I told you. I was so embarrassed I wanted to die. I signed up to repeat my neurology rotation at another hospital. And, not that this would matter to a person such as yourself, but I was going through a horrendous divorce at the time."

"Why didn't you speak with me after you found out your grade?"

"What for? To hear the same kind of lame excuses and denials I'm hearing now?"

"You weren't the only student I had with a personal problem. I think I was always understanding and fair."

In a droll voice she said, "You're right, Jack. You were very understanding—right up until the time you fed me to the lions." She picked up a napkin, crumpled it up and tossed it back on the tray table.

In spite of his best efforts, Jack was not recovering from the free fall.

He could understand Madison's anger, but they were debating something that had happened a long time ago. And as it turned out, failing her third year neurology clerkship had no negative effect on her career. She had successfully climbed the academic ladder and was now the chief of perinatology at a prestigious medical school.

But Jack was politically seasoned and knew the facts of a disagreement were not always what mattered. Who was right and who was wrong were oftentimes irrelevant. Sometimes, simply apologizing in the blind was the easiest and quickest solution to a problem.

"I'm very sorry for what happened," he began in a calm tone. "I can honestly say I have no recollection of failing you on the final exam. But if the time you spent on the neurology service caused you any personal difficulties, I apologize."

She grinned at him. "Does that lame sorrygram really make you feel any better? Because that's the most oblique apology I've ever heard."

"I can't make you accept my apology. If you have a problem with me—fine. But I would like to get past it so we can work together."

"While I appreciate that—"

"Look, it's going to be tough enough for us to figure

what's going on with these women. Dr. Morales expects us to work together in a productive manner. Certainly what we're facing with respect to GNS is a lot more important than any misunderstanding that took place between us umpteen years ago. Being at odds with each other will only make things more difficult. I'm asking you to accept my apology so that we can move on."

Madison's expression changed slightly. From the loss of conviction on her face, Jack suspected she was giving serious consideration to his proposal.

"You're right," she told him with conviction. "Dean Morales has certain expectations. I'm sure I can put my personal feelings aside so that we can work together."

He nodded politely and said, "I appreciate you being so open-minded and accepting my apology."

"I didn't say I accepted your apology. I said I'd work with you. If you're expecting a group hug and a chorus of 'Kumbaya' around the campfire, you'll be waiting a long time." Jack sat in guarded silence, taking in Madison's self-satisfied grin. It was as if she were happily basking in a bit of long-awaited payback. He actually found himself forced to hold back an optimistic smile. If a few verbal lashings at his expense were all Madison needed to square things between them, it would be a small enough price to pay. His ego had endured worse.

With a circumspect expression, he raised his glass in a mock toast.

"Even if you see it as a descent into the depths of hell—I appreciate your willingness to put your feelings aside and agree to work with somebody you truly despise."

"I never said I despised you. I don't despise anybody. I just think you're an asshole—that's all."

He took a swallow or two and then set his glass down.

"Did you really just call me an asshole?"

"Absolutely."

Grinning on the inside, he shook his head. "I can't remember the last time a colleague called me an asshole."

"Not to your face, maybe," Madison said with a laugh. It was a response Jack deemed a minor breakthrough, even if it was only a small breach in her glacial exterior.

18

It was just after six P.M. when Jack and Madison's flight touched down in West Palm Beach. With no luggage to claim, they made their way directly through the terminal and then to the same-day parking lot.

"I understand that most of the key treating physicians will be at dinner tonight," Jack said, buckling up his seat belt. "Have you worked with Dr. Sinclair very much?"

"Our specialties don't really overlap, but we've consulted on a few cases together."

"How have you found working with him?"

With an intrigued look on her face, she said, "That's kind of a strange question."

"Really? In what way?"

"I'm not sure, but I'm getting the feeling you and Marc must be getting pretty chummy. So what it is that you're really asking me?"

"Nothing," he insisted, trying to deflect her question by sounding as vague and nonchalant as possible. With Madison already having misgivings about his integrity, the last thing he wanted was to be caught flirting with the truth.

"It sounds more to me as if you already have a pre-conceived notion about him."

"I wouldn't exactly put it in those terms."

"Really? Then what terms would you put it in?"

"From what little I've heard, I get the impression he feels comfortable managing the GNS cases without a great deal of assistance."

"Hollis Sinclair's a well-trained neurologist, and he's an excellent clinician. There are some who think he's a tad inflexible and self-important at times." She paused just long enough to cast a cautionary glance his way. "I guess we've all been guilty of that from time to time in our careers."

A few more minutes passed and they pulled up to the hotel. With no further mention of Dr. Sinclair, they strolled past the concierge's desk and down a carpeted hallway. The walls were decorated with grainy photographs of Boca Raton's high society and dignitaries from the turn of the twentieth century.

They reached a group of meeting suites. A cardboard announcement resting on an easel identified the dining room reserved by Helen Morales. Jack opened the door for Madison and they walked into a room heavily steeped in history. The royal blue carpet was as thick and lavish as the antique satin drapery. But the showpiece of the room was an eighteenth-century exquisitely crafted crystal chandelier. Helen Morales greeted them immediately and began introducing Jack and Madison to the fifteen other physicians in attendance.

After a few minutes, Helen left Jack and Madison to chat with a few of the latecomers. It was at that moment that Hollis Sinclair strolled up.

"Good evening," Madison said. "Hollis, I'd like you to meet Jack Wyatt."

"Ah, the prophet from Ohio State," he said, removing the two impaled olives from his martini and popping them into his mouth. Jack extended his hand. Sinclair stared at it for a few seconds before giving it a hasty shake. The limp-wristed greeting had all the warmth of a get-well card from one's worst mortal enemy.

"It's nice to meet you," Jack said.

"I haven't had the opportunity to ask you, but when exactly did you arrive?"

"Yesterday morning," Jack said, suspecting Sinclair already knew the answer to his question.

Appearing uninterested in Jack's answer, Sinclair held up his glass and motioned the bartender.

"Have you got it figured out yet?" he asked Jack.

"I beg your pardon?"

"Do you have any idea what's causing GNS?"

"I'm afraid not, but I'd certainly like to compliment you and your team on the way you're managing these difficult cases."

"Speaking on behalf of all the second-stringers," he

said with a smile that displayed thirty-two perfect teeth, "we thank you."

Jack could recall getting off to a stilted start with a colleague a couple of times in his career, but the last two days had been unprecedented. He wasn't one to make snap judgments about people, but in the case of Hollis Sinclair he was ready to make an exception. He found his pompous and sarcastic manner repugnant. Jack had no way of being certain but he strongly suspected Sinclair had a privileged life growing up and believed pedigree trumped civility. "So, Dr. Wyatt. You were about to share your impressions of GNS with me."

"Hollis," Madison said, "this is supposed to be the social part of the evening. There'll be plenty of time to discuss GNS after dinner."

The bartender walked over and handed Sinclair another vodka martini.

"Nonsense. You don't mind talking about the cases now, do you, Dr. Wyatt?" he asked, taking two swallows of the premium alcohol.

"Not at all but I'd prefer hearing your thoughts first. And please, call me Jack."

"Okay, Jack" he said, raising his glass in a pseudo toast. "Everybody has made two assumptions, both of which I believe to be totally erroneous and both of which have led all of the investigators down the path of misdiagnosis."

"Interesting," Jack said. "What assumptions are those?"

He raised his hand and with a wry smile wagged his

finger. "I'm close to finalizing my theory regarding the cause of this disease, so I'd prefer not to say anything at this time. I will mention, however, I've been speaking to some of the brightest minds on three continents. I find it interesting that nobody besides myself appears to be intrigued by the fact that there are no cases of GNS reported outside of the United States."

"Will you be recommending a treatment plan?" Jack asked.

"Naturally."

"I hope it doesn't include termination of the pregnancies," Madison said.

"I'm a doctor. I don't have the luxury of addressing the moral and religious matters of this disease. I'm far too busy trying to cure it. I suggest we leave the spiritual issues to the clergy. The plan of treatment I'll be suggesting will be both unconventional and aggressive." He shifted his gaze to Madison. "With respect to termination, I'm not ruling out any possibility. But I think you would have to agree that common sense would dictate there's no point prolonging a pregnancy if it means certain death for the mother and baby. In any event, termination is a matter for the families to decide, not their doctors." The conversation was rapidly heading south. Jack had enough political savvy to remain a listener. Sinclair was acting as if he had just shared a point of profound wisdom with them that neither of them had the insight to see on their own.

"We're physicians, Hollis. There's a humanistic side to what we do. I could agree with you on your theory of termination, but then we'd both be wrong." Madison took a few seconds to regard him with a glassy stare. "If you'll excuse me, I'm going to join the others."

Sinclair didn't respond to Madison's comment. Instead, he continued to hold Jack captive, droning on endlessly about his accomplishments and the inevitability that he'd be named the new chief of neurology at Southeastern State School of Medicine. Every minute or so Jack found himself glancing over at the table. Madison was seated between two colleagues, apparently involved in an amusing conversation. She never once looked in his direction.

A few more minutes passed and at Helen Morales's behest everybody began to find his or her place at the table. A young woman entered the room and handed Helen Morales a folded note. She took a moment to read it, sighed deeply and then raised her eyes.

"Excuse me," she began, "but I'm sorry to have to report that I just received word that there's been another death. A twenty-five-year-old woman in Reno, Nevada, suffered a cardiac arrest approximately an hour or so ago. They were able to deliver the baby by C-section. The infant weighed three pounds and was transferred immediately to the neonatal ICU." After a hushed pause, she added, "As soon as additional information becomes available, it will be posted on the National Patient Data Record."

The dining room was noticeably quiet for the next few minutes. But eventually, the conversation picked up and Jack found himself inundated with questions from his colleagues. He didn't particularly mind, but he was relieved when Helen stood up and reminded everybody there would be plenty of time to discuss GNS and any other medical topics of interest later. Before retaking her seat, she strongly suggested a brief moratorium on the topic of GNS in favor of lighter conversation and enjoying their dinner.

19

Army War College
Carlisle, Pennsylvania

Dr. Benjamin Milton was a career-hardened military physician. Holding the rank of colonel, he had served as the director of the Army's Strategic Studies Institute Center. His specific area of interest was the study of biological weapons. Having chaired numerous national and international committees, Colonel Milton had published dozens of scientific papers and had lectured all over the world. Of all the bioterrorism experts in the country, it was Milton that President Stephen Kellar wanted at this evening's meeting.

Renatta Brickell was met at the entrance to the college by two security personnel who escorted her to a small private dining room on the second floor. Glancing over at the table, she was surprised to see it had only been set for three people. When she heard voices, she shifted her gaze to the far side of the room to a rawboned man with a grainy complexion wearing a tweed sports coat. She pushed a smile to her face, filled her lungs with a cautious breath and walked toward the man who had appointed her to the position of United States surgeon general.

"Good evening, Mr. President," she said, extending her hand.

"Happy holidays. It's nice to see you," he answered taking her hand in both of his with the same winning grin that had paved his way to the White House. At forty-seven and only halfway through his first term, the former governor of Rhode Island had moved from a charismatic upstart with a marginal amount of political experience to a seasoned pro. "I don't believe you've had the pleasure of meeting Dr. Milton."

She turned toward the unimposing man with a snub nose and shook his hand.

"It's a great pleasure to meet you. I'm quite familiar with your outstanding contributions to the field."

"Let's sit down," the president suggested, gesturing toward the table. "I considered a larger meeting, but then I thought it might be better if just the three of us chatted." A tall server wearing a white vest entered and placed a garden salad in front of each of them. As soon as he exited, the president continued, "I've spent most of the afternoon being briefed on certain aspects of GNS. I've spoken to several key members of the scientific community and . . . well, my sense is that these young women are not the victims of bioterrorism." He turned to Milton. "Do you agree?"

Milton didn't answer at once. Instead he placed his salad fork down and patted the corners of his narrow mouth with his napkin. Brickell was familiar with his reputation as an articulate man, measured in his responses and one who never presented information he couldn't back up with the facts.

With little inflexion in his voice, he answered, "GNS has an unusual and distinct set of symptoms. Considering what we know about the development of biological weapons, I'd say that the likelihood this disease is a weaponized virus or bacteria is small."

"How small?" Kellar asked in a cautious tone.

"To manufacture a biological weapon of such sophistication is probably beyond the capability of any terrorist group we are currently familiar with."

Kellar smiled but appeared circumspect. "You said probably, Colonel."

"Unfortunately, sir, I can't give you an unqualified guarantee."

The president laced his fingers behind his neck and pushed back in his chair. His salad remained untouched.

"I hope you're simply speaking with an abundance of caution, because as president, I have to know if our country could possibly be under a biological attack. You sound to me like a man with something on his mind. So, irrespective of how remote your concern is, I'd like to hear about it in detail."

"Of course, sir. As soon as the first cases of GNS were

reported, we began looking into the possibility we were facing an act of bioterrorism. In conducting that review, we came across several political groups and individuals of interest. We were able to dismiss most of them fairly quickly, but there was one who stood out. His name's Alik Vosky. He was a Russian scientist."

"The Russian biological weapons research program was dismantled in the 1970s. How does Vosky tie into GNS?"

"As you know, the Russian research program into biological weapons was by far the most extensive and sophisticated of its time. Because of the political upheaval surrounding its termination, we've never had more than a hazy understanding of just how far their research had taken them, and if any of their technology might have fallen into the wrong hands." Milton stopped for a few seconds. Before continuing he took a couple of breaths and fiddled with one of his gold cuff links. "Several years ago, information reached us via the Canadian authorities that prior to its closing, a research facility in the Ukraine had been working on selective acts of biological warfare."

"What do you mean by selective acts?" the president asked.

"It's a term that describes biological weapons that target a specific segment of the population."

"Such as pregnant women."

"I'm afraid so, sir."

"Is there reliable information that such a weapon was ever developed?"

"None that's definitive."

"What else to you know about Vosky?"

"It appears he was a brilliant scientist. Before he reached the age of twenty-five, he had already earned both an M.D. and Ph.D. from Kiev University. He then served three years in the military before being recruited into the biological weapons program. After the program was shut down, he spent almost a year in North Korea before moving to the Middle East. We don't have a lot of information about the time he spent there, but we do know that he became rather wealthy, and he adopted some radical political views. The intelligence we have is a little sketchy, but it seems probable that he didn't acquire this sudden wealth by legitimate means. Eventually, he left the Middle East and made his way to Canada."

"Did the Canadian authorities have any idea who he was?"

"Not at first, but when his prior employment history came to the attention of the Royal Canadian Mounted Police, they invited him in for a chat. A copy of the transcript of that interview was forwarded to our office this morning. In a nutshell, Vosky confirmed there was a pilot program investigating a biological weapon which would control populations. He told the Canadians that the project had a number of start-up delays, but after two years, they had made progress. It was the interviewer's impression that Vosky was probably more knowledgeable than he was letting on."

With a pained stare, Kellar asked, "Just how high up on the food chain was Dr. Vosky?"

"We don't think he served in a supervisory role. He was probably an upper-level scientist on the project."

"What about his mental state?"

"We've asked ourselves the same question. Unfortunately, the interviewer didn't cover that area very well. So, the best we can say is that Vosky was mentally impaired. Where he might fall on the spectrum from mild depression to frank schizophrenia is impossible to say."

"What about the research itself? Did Vosky reveal any of the specifics?" the president asked.

"He disclosed that the program focused on several areas," Milton answered as he set his fork down. "One of the main areas was targeting pregnant women. Their theory was that only a relatively small percentage of the population needed to be affected because such an outbreak would cause a major societal disruption."

Kellar slid his glasses down and looked over the rims. "I suggest we contact the Mounted Police and ask them to get Comrade Vosky back in for another chat."

"That may be a little difficult. They've already made some preliminary inquiries. It seems Mr. Vosky went missing about six months ago."

"How hard has anybody looked for him?" the president asked.

"Not very, but until today there wasn't really a reason to."

"I certainly hope all that's about to change."

"The director of the RCMP asked me to assure you personally that locating Vosky is now on their short list of highest priorities."

"I'd like to see a copy of the original transcript, Colonel."

"It will be on your desk by nine A.M., sir."

The server cleared the salad plates and began serving the main course. Renatta didn't even have to look. Having had many dinners with the president, she was quite familiar with the aroma of pine nut pesto, his favorite sauce.

"I'm not a scientist, Colonel, but wouldn't thirty years give somebody or some group ample time to bring almost any biological weapon to fruition?"

"It seems like a long time but when you consider the necessary brain power and resources . . . well, I still think it's unlikely."

The president smiled knowingly. "One of the first things I learned after winning the election was to be mindful of the word *unlikely*. My predecessor, a man of uncommon wisdom, told me the road to presidential hell is bricked with similar words. A better way to look at all things is that they're all fifty-fifty. Either they'll happen or they won't. As a result of our meeting tonight, I'm far from convinced GNS is a mere act of God."

"Yes, sir."

The president reached for his fork. "As soon as you're notified Vosky has been found, I'd like to know about it."

For the next hour, both the president and Dr. Brickell asked Milton a number of tough questions regarding the possibility that GNS was an act of bioterrorism. He was informative, but measured in his responses. After coffee and dessert, Kellar thanked Brickell and Milton and ended the meeting.

"May I offer you a ride back to Washington?" he asked her. Brickell had made the trip to the War College by car with two of her aides. She would have preferred to ride back with them, but for reasons far too numerous to count, turning down the president of the United States' offer to accompany him back to Washington was definitely not an option.

20

Jack was accustomed to boring medical dinners. When the crème brûlée and hazelnut coffee were finally served, the conversation shifted from informal and innocuous to a discussion of Southeastern State's enigmatic group of GNS patients.

Jack was asked several general questions, which he answered with a mixture of caution and guarded optimism. The participation was excellent, so when Sinclair didn't utter a single word, it left Jack wondering at first. But as he gave it more thought, he understood. Sinclair believed he had the solution to GNS. To contribute to a conversation held by a group of bumbling, less-enlightened physicians than he would be intellectually beneath him. Jack had little doubt that when Sinclair felt the time was right, he wouldn't hesitate to move center stage and announce he had discovered the cause of GNS and how to cure it.

After another thirty minutes had passed, most of the guests had left. A few, including Sinclair and Madison, remained.

"We've scheduled you to host our noon conference tomorrow," Helen informed Jack. "The residents have prepared a couple of cases to present to you. I should warn you, they're pretty tough ones."

"I'll look forward to it."

She took a sip of her red wine and added, "Under the circumstances, I thought it might be better if we didn't discuss the GNS cases at the conference. We've already had a problem with some members of the press sneaking into the hospital. There will be a large number of people there and I'm not sure our security department has the resources to monitor everybody entering the auditorium."

At that moment, Madison approached with an ominous look on her face.

"Excuse me for interrupting but I've just had a call regarding a new patient with GNS."

"We should check with the ICU to make sure we have a bed available," Helen suggested. Sinclair, who was seated a few feet away, turned in his chair but said nothing.

"Actually, she's in the children's hospital emergency room. She was transferred down from Cocoa Beach about two hours ago."

"How old is she?" Helen asked.

"She'll be fourteen next month," Madison answered, hoisting her purse on her shoulder. "I'm going over there."

"Any doubt about the diagnosis?" Helen asked.

"It doesn't sound like it. She has all the symptoms."

"I guess I should go as well," Sinclair grumbled without coming to his feet.

In addition to the two vodka martinis he'd seen Sinclair drink before dinner, Jack had also noted he had consumed several glasses of wine with his meal. He scanned the faces of those around him. It was obvious the only person amongst them who felt Sinclair was in any shape to see a patient was the acting chief of neurology himself.

Madison stepped forward. "There's no reason for both of us to go, Hollis. I'll make sure everything's taken care of. I'll fill you in first thing in the morning and give you a thorough briefing."

Sinclair shook his head and smiled sardonically. "Why do any of us need to see her tonight? Is there some pressing reason she needs to be seen urgently? The children's hospital has an intensive care unit and neurologists on staff."

"She's a child," Madison replied. "I'd feel more comfortable if I examined her tonight."

"Seems ludicrous. There are a couple of thousand other pregnant women in the country just as sick. The problem's that teenage pregnancy is rampant in this country. If her parents had done their job, she wouldn't be in a hospital."

After a few moments of silence Jack asked, "Would you mind if I tagged along?"

"I don't think that's such a good idea," Sinclair was quick to say.

"That's very kind of you to offer," Helen said, ignoring

Sinclair's objection. She looked over at Madison. "I assume that's okay with you."

"Of course," she answered the dean's rhetorical question without hesitation.

"She'll be the youngest patient we've cared for," Helen said.

"Actually, I suspect she's the youngest patient in the country."

Helen removed her purse from the back of her chair. "I'll walk you two to the lobby," she said, pointing in the direction of the door. Jack anticipated Helen would offer a third-party apology for Sinclair's remarks but she said nothing as she escorted him and Madison to the hotel exit. "If you had asked me a half-hour ago if it were possible for the mood of the country to be any worse, I would have said no. But if we are on the verge of discovering that GNS is capable of attacking children, there's no telling what the catastrophic consequences might be. For starters, we may see every school in the country closed." Her eyes dropped for a moment. "Please call me as soon as you've assessed this young lady's condition."

"We will," Madison assured her.

21

Five minutes after they'd boarded Marine One, Kellar and Brickell were airborne. They sat across from each other in wide leather chairs. They barely had time to review the events of the meeting when the helicopter settled on the south lawn of the White House. With the sound of its engine fading into the evening sky, they walked across the lawn.

"How fast do you think we'll see the death rate escalate?" he asked her.

"It's impossible to say, but in the continued absence of any real progress, I would expect it will be pretty rapid."

"My understanding is there haven't been any infant deaths as yet."

"That's correct, sir. All of the women we've lost underwent urgent C-sections and the babies were saved. They're obviously all very ill, but it's impossible to tell whether they have GNS or just severe prematurity."

The president shook his head slowly as he looked overhead at a full moon that had just emerged from behind a stack of clouds. For the first time since she'd met him, his face was painted with anguish.

"Have you been watching much TV of late?" he asked.

"Excuse me, sir?"

"It may not be what most people imagine their president does in his limited leisure time, but I enjoy watching a little TV at night. I especially like it this time of year because of all the holiday specials." Renatta smiled, wondering where one of the brightest and most insightful men she'd ever met was going with this. "Since the GNS outbreak, there hasn't been too much else on except the coverage. Most of it is understandably depressing. The tearful interviews with grieving friends and family members betray the terrified mood of the country. Millions of Americans, whether they have a loved one with GNS or not, are in mourning." Kellar's face went slack, and after a weighty sigh, he said, "Good night. Let's talk in the morning."

She watched as the slump-shouldered chief executive made his way across the lawn and past the Rose Garden. She suspected there were things Kellar had left unsaid because that was his style when facing difficult problems. But she knew the events of the meeting at the War College weighed heavily upon him. She was also sure they shared the same dreaded fear: If GNS was an act of biological terror, it could easily become the greatest medical catastrophe in modern history.

22

Although it had only been four years since the ribbon-cutting ceremony, the Stenson Family Children's Hospital had matured into an outstanding facility. An eight-story architectural triumph, the hospital incorporated multiple inspirational themes that successfully captured what modern children's hospitals strove to achieve. Its construction would not have been possible without the efforts of Southeastern State University's charitable foundation, which had raised ninety million dollars for the project. Although Madison served on many hospital committees, she was most proud of being asked to serve on the foundation's board of directors.

Avoiding the packed waiting room, Madison led Jack into the emergency room through the staff entrance. Having been there several times to consult on teenage high-risk pregnancies, she was familiar with the ER's layout. Jack, on the other hand, could barely remember the last time he'd been in a children's hospital. The voices of harried personnel barking orders while wailing children clutched at their parents was a stark reminder to Jack why he never gave serious thought to going into pediatrics.

Following Madison down a hallway crowded with equipment and staff, he glanced back and forth into the examination rooms. Not a single one was empty, and the patients spanned the gamut from infancy to adolescence. Approaching the nursing station, they walked past a six-bed pod specially designed for the treatment of asthma. Even from the hall, his eyes fixed on the anxious face of a father cradling his squirming daughter. He struggled to hold a plastic mask that spewed a medicated aerosol over her mouth and nose.

Just as they reached the central station, Linda Haise, a veteran nurse with a skeletal frame and a pair of tortoise-shell reading glasses that teetered on the tip of her nose, emerged from the trauma treatment area.

"Hi, Dr. Shaw. I heard they called you to come to see Isabella Rosas."

Madison nodded. "How's she doing?"

"Not great. Her vital signs have been all over the place and she's pretty out of it. When the paramedics first brought her in we thought she had suffered an unwitnessed head injury, but when we saw the dancing eye syndrome . . . well, it didn't take too long to figure out she was the first case of pediatric GNS."

"Is Dr. Effratus still in there?"

"Yeah," she said, brushing a few obstinate strands of

auburn hair from her forehead. "When I left the room a few minutes ago, he was still scratching his head. Sam's been in there with her for a while," she said. A nurse's aide walked up and handed Linda a printout of lab results. "I gotta go. I have a two-year-old who decided to eat his toy soldiers and their cannons for dinner. I think it's affecting his digestion."

"That sounds terrible," Madison said.

"There are a lot worse things. I'm sure if we wait a day or so the entire army and their artillery will come out in the wash."

Madison and Jack made their way down to Isabella's room. When they were a few feet away, they noticed a sign on the door indicating isolation precautions. They each slipped on latex gloves, a yellow paper gown and a mask.

Dr. Samuel Effratus was hunched over the bed listening to Isabella's heart. He was a placid man who maintained an optimistic outlook on most things and who waged a never-ending war to keep his weight down. If asked, he'd be the first to admit he'd lost the last few battles. His usual engaging smile absent from his face, he glanced up at Madison and shook his head.

"Sam, this is Jack Wyatt," Madison said. "He's a visiting professor of neurology from Ohio State."

"Nice to meet you," he said, strolling over to shake his hand.

"How's she doing?" Madison asked, glancing up at the cardiac monitor.

"I'd say fair at best. Her blood pressure and pulse are

finally okay. She's still conscious but she's not responding to verbal commands. She has muscle twitching in both legs and dancing eye syndrome."

"Doesn't sound like there's much doubt about the diagnosis. Are her parents here?"

"Unfortunately her father's been MIA for the past five years and mom's been in and out of rehab so many times the court awarded permanent custody to the grandmother. She brought her in. She seems very concerned. She needed a break so I sent her out to the waiting room."

"Have you done a CT scan of her head yet?" Jack inquired.

"It was normal," Effratus answered. He then turned to Madison and added, "I spoke with a pediatric neurologist and went over the case with him in detail. Because you guys have all the experience dealing with GNS, he suggested we transfer Isabella to the main hospital. He slung his stethoscope around his neck. "What do you think?"

"I think it's a good idea," Madison said. "When were you planning on sending her over?"

"I wanted to get your approval first. I'll give our transport team a call. They'll have her over there within the hour."

Madison walked up to the head of the bed. She reached under the covers and gently palpated Isabella's tummy. She looked over at Marc. "Pretty normal abdomen. What did her ultrasound show?"

After a brief silence, Marc said, "We didn't do one."

"Why not? What are you waiting for?" she asked with an impatient huff.

"Her physical examination shows no signs of her being pregnant. We sent off both urine and blood. They both came back normal, so we repeated them and they both came back normal again." With a furrowed brow, he turned away and covered his mouth for a few seconds. Finally, he said, "There's no way she's pregnant."

Madison took a step back from the bed.

"The only factor these patients have in common is that they're all pregnant. It's the only damn clue we have . . . or should I say, had." She gazed overhead with disbelief fixed on her face. "Now what the hell do we do?" She exhaled sharply and, then, in a more controlled voice said, "Thanks for everything you've done, Sam. We'll check on her as soon as she gets over to Southeastern State."

Jack could well appreciate Madison's mounting frustration. He'd been in the same situation many times himself, chasing an elusive diagnosis. The problem was that Madison was right. In a clinical investigation already fraught with one dead end after another, losing the one glimmer of hope that could lead to a major breakthrough was hardly a trivial setback. They retraced their steps out of the emergency room. This time Jack was lost in thought and oblivious to the commotion around him. They stepped outside and continued in silence toward the parking lot. They waited for a minute while an ambulance with its red and green lights flashing backed into one of the four bays.

"This may not be as bad as it looks," Jack said, trying not to dampen her resolve any more than it already had been.

"For God's sake, Jack. The only clue we had just evaporated in front of our eyes. From where I sit, we're back to square one. How much worse could this be?"

"It's just a matter of expanding the possibilities. Even though Isabella's not pregnant, there still has to be one or more factors she shares with the other GNS patients."

"Your optimism is commendable, but if you look at things objectively, you don't have to be a Jedi Master to see we're screwed. You'll have to excuse me for not breaking into a victory dance over the events of the evening."

Madison picked up her pace, leaving Jack a few steps behind. He sensed any further pep talks would be as useful as shouting at the rain. He reached the car a few seconds after she did, climbed in and sat in silence.

23

They both remained silent on the drive back to Jack's hotel. By the time Madison dropped him off, he was exhausted. Unfortunately, with his divorce had come a nagging case of insomnia. Even though he was half-dead on his feet, he suspected a restful night's sleep was not in his future.

He was making his way across the lobby when he noticed a squat man with his shirttail draped across his lumpy paunch coming directly toward him. Instinctively he averted his eyes, but it was to no avail. Without breaking stride, the man walked up to him.

"Excuse me, Dr. Wyatt. I know it's kind of late, and I really hate to bother you like this, but I was hoping for a minute of your time to talk with you."

Jack slowed down, taking note of the man's mismatched, shaggy eyebrows and sagging jowls.

"I'm sorry. Have we met?"

"We've never been formally introduced. My name's Kazminski," he said with the corners of his mouth creasing into a cordial smile.

"I'm sorry, but it's kind of late and I—"

"Somebody told me you grew up down here. Maybe you remember me. I've been a reporter with the *West Palm Beach News* for nearly thirty years."

Jack didn't recall the name, and having attended more than one hospital-sponsored seminar regarding the media and medical privacy, he was instantly leery. It didn't take a Rhodes scholar to figure out why Kazminski had ambushed him.

"I'm not trying to be rude, Mr. Kazminski, but if you don't mind I'd really—"

"Most people call me Kaz, but my real first name's Arnold. I guess my mother was in a bad mood the day she named me," he explained, hiking up his pants with a quick tug on his cracked black leather belt. "Thank God my father had the brains to nickname me Bud two days before I started kindergarten."

"As I said, Mr. Kazminski, it's been a long day and . . ."

"To tell you the truth, Doc, I've had the same kind of rotten day myself. I'll tell you what. If you don't mind, I'll just walk you to the elevators." Jack looked toward the far side of the lobby. It seemed hopeless trying to dissuade the pushy reporter, so he decided a controlled dash was his best hope of escape. Jack nodded and started for the elevators. "I was told by a pretty reliable source that you're here to consult on the GNS cases."

Not having been the victim of a fool's mate since the

first day of his junior high's chess club, he said, "No comment, Mr. Kazminski."

"I checked you out, Doc. You're an expert in diagnosing tricky neurologic cases. You run the neurology department at Ohio State and you travel all over the place lecturing on the topic." Jack looked at him askance. Kazminski held up his hand and smiled. "I know what you're thinking. How do I know who you are? Well, I guess after nearly three decades in the newspaper business, you make a lot of friends in all kinds of places—including hospitals." They stopped in front of the elevators. Jack wasted no time giving the Up button three quick taps. "Do you have any idea what's causing GNS?"

"Look, I'm the last person who'd want to disappoint your readers but I don't think this is the right time or place to—"

Kazminski stepped between the elevator door and Jack. His face suddenly filled with grief. He looked past Jack with a distant stare. "I'm not asking for my readers, Dr. Wyatt," he began in a cracked voice. "I'm asking for my daughter. She was admitted to Southeastern State a few days ago with GNS." He cupped his mouth with his hand. "Five minutes of your time, Doc. That's all I'm asking."

24

The elevator door rumbled open. Instead of moving forward, Jack glanced overhead. A few seconds passed and the doors closed. He looked at Kazminski and pointed to an empty couch a few feet away.

"Sherry's six months pregnant," Kazminski began. "My son-in-law, David, works for the State Department. He's on his way back from the Far East right now—a little frantic to say the least." Kazminski waited while a woman in environmental services picked up an empty coffee cup from a nearby end table. "He told me the news of the epidemic has already reached every major city in Asia."

"Apart from this illness, has she always been healthy?" Jack asked.

"She's never had anything more serious than a cold. She's a social worker assigned to young teenagers in trouble with the law. She's never missed a day of work because of illness."

"How familiar are you with the symptoms that led up to her hospitalization?"

"I'm a reporter, Dr. Wyatt. I'm a walking sponge when it comes to accumulating facts. I'll answer anything I can."

For the next twenty minutes, Jack gathered every drop of information Kazminski could recall regarding his daughter's illness. Her symptoms were identical to all the other women with GNS. Kazminski's claim that he was a fountain of information wasn't an exaggeration.

With his eyebrows gathered in, Jack said, "I'm sorry. I wish there was something I could say to reassure you but I'm afraid, at least from right now, there just isn't a lot of information. We're just starting into this thing. The best minds in the country are all working together trying to find a cure."

Staring down at his hands, he said, "Two years ago, my wife noticed a little mole on her arm. We saw our family doctor who arranged for a dermatologist to remove it. He told us it was a melanoma but he was certain she was cured. Eight months later she was gone." He raised his eyes. And then with a blank gaze, he added in just above a whisper, "I'm not sure I can go through losing another . . ." He pulled a business card from the inside pocket of his sports coat and wrote his cell phone number on the back. "My daughter's one of those rare people who everybody loves. She's never done a self-serving thing in her life." He rolled his lips back and forth a couple of times. "Until a few days ago, I never questioned the absence of justice. I just thought it was the way things were."

Lost for words, Jack said, "I'll have a look at her tomorrow."

"I'd appreciate that, and thanks for listening." Kazminski handed him the card and shook his hand. "I'd wish you a merry Christmas, Doc, but I don't think too many people are feeling that way."

Jack waited a few seconds for Kazminski to walk away. He then looked down at his watch. It was close to midnight. He rode the elevator up to the ninth floor and went to his room. Needing a few minutes to gather his thoughts, he walked out on the balcony and looked south along the Intracoastal Waterway.

Beneath the splash of the hotel's floodlights, he followed a sleek catamaran slip under a towered drawbridge. He thought about Tess Ryan and Sherry Kazminski. Then he thought about all the women who were lying in intensive care units across the country. None of them was really just a case of GNS: Each was a victim, a victim whose desperate family members were consumed with terror about what the future held for their loved one.

25

Jack opened his eyes and shook the sleep from his head. He was just about to throw back the covers and climb out of bed when his phone rang.

"Dr. Wyatt, it's Marc. I'm sorry to call you so early but I'm in the ICU with Dr. Fuller." From the foreboding tone of Marc's voice, Jack was certain he wasn't calling to tell him Tess and the other patients were showing signs of recovery.

"What's going on?"

"Tess had a major seizure. She's been completely unresponsive to any form of stimuli ever since. Dr. Fuller called the neurologist on call for a stat consult. She agreed that Tess meets coma criteria." Marc paused for a moment before adding, "I think things may be going south faster than we anticipated."

Thumbing his eyebrow, Jack said nothing at first. He wasn't stunned by the news. He suspected things would get worse before they got better, but he was hoping it wouldn't be this soon. It was obvious the slower GNS progressed, the better the chances were of finding a cure. "How is the baby doing?"

"I'm just about to begin a complete evaluation. Madison's on her way in."

"Has anybody spoken to Mike yet?"

"No. Dr. Fuller thought you might want to be the one to make the call."

"Do you know if he's in the hospital?" Jack asked, looking down at his watch.

"I haven't seen him as yet. He usually comes in at around eight."

"I'll call him after I've had a chance to look at Tess. I should be there within the hour."

Jack showered and got dressed as quickly as he was able. Forty minutes after receiving the phone call from Marc, he was at Tess's bedside. She still had the splotchy red rash, but it was now weeping a thick orange-black colored fluid from the edges. All spontaneous movement was gone. Her face was absent any animation and a gray crescent arc of puffy tissue had developed beneath her eyes.

Jack barely noticed when one of the nurses approached.

"Dr. Wyatt, Mr. Ryan just called. He said he'd meet you in the lobby in ten minutes."

"Thank you."

Dreading his impending conversation with Mike, Jack sat down on the far side of the room to gather his thoughts. There was no question in his mind that Dr. Fuller was right: Tess was in a profound coma. With the death toll rising every day, Jack had no idea how long Tess could hold on. He had too much respect for Mike to try to conceal the truth from him. Feeling his options melting faster than a baby's birthday candle, Jack started for the exit.

26

"It's a nice morning," Mike said, motioning in the direction of the exit. "How about taking a walk? There's a park on the other side of the hospital. It seems like I'm spending more and more time there."

"Sure," Jack answered.

They left the hospital and followed a brick-paved path that took them around to the west side of the campus. Similar to Mike, many other family members had discovered the small green space, using it as a respite from the stress and fatigue of the hospital. They sat down on one of a dozen steel benches.

Their conversation began with Jack providing Mike with a detailed update on Tess's condition.

"So, you'd agree with the other doctors that she's worse," Mike stated flatly.

"Yes."

"I'm getting the feeling you're struggling to find some way to tell me Tess isn't going to make it."

"I know I keep saying the same thing, but I need more time."

"And you still have absolutely no idea what might be causing the illness."

"Not yet."

Mike's manner and tone reflected a growing sense of both doom and contrition.

"I got a call from Dr. Sinclair. He told me he thinks he's within a few days of proving what's causing GNS and how to cure it. He wants to set up a meeting with me as soon as possible to discuss his treatment plan."

"What else did he say?"

"That he believed GNS was a viral disease that was very treatable. He also mentioned that most of the doctors in the country had their heads up their collective asses regarding GNS, and unless they opened their eyes, they had no hope of finding a cure." Mike waited for a young couple to walk past before going on. "He didn't say it in so many words, but I got the feeling he was counting you amongst those unenlightened physicians."

Considering the source, Jack wasn't bothered by the comment.

"Over the years I've been called everything from uninspired to intellectually reckless. I guess I've developed a pretty thick skin."

"Do you think he's right about GNS being a viral disease?" Mike asked.

"My gut feeling is no, but I can't prove he's wrong."

"So you're saying you don't know?"

"That's right," Jack answered in a quiet voice. "I'm saying I don't know."

"On the phone you said you had something to tell me."

"It wasn't anything specific. I have some understanding of what you're going through and I just wanted to make sure you didn't make any rash decisions. I don't foresee any choices that have to be made on an urgent basis. We should have time to calmly discuss any treatment plans that . . . that are proposed."

"Since Sinclair's the only one proposing any, I assume you're referring to him."

"His plan would be included in what I'm talking about."

"Don't worry. That's why you're here. If you think putting Sinclair off for a few days is the way to go, that's what we'll do." Mike lifted his eyes, staring off at nothing for a few seconds. "I'd rather not talk about this anymore," he said, coming to his feet. "Do you mind if we head back to the hospital?"

As they started back toward the hospital, Mike's silence spoke volumes. Jack knew he was doing everything he could to disguise his dismay and fear. Going all the way back to their childhood, one of the first things Jack had learned about Mike was that timing was everything. Now was not the time to try and allay his concerns or look for a silver lining. Jack knew if he tried, it would only make matters worse.

27

The noon conference at Southeastern State Hospital was the medical school's most important teaching conference. It was always well attended by a host of specialists who took turns presenting topics of medical interest to the entire staff. The conference took place in the hospital's newly constructed auditorium, which boasted a thirty-foot ceiling, stadium-type seating and a state-of-the-art audiovisual system.

Jack arrived a few minutes before twelve and was escorted onstage by one of the senior neurology residents. Helen Morales stood up from a table she shared with several senior physicians and greeted him with a warm handshake.

"I hope you're ready. I saw the cases the residents have chosen to present to you. They're pretty tough."

"I'll do my best," he replied, knowing he'd been in the

same situation dozens of times. He was an adept speaker and had never had a problem thinking on his feet, especially in an impromptu venue.

The conference began on time with the chief resident in neurology presenting an unusual case of an elderly man with a sudden loss of his sense of smell. Jack led a discussion on the topic, which included commenting on the principle causes of the man's symptom. He then went over the possible causes of the illness until finally coming up with the correct diagnosis.

About halfway through the conference Hollis Sinclair ascended the stage and took the final seat at the table. Jack couldn't figure out if he was trying to make an entrance or he was simply being his usual ill-mannered self.

Jack had no problem figuring out the illnesses being presented to him. The final part of the conference allowed questions from the audience. When Jack had answered the last one, he stepped away from the lectern. Hollis Sinclair stood up and walked over. As Southeastern State's chief of neurology, Jack assumed he was about to thank him and close the conference. His assumption couldn't have been further from the truth.

28

After making a grand gesture to look at his watch, Sinclair said, "I see we still have ten minutes. As some of you may already know, Dr. Wyatt has kindly agreed to serve as a guest professor so that he might offer his expert opinion regarding our GNS patients."

Jack inhaled sharply and then shifted his eyes to Helen Morales. The solemn look on her face betrayed what she was thinking. She had made her feelings clear to him that there would be no discussion of GNS. He was sure she must have told Sinclair the same thing. Already having a sense for her astute political skills, Jack wasn't surprised when she didn't rise to put a stop to Sinclair's uninvited commentary.

"With this growing national epidemic," Sinclair continued, "I was hoping our distinguished guest from Ohio might offer us his insight into these very intriguing and challenging cases?"

As soon as Sinclair stepped aside, Jack returned to the lectern.

"Unfortunately, I find myself in the same position as my colleagues are across the country. I have no theory as to what's causing GNS. Hopefully, that will change in the days to come. I would mention, however, that Dr. Sinclair and his team have done an outstanding job in caring for these patients."

Sinclair moved toward the edge of the stage. He scanned the front row of seats.

"I see Dr. Lewis is with us today. I'm sure we'd all like to hear her opinion on a possible cause for GNS."

Carmella Lewis was Southeastern State's longstanding chief of infectious diseases. She had been involved since the first GNS patient had been admitted. She and her team had consulted on every case and were in constant communication with the CDC.

She stood up and waited for one of the audiovisual technicians to trot down the center aisle and hand her a microphone.

"We have done extensive diagnostic tests but to date we've not been able to identify either a bacterial or viral cause for GNS. Although we haven't entirely excluded the possibility, we have no evidence at this time that GNS is a contagious disease. I believe the CDC has reached a similar conclusion."

"Have you considered that this disease might be a new strain of parvovirus?" Sinclair asked.

It wasn't hard for Jack to understand the astonished look that instantly swept across Carmella's face. Sinclair cared for patients with neurologic problems. He had no training or expertise in the specialty of infectious diseases. His question was at the least inappropriate and at the most insulting. Jack's eyes shifted to Helen. From the perturbed look on her face, he assumed she shared his sentiments.

Ever the diplomat, Carmella responded, "We certainly considered a parvovirus infection but all of the blood tests were negative. We therefore dismissed the diagnosis. I believe the CDC followed a similar protocol and arrived at the same conclusion."

"I'm aware of those results, but based on the extraordinary nature of this illness, I contacted Carson McPherson." Jack was quite familiar with Dr. McPherson. He was a nationally renowned professor of infectious diseases with particular expertise in viruses. He had spent most of his career at Yale Medical School but was now at the National Institutes of Health in Washington. "Dr. McPherson and I had a lengthy discussion and we both feel that the symptoms of GNS are quite consistent with a new strain of parvovirus that's never been seen before."

The pained look on Carmella's face was understandable, considering she had just been thrown to the curb by a fellow physician. Basic professional courtesy would have dictated that Sinclair share his parvovirus infection theory with Carmella before publicly asking for her opinion.

"I haven't spoken with Dr. McPherson, so it would be difficult for me to comment on his thoughts. That being said, Dr. Sinclair, I will again state that based on these patients' natural immunity and the tests we conducted, we have ruled out a parvovirus infection as a possible cause of GNS. And if I'm not mistaken, the CDC has done the same thing."

Sinclair wasted no time returning to the lectern, where he took up the position as the self-appointed principle speaker.

"Thank you, Dr. Lewis. In response to your comments, I would like to point out that Dr. McPherson feels it's a strong possibility we may be dealing with a new strain of parvovirus that our current tests wouldn't detect."

Sinclair's comments were met with a flurry of raised hands. He recognized Kenton Biggs, the chief of internal medicine.

"Are you saying the CDC and most of our leading experts in the area of contagious diseases are wrong?"

"That's precisely what I'm saying. And the sooner we realize it, the sooner we can shift our focus in the right direction and begin helping these women and their unborn infants. There's credible data suggesting that certain drugs are quite effective in treating parvovirus."

Helen had already come to her feet and was quick-walking toward the center of the stage. Before Sinclair could make any further comments, she reached the lectern.

"It's already a few minutes past the hour, so I'm afraid we'll have to end the discussion here. I want to again thank Dr. Wyatt for agreeing to lead today's conference. This has certainly been one of the more lively discussions we've had in quite some time." She turned toward Jack and began to applaud. The audience followed. Sinclair wasted no time in descending the stage and falling in amongst the physicians who were quick to barrage him with questions.

"That was very well done," she told Jack, motioning to Madison to join them.

"Thank you," he responded, seeing no reason to offer any thoughts on Sinclair's inappropriate behavior.

"Maybe it would be a good idea for us to get together later today," Helen suggested. "Say about four in my office? I'm going to ask Dr. Sinclair to join us. I want to hear more about his parvovirus theory."

At that moment, Paul Boland, one of the senior radiation oncologists strolled up.

"That was an excellent presentation," he told Jack in a South African accent that hadn't faded a drop since he'd moved to the United States twenty-seven years earlier. Boland then turned his attention to Helen. "I wonder if I could have five minutes of your time. I'm afraid my department is in dire need of your help."

"Of course, Paul. We can talk in my office."

Helen turned to Jack and Madison. "I'll plan on seeing you two at four."

Jack was well aware Helen Morales hadn't reached the position in academic medicine she had without learning how to sidestep a few politically charged landmines. This was one of those situations. Jack suspected she was seething but her manner was controlled and diplomatic. He wondered if she would be as calm at their four o'clock meeting.

29

Malcolm Athens quick-walked through the West Wing of the White House. Clutched in his hand was a report he'd received five minutes earlier from the Royal Canadian Mounted Police. Athens had been a White House liaison to the CIA for the past four years. It was his principal responsibility to brief the president regarding matters of national security.

He walked past two Secret Service agents standing like pillars on either side of the entrance to the Situation Room, a five-thousand-square-foot chamber consisting principally of six flat-screen televisions and a large conference table. An eight-foot ornately decorated Christmas tree brightly lit with a ceiling-mounted floodlight stood in the near corner.

Casually dressed in a plaid shirt, President Kellar was

seated at the table. The only other person in the room was Zachary Carlton, his chief of staff.

"I just received this report from the RCMP," Athens began. "It seems our Canadian colleagues have been able to determine that Alik Vosky took a job with Bitrax Industries in Winnipeg a little over a year ago. They are a small pharmaceutical company."

The president frowned. "With his immigration history, how in the world did he get a job like that? I thought drug companies were more cautious in their hiring practices."

"I'm sure they are, unless somebody applies under a false name. Vosky's no amateur. The documents he used in support of his application were all excellent forgeries. He even had three phony letters of reference."

Kellar steepled his fingers. "In what capacity did this drug company hire him?"

"As a senior laboratory technician."

"In what area?"

Athens fidgeted in his chair. "He was assigned to the research and development department. He participated in several areas. One of them was developing new antibiotics for the treatment of serious obstetrical infections."

"Great," the president muttered. "Does anybody have an idea how all of this might tie into Mr. Vosky's disappearance?"

"There was an . . . an incident at the company. Vosky's computer skills were exceptional. The IT department at Bitrax discovered he had acquired certain sensitive files that contained information that went light-years beyond his pay grade. Their first thought was he was involved in an industrial espionage scheme, but before they could sort things out, Vosky must have realized they had nailed him. He never showed up for work again. The company pressed charges but it wasn't the type of case that was going to receive a lot of resources. As of today, Vosky's whereabouts are still unknown and the case remains open."

"Has anybody considered that perhaps it wasn't his intent to sell the information to a competing pharmaceutical company?" Turning his palms up, he continued. "Maybe he had more personal plans for the information."

"We agree with you, sir. The Canadian authorities have undertaken a major initiative to locate Vosky. I'll be receiving daily briefings from them."

"Perhaps you and I should have a similar arrangement," Kellar suggested with a manufactured half smile.

"Of course," Athens said. "I'm sure they'll locate him soon, Mr. President. They're putting their best agents on it."

The president pushed back in his chair and stood up. With a stiffened posture, he said, "Optimistic predictions are not what I need at the moment. What I want is for somebody to locate this son of a bitch. If the American people should even get an inkling that GNS might be an act of bioterrorism, it's going to touch off a national panic the likes of which this country's never seen before."

30

After the noon conference, Jack caught up with Madison and accompanied her to the auditorium exit. Most of the physicians had dispersed but a few remained in the expansive atrium talking in small groups.

"What do you think about Sinclair's parvovirus theory?" Madison asked.

"I'm a neurologist. What I know about parvovirus infections wouldn't fill a thimble."

"The most common one is called fifth disease and is seen mostly in children. It's generally a mild flu-like illness that's frequently accompanied by a very distinctive rash. It's called a slap-cheek rash because it's bright red and looks like the patient's been smacked. Most women already have natural immunity to the virus before they ever get pregnant. If not, there's a vaccine. The few who do get the illness usually have a pretty mild case, and there's only a very small chance they can pass it along to the baby."

"What happens if the virus does reach the baby?"

"They generally do okay," Madison explained. "But a few will develop serious heart and liver problems, and very occasionally, the disease is fatal."

"I'll ask you the same thing you asked me. Do you think there's any chance Sinclair's right about some new strain of parvovirus being the cause of GNS?"

"Hollis is an extremely well-read, talented doctor. But I don't know if he's truly convinced GNS's a viral infection or he's just showboating for the hospital board hoping to find a shortcut to the chief of neurology's office. He's made no secret that he sees himself as the only logical choice for the position."

"His personal agenda aside, sometimes a physician can have a vague hunch about a disease that turns out to be right on the money."

"I guess anything's possible," she said, "But I prefer to practice medicine by sticking to proven scientific facts. At the moment, this parvovirus theory has all the scientific basis of an Ouija board prediction."

"You said the rash was very distinctive. It almost sounds a little like the one Tess and the other women developed. Maybe that's why Sinclair's convinced GNS is a parvovirus infection." They exited the stairwell on the second floor and then made their way toward the ICU. They continued to talk about the cases, focusing on what further diagnostic steps could be taken that might lead to an answer. "I'm supposed to meet with Isabella's grandmother in a few minutes," Jack said, stealing a glance at his watch. "Do you think we should touch base before our meeting with Helen?"

She shrugged. "I don't but if you think it's necessary, I will—"

"No. I just thought it might be a good way to . . ."

"I have a lot to do, so unless there's anything pressing, I'll see you at the meeting."

He cleared his throat twice and said, "Absolutely, sounds good."

With slumped shoulders, Jack watched Madison disappear down the hall. He felt as if he were in eleventh grade and had just been turned down cold for a date. Although she'd been a little more civil to him since they spoke on the plane, it was apparent she had no intention of forgetting the past. After an inward sigh, he told himself that Madison's opinion of him had no bearing on anything. She had promised to work with him in a collegial and productive manner, and that was all that mattered. Jack started down the hall toward Isabella's room. He hadn't taken more than a few steps when he made a firm promise to himself to accept the way Madison Shaw felt about him, and give up the ghost trying to convince her he was a decent guy.

31

Hollis Sinclair strolled into the ICU family conference room for the urgent meeting his administrative assistant had set with Bud Kazminski and his son-in-law, David Rosenfelt.

The moment Sinclair entered the room, Kazminski and David rose from the couch. With a quick gesture, he invited them to retake their seats while he sat down in a plaid upholstered chair across from them.

"I assume I have your permission to speak freely in front of your father-in-law."

"Of course," David responded.

"As you know, I've been very much involved in your wife's care since she was admitted. For many reasons, it's my belief that her illness is being caused by a new strain of a powerful virus. My suspicion is that both mother and baby are infected with the virus." He paused for a moment and then with a hard stare added, "I feel certain if we don't begin treatment soon, this illness will ultimately prove to be fatal to both of them. I am, therefore, recommending to you that you consent to a test that will very likely lead to a diagnosis."

Kazminski stole a peek at David. The skin bunched around his eyes in a pained stare. From the time he and Sherry began dating it was clear that she was the alpha member of the relationship. David was a considerate and caring husband, but he was short on confidence, and predictably indecisive relating to matters of importance.

"Dr. Sinclair," Kazminski began, "before we agree, I think both David and I would like to hear something of the specifics of this test."

"I'm proposing that your daughter undergo a brain biopsy. I believe a microscopic analysis of her brain tissue will confirm conclusively that a virus is causing her illness. And, as I mentioned, such a confirmation will open the doors to beginning treatment for her and the baby."

Over the course of a very long career as an investigative reporter, Kazminski had interviewed all types of people. Anybody who knew him professionally would say he'd been around the block more times than the UPS truck and that he had developed an astute sixth sense about people. He combed the stubble under his chin with his finger for a few moments. David remained expressionless, his eyes frozen open.

"Dr. Sinclair, are you suggesting we perform brain surgery on my daughter?"

"Technically, yes."

"This whole thing sounds a bit risky to me," Kazminski said.

"I assure you, it's a very routine procedure performed by neurosurgeons across the country every day. It's done with a needle using a CT scan for guidance. It's called a stereotactic biopsy. I believe the benefits far outweigh the risks. And, as I've already mentioned, I'm convinced the biopsy will reveal the cause of Sherry's disease."

"Would she feel any pain?" David asked.

"Absolutely not."

Kazminski asked several more questions, most of which Sinclair answered in a manner somewhere between off-handed and overly confident. As he expected, David was unable to give his consent for the biopsy even when pressed by Sinclair.

Finally, when Kazminski sensed Sinclair's patience was going from thin to exhausted, he said, "I think my son-in-law and I need a little time to consider your recommendation. When do you need an answer by?"

"The sooner the better," he said, getting up from his chair. "I've already discussed the matter with the chief of neurosurgery, Dr. Constantine. He agrees fully with the need for a biopsy and is ready to do it as early as tomorrow."

"What if the biopsy doesn't provide the information you're looking for?" Kazminski inquired.

"I don't believe that will be the case, but even if it is, we'll be no worse off than we are now."

"Except that my daughter would have undergone an operation that did her no good."

"We are under considerable time constraints, gentlemen. Thousands of families from here to California are in a panic, demanding we find a cure for this disease. Your daughter's in the unique position to be instrumental in ending this horrible epidemic."

Kazminski massaged the knots that continued to tighten in his neck muscles. "May I ask you one last question, Doctor?"

Sinclair nodded.

"Why Sherry? There are thousands of young women in the country with GNS. Why her?"

"I can't speak to what physicians in other parts of the country are doing. I practice medicine here at Southeastern State. I believe we're way ahead of the curve when it comes to finding a cure. From my perspective, Sherry's one of our stronger patients. I believe she would tolerate the procedure well. But you are correct, there are other women who are potential candidates for the biopsy."

"How many other families have you already asked?"

"I'm afraid that's a private medical matter."

"Of course, excuse me for asking," Kazminski said, not believing Sinclair for a minute.

Sinclair started for the door but after a few steps he turned and looked squarely at David.

"I should also mention, when the biopsy does confirm GNS is a viral illness, there will be an enormous demand for the drug that will cure it. It's likely the supply will be woefully inadequate. If you do agree to the biopsy, Sherry would, of course, be amongst the first treated."

With his lips pressed together to help disguise his

disdain, Kazminski forced a polite nod in Sinclair's direction. "Thank you for taking the time to meet with us." An empty stare covered his face. He felt he had acquired a sense for the man. And, it wasn't a flattering one. He didn't question his ability as a physician. He did, however, wonder if his personal agenda trumped the well-being of his patients. Kazminski had no proof but he was suspicious Dr. Hollis Sinclair viewed the care of his daughter, Sherry, as a bridge to personal gain.

32

Jack arrived for the meeting with Helen Morales a few minutes early. He barely had enough time to leaf through an outdated hospital administration journal when Helen's assistant stepped out from behind her desk and escorted him into the her office. Helen, who was seated behind an ornate antique desk, stood up and met him in the center of the room.

She shook his hand. "Thank you for coming."

She then gestured to the other side of the office and led him over to a richly carpeted adjoining area that contained a racetrack-shaped conference table and an oak bookcase. A curved bay window provided a spectacular view of the coastline.

Jack had just taken a seat when the door again opened. Madison and Sinclair entered the office together.

"I hope I'm not late," she said, sitting down directly across from Jack.

Taking the chair next to Helen, Sinclair said nothing.

"You're right on time," Helen assured her. "I wanted the four of us to get together, so we might discuss Hollis's parvovirus theory. I was a little taken back when you announced your possible discovery at the noon conference. I wasn't aware we were seeking any outside opinions."

"You mean apart from Dr. Wyatt's?" he responded with a note of sarcasm in his voice. "We are in the middle of a national emergency. As a department chief, I naturally assumed I had both the authority and academic freedom to discuss these cases with any colleague whom I felt might help shed some light on finding a cure."

"Of course you do, Hollis. I just would have preferred to have been briefed on your conversation with Dr. McPherson before the conference." With arched eyebrows, she added, "I suspect Carmella Lewis and her colleagues in the infectious diseases department share my sentiments."

"With all due respect, Dean Morales, either we have a transparent system regarding academic freedom or we don't, and if—"

She raised her hand in restraint. "I think academic freedom at Southeastern State University, while interesting, is a conversation for another time. At the moment, we have important matters to discuss and limited time to do so, so perhaps we should move on."

Jack had to push his lips together to avoid grinning.

Helen had just done a nifty job of dealing with a difficult faculty member. Perhaps Sinclair hadn't learned it as yet, but diplomacy was an essential part of being an effective department head.

Helen reached for a white legal pad and slid it in front of her. Uncapping her silver fountain pen, she said, "I'm very intrigued by your theory, Hollis. I'd like to hear more of the details."

Drumming the glass tabletop, he said, "As I've mentioned in conference, I'm convinced GNS is being caused by a new strain of parvovirus."

"There are many strains of parvovirus, but to my knowledge, there's only one that infects humans, and that's the B-19 strain," Madison said.

"That's old information. Right now as we sit here, groundbreaking research is being conducted that will show new strains of parvovirus do exist, and that they can infect humans."

With a slight shake of her head, Madison said, "I'm pretty compulsive about keeping up with the most current scientific journals, and I haven't seen anything about that."

"It's cutting-edge work. It will be months before the results of this research appear in any of the medical journals. If doctors waited until every medical breakthrough appeared in a scientific journal, they'd all be twelve to eighteen months behind the most recent advances."

Helen said, "I'd like to hear more details about these studies."

Sinclair pressed his palms together. "Dr. McPherson

advised me there are several studies ongoing in Canada and Europe which have identified two new strains of parvovirus that infect humans. There's a group in Leuven, Belgium, who has taken the research one step further and is working on a plan to treat these new strains." Sinclair moved forward in his chair. "I called the principal investigator, Jacques Aaron. He firmly agrees with the group in Canada regarding the existence of these two new strains."

"Did you speak with the group in Canada?" Helen asked.

"Of course. They believe these strains are treatable with Vitracide, which is an FDA-approved antiviral drug."

"They think? I'm quite familiar with Vitracide," Madison was quick to point out. "It's recommended only for severe viral infections."

With a smug grin, he responded, "I think GNS would fall into that category."

"Are you aware that Vitracide can be extremely toxic to the heart muscle of both mother and baby?"

"Of course I'm aware. I feel quite well versed regarding all aspects of the drug."

"In that case, I'm sure you know that this toxicity has been scientifically documented and is not based on guesswork or half-completed research."

With a face now filled with boredom and annoyance, he said, "All drugs have side effects, Madison. What's your point?"

"Do I really need to answer that?"

"Let's stay calm," Helen suggested. "I'd like to go off in another direction, Hollis. Can you offer an explanation why, with one exception, GNS appears to affect only pregnant women?"

"Viruses flourish in different environments. Obviously, there's something unique about pregnancy that makes these women vulnerable. Maybe the virus was already present in a dormant state and became activated for some unknown reason—a situation similar to shingles perhaps." He exhaled sharply and added, "We're embarking upon new ground here. We can't be held hostage by conventional, uninspired thinking. Without going into great detail at this time, I will tell you that I expect to have irrefutable proof that GNS is being caused by a parvovirus in a matter of days. The moment I do, I'll make a national plea that every woman stricken with this catastrophic illness be urgently treated with Vitracide." Sinclair made a grand gesture to look at his watch and then started to stand up. "I'm sorry but you'll have to excuse me. I have another commitment. I think we should all bear in mind that the more time we spend on unproductive meetings, the more time we take away from helping our patients. Left untreated, I assure you GNS will make SARS and H1N1 flu look like a mild case of the sniffles."

Without waiting for a response, he turned and left the room. Jack's gaze shifted to Madison. Her eyes were flinty from anger.

Helen was the first to speak. "I already know how

you feel, Madison. Jack, you're a nationally recognized expert on uncommon neurologic diseases. Do you think GNS is being caused by a virus?"

"I'm not an infectious diseases expert, but from what I've been able to gather to this point, I'd say it's unlikely."

"I know you've only been here a short time and that you didn't want to say anything speculative at the conference today, but do you have even an inkling of what might be causing GNS?"

"I'm sorry, I don't."

They spoke for a few more minutes. When they were finished, Helen escorted Jack and Madison back to her outer office. Helen's silence did little to conceal her frustration. Jack sensed she was disappointed he hadn't a clue what was causing GNS.

Walking back to the ICU, he wondered if Helen Morales was developing second thoughts about inviting him to Southeastern State.

33

Hollis Sinclair strolled through Southeastern State Hospital's main lobby. A choir of students from a local high school stood behind a white baby grand piano filling the lobby with melodious Christmas carols. He walked over to the Family Welcome Center and randomly reached for one of the many brochures describing the hospital's special programs. He opened the pamphlet but instead of reading about Southeastern's advanced program of knee and hip replacement surgery, he peered above it to the area in front of the hospital. As he expected, the sea of reporters that had been congregating outside all day was still there.

Replacing the brochure, he buttoned his freshly pressed white coat, straightened his tie and, finally, made sure his identification badge was in clear sight. Because of the unrelenting presence of the media, the administration had advised all physicians to use alternative hospital exits to avoid an ambush—an advisory that Hollis Sinclair fully intended to ignore.

He gave a final tug on the lapels of his coat and then made his way out of the hospital into an early dusk. Having participated in two of the regularly scheduled hospital press briefings, he was immediately recognized by the reporters. They scampered forward en masse, gathering around him like frenetic autograph seekers at a rock concert. Above the clamoring of their questions, he held up his hand.

"I'm sorry. I would prefer not to answer any questions at this time."

"Can you just tell us if you're still involved in the care of these women?"

"GNS is a neurologic disease. I'm the chief of neurology. Naturally, I'm involved."

The same reporter again made his voice heard above the others. "Can you share with us your impression of the overall condition of the victims of GNS?"

"As I just mentioned, I'd prefer not to make any specific comments at this time."

A second reporter, waving his notebook in the air, asked in a booming voice, "Are the doctors any closer to discovering the cause of GNS?"

"Without going into detail, the answer to your question is yes."

A television anchorwoman from one of the local channels had managed to weave her way to the front and was now flanking Sinclair.

"Does that mean you're also getting closer to finding a treatment?"

"I'll make one comment because I think it's important the American people understand that there's a small group of forward-thinking doctors who are convinced GNS is a curable disease. Even as we speak, I am planning on a bold diagnostic test that will answer a great many questions about this dreaded disease and lead to a treatment plan." Sinclair's prediction prompted an immediate cacophony of fever-pitched voices. He started forward and again raised his hand. "I'm sorry. That's all I can say at this time. If you will excuse me, I have important patient-related matters to attend to."

Sinclair made his way slowly through the reporters, who, for obvious reasons, were not deterred by his insistence he would make no further comments. But Sinclair had already accomplished what he had set out to do. He picked up his pace and ignored all the questions being posed to him.

By the time he reached the main medical office building, the reporters had retreated. With a satisfied grin, he looked back at the group and then continued on his way toward the doctors' parking lot. His less than impromptu meeting with the press went exactly as he'd planned. He knew there would be a price to pay, and it would come in the form of an urgent summons to Dr. Helen Morales's throne room—but he didn't care. In matters with such profound life-and-death consequences, the ends always justified the means.

34

DECEMBER TWELFTH

NUMBER OF CASES: 2,654
NUMBER OF DEATHS: 13

Jack's first stop when he arrived at the hospital was Tess's room. He took over a half an hour examining her and reviewing her medical record. His conclusion was that there was no improvement in her neurologic condition. He was also concerned her ability to breathe on her own was deteriorating.

When he had finished his evaluation, he called Mike to give him an update. He was honest but chose his words carefully to avoid eroding the small amount of hope his friend was still clinging to. After arranging to meet him for lunch, he started down the hall to visit Isabella Rosas. Even though she wasn't pregnant, her medical condition continued to worsen, making her no different from the other women with GNS.

"Her grandmother's in the waiting room," Peter McLeod, the ICU nurse caring for Isabella, said. "She's been here for the past ten hours. She's pretty anxious to speak with you. Would you like me to get her now or do you need a little time?"

"Now's fine," Jack answered.

Peter left the room. For a time, Jack studied the monitors. The flashing colors of the various displays were hypnotic, and he soon found himself lost in thought. One of his favorite mantras regarding the art of diagnosis came to mind: *Focus, simplify and execute.* Each failure along the way was no different than a false start in a hundred-meter dash. The only way to deal with it was to reset yourself in the blocks, wait for the crack of the starter's gun and explode out of the gate again. He smiled when he thought about the corny poster on the wall of his college dormitory room that advised, *It's not how you fall that's important. It's how you get up.*

The sound of Peter clearing his throat snapped Jack back to the moment. Standing just inside the door was an elderly, square-chinned woman with wiry gray hair and a slight droop at the corner of her mouth.

"Dr. Wyatt. This is Audrey Phillips; Isabella's grandmother."

Jack moved toward her and shook her hand, the back

of which was crisscrossed with a nest of tortuous veins. Her skin was craggy and furrowed from years of working in the sun caring for and training horses.

"It's nice to meet you," he told her. "I'm one of the neurologists looking in on Isabella."

"I know who you are, Doctor. You were brought in from Ohio to help with the GNS cases. How's my granddaughter doing today?"

"The best I can tell you is that she's stable and no worse."

"That doesn't sound very encouraging," Audrey said, reaching into her purse. She fished around for a few seconds and then pulled out a pair of plain black glasses with smudged lenses. She put them on and said, "To me, Isabella seems worse every day. Do you have any idea when we might start to see some improvement?"

"That's very difficult to say."

"I was hoping she might be home in time for our big spring horse show."

"Ms. Phillips," Jack began slowly, suspecting Audrey was either in denial or simply didn't comprehend how sick her granddaughter was. "I'm sure you understand that Isabella's very ill. It would be impossible for me to offer an opinion as to when she might be going home." Jack waited a few moments for her to gather herself before going on, "I know you've spoken to a great number of doctors, but I was hoping you might be willing to answer just a few more questions."

With a tense face and a downward gaze, she nodded in agreement. "Of course, Dr. Wyatt."

"Do you remember how Isabella first got sick?"

"She plays on her junior high school softball team. A few weeks ago they were getting ready for a Christmas tournament and she told me her stomach was hurting."

"Where exactly?"

Isabella pointed to her own abdomen. "Down low, on the right side. I spoke to our family doctor about it. He said it was a woman thing and not to worry about it."

"What about her mental function. Did you notice anything different?"

"Maybe she was a little forgetful. I do remember the day before she was admitted, she said something about being dizzy."

Jack continued posing questions on a wide range of topics. To his dismay, there was nothing new or helpful in Audrey's answers. It was remarkable how similar her responses were to those of the other family members when asked about their loved ones with GNS.

His frustration was mounting rapidly. "I'm going to ask you to forget about the idea of an illness for the moment. Was there anything . . . anything at all over the last several weeks or even months regarding your grand-daughter's health that was . . . out of the ordinary?"

A pensive expression came to her face. It remained there for a few seconds before the corners of her mouth lifted into a tender smile.

"There was one thing . . . but I'm not sure it matters. I hadn't thought of it until now. It was a little personal and I think Isabella was embarrassed about it." Jack got the sense Audrey knew what she wanted to say but was searching for the right words. "Her breasts were getting bigger way too fast."

Jack sighed silently. "I guess at her age it's not too unusual for—"

"I raised two girls that now have kids of their own, Dr. Wyatt. Neither of them matured that quickly. It was almost like she really was pregnant. You asked if . . . well, I just thought it was a little unusual." Peter moved forward and held a box of tissues out to her. In just above a whisper and with despair mirrored in her face, she added, "Isabella's only fourteen . . . and she's not pregnant, so there's something different about her than all of the other women. Surely, you must have some idea what might be wrong with her."

"We have some theories but we don't have a specific diagnosis as yet." Seeing her pained stare, he took her hands in his and added, "I promise you nobody's going to give up until we figure this thing out."

Audrey didn't say anything. Jack released her hands and she walked to the head of Isabella's bed. With the tear-soaked tissue clenched in her fist, she reached down and gently stroked her granddaughter's hair as a sob escaped her lips.

35

Port-Menier, Anticosti Island

Located in the province of Quebec, Anticosti Island was home to 150,000 deer, a population that well outnumbered the 280 permanent residents. Called the graveyard of the Saint Lawrence, the treacherous gulf had claimed the lives of thousands of mariners over the years.

Alik Vosky sat on the end of his bed, staring at the blank screen of the television sitting atop his chest of drawers. He was pigeon-chested, and his stubby hands ended in fingernails that were buttery in color from years of smoking filterless cigarettes down to the last few millimeters. His father, an inconsequential bureaucrat whom Vosky had never come to love or admire, was completely bald. It was a fate he had managed to escape, having thick black hair that he wore combed hard against his craggy forehead hoping to conceal a nest of cross-hatching wrinkles.

The master bedroom of the small guesthouse he'd rented on the island bore little resemblance to its spartan appearance the day he'd moved in. In less than a week, he had covered all four walls with bulletin boards of various sizes and shapes. Each was cluttered to capacity with dozens of multicolored papers and documents. The papers were a hodgepodge of handwritten and printed documents ranging in size from small Post-it notes to legal pad pages. Between the bulletin boards, Vosky had thumbtacked dozens more randomly overlapping papers to the walls. The floor, covered with a dreary olive carpet stained dark from age, had become a veritable obstacle course due to the numerous stacks of textbooks and scientific journals littering the space.

Ever since he was a child, Vosky had a strong belief in God. But in spite of his prayers, the exquisite pain he would occasionally suffer had now become a daily occurrence. Beginning as a dull ache across his entire forehead, it would quickly reach a fever pitch and then settle in as a relentless ring of pain around each eye. He massaged the bridge of his nose, but he did so more as a reflex than a remedy. His gaze shifted to his night table. An unopened pill bottle sat next to his lamp. He had placed it there the same day he'd picked it up from the pharmacy. For years he took them religiously, but now the bottle served only as a reminder of his prior life and how the medication had reined in the creative processes of his mind. It was on that same day he vowed never to push another one past his lips.

As he often did to distract himself from the endless throbbing, his thoughts drifted to his former life in Russia . . . a life he yearned to return to. But the large sum of ill-gotten money he had fled with made returning to his homeland impractical. He stood up and walked over to the small desk and sat down behind his computer. He brought up his project's main file, which was a detailed timeline of events. To date he had achieved every milestone precisely on schedule.

Earlier in the day, he had decided to spend the evening going back over all the key calculations he had made. As his mentor at Kiev University had advised him, a great scientist steps out from amongst the trees every so often to study the forest. Vosky realized it was an observation that was uninspired and hackneyed, but he overlooked it because of his tremendous admiration for his professor.

What Vosky had created from nothing, what his colleagues in Russia had told him was impossible, he had accomplished and now had taken on a life of its own. He picked up the remote control to his television and turned on his library of video recordings. Although he had already watched it countless times, he brought up the story from the United States that featured Dr. Hollis Sinclair's impromptu news conference. He watched the video twice before turning off the television.

In addition to being an insightful physician and

researcher, Dr. Hollis Sinclair possessed charisma. Other doctors working on GNS in the U.S. would look to him for guidance and leadership. That was something Vosky knew he couldn't allow. As proud as he was of what he'd accomplished on his own, he wasn't naïve enough to think he could achieve ultimate success without some obstacles and setbacks along the way. What he needed to do with respect to Dr. Sinclair first entered his mind as nothing more than an intriguing idea; now, it was a moral absolute.

He got up, walked past the iron-framed double bed and stopped in front of a night table. Opening the drawer, he pushed a few envelopes and magazines aside and removed three passports. Each had cost him a small fortune, and each was an expert forgery. With a confident grin, he selected one. He then walked back to his computer and brought up his preferred travel website.

36

Jack walked slowly around the hospital gift shop, browsing for another Christmas present for his daughter. Being apart from her, especially during the holidays, was becoming increasingly difficult. He had even contacted the American Hospital in Paris to see if a consulting position could be arranged for a few months, but the amount of bureaucratic hurdles to leap over made the prospect near impossible.

After a few more minutes of perusing the store's inventory, he decided on a rainbow unicorn stuffed toy. He was just about to sign the credit card receipt when he noticed Madison walk into the store.

"How did your meeting with Isabella's grandmother go?"

"No revelations," he answered, handing the pen back

to the volunteer. "She did mention Isabella was having some lower abdominal and pelvic pain for the past few weeks. She spoke to her family physician about it, but he wasn't concerned."

"Did he order an ultrasound or a CT scan?"

"No. He didn't think any tests were necessary." Jack grinned.

"What?" she asked.

"It was nothing. I asked her if she had noticed anything at all out of the ordinary and she told me Isabella had been experiencing very rapid breast development of late." He added, "I assured her that wasn't what was making Isabella sick."

Staring steadily at Jack, Madison eased the container of coffee away from her lips.

"You're sure about the pelvic pain?" she asked.

"Yeah."

"And the rapid breast development?"

"Of course I'm sure. I may be getting a little senile, but I still remember how to take a medical history." A little taken back, he asked. "What's going on?"

Madison handed her coffee cup to Jack, grabbed her cell phone and dialed Marc.

While she waited for him to answer, she paced back and forth.

"C'mon, Marc, pick up your damn phone." Finally, on the sixth ring, he answered. "Marc, find an ultrasound machine right now and meet me in Isabella's room. Don't ask me any questions. I'll explain everything when I see you." She drew a sharp breath, gestured toward the lobby and said, "C'mon, let's go."

"What's going on?"

With a smile that couldn't be contained, she answered, "Well, if I'm right, you may have just stumbled across our first real clue for finding out what's causing GNS."

37

One year ago, quite by chance, Dr. Mary Grandeson, director of toxicology services, stumbled upon the perfect hideaway. The small library in the old rehabilitation unit had, for all intents and purposes, been forgotten and abandoned. The furnishings were sparse, consisting of a black metal desk, two upholstered chairs and a saggy corduroy couch. In spite of the hint of must in the air, the small library was the perfect escape from the constant barrage of interruptions, and for Mary, the perfect place to work.

As all of the physicians who had been asked by the surgeon general to serve on the elite GNS task force had done, Mary had shelved all of her other projects in order to devote herself entirely to the current GNS crisis. After her presentation at the CDC in Atlanta, she had heard from many of the attendees who expressed their strong conviction that the cause and the cure for GNS might very possibly come from her work in nanotechnology.

One of the few people who was aware of Mary's hideout was her senior research associate, Wright Zarella. Prematurely bald with curled shoulders, Wright had earned his M.D. and had completed a pathology residency in Minneapolis. Because of his special interest in the threat of nanotoxins and e-waste products, he applied to and was accepted to Mary's department as a Ph.D. candidate.

Working on her laptop, she barely noticed when he strolled into the library.

"I think I've come across something that might interest you," he told her, pulling up a chair.

She barely looked up from her laptop. "I'm listening."

He slid a manila file across the desk. She picked it up and shook her head. "Just how many of those awful sweater vests do you own?"

"I don't know," he answered looking down at the sweater. "About a dozen I guess. You never said anything before."

"That's because they're terrible," she said with a quick roll of the eyes as she opened the file. "Toxicity of cosmetic skin care products? C'mon, Wright, we've been over this ground so many times it's trampled beyond recognition."

"Well, there may be one small patch we missed. Keep

reading." She looked at him with a measure of skepticism as she waited for him to continue. "A few years ago, when certain skin care product manufacturers began using nanoparticles, concern was raised that these particles could theoretically penetrate the skin and be toxic to the user."

"I'm familiar with the theory. As you may recall, I'm the one who taught it to you. But the key word is *theoretical*, and as far as I know, nobody's ever been able to prove it."

"That's true, but all of those studies were done on normal skin."

"What other kind is there?"

"Well, being pregnant changes the hormonal balance in the body. Maybe that includes the skin," he said with arched eyebrows. He pointed to the file in front of her. "Last month an article appeared in an obscure European medical journal. The research group is from Magdeburg, Germany. They studied skin penetration of nanoparticles, but with a slightly different slant. Instead of normal skin, they studied it in a number of different situations."

"Like what?"

"Well, amongst others—pregnancy. Their conclusion was that these particles easily penetrate the skin."

"Did they offer an explanation as to why?"

"Nothing definite. They can only speculate that the hormonal changes during pregnancy affect the normal skin barrier in some way that allowed these particles to pass through and get into the bloodstream."

Mary slid the article from the folder. "What type of nanoparticles did they use?"

"They chose three; all of which are commonly used in cosmetic skin creams."

Grandeson pushed her chair closer to the desk and then read every word of the article.

"This is a pretty small study group but it seems well done from a scientific standpoint." She tossed the article back on the desk. "Assuming the study is correct and some of these nanoparticles can penetrate the skin. Even if they do, there's still no evidence they cause any harm."

"But there's no evidence they don't."

Grandeson exhaled gradually, stood up and strolled over to the only window in the room.

"So, you're postulating that a nanoparticle that has never been proven to be harmful can penetrate the skin of pregnant women and cause GNS."

"I'm simply saying it's a possibility."

"Okay, let's follow your logic pattern for a moment. I have two questions. The nanoparticles used in this research have been around in cosmetic products for the last five years or so. If they're the cause of GNS, why has it taken this long for the first cases to appear?"

Wright remained silent for a few seconds and then with a wrinkled forehead asked, "What's your second question?"

"Why have all of these cases presented within days of each other?"

"I have no answer for that one either," he responded.

"Any idea of the type of cosmetic product we might be looking for?"

"Nope, but there are just so many new skin care lotions and other products hitting the market monthly. If we go back six months, it shouldn't be too difficult to come up with a list."

Mary leaned forward and replaced the article in the folder. "I don't suppose we already have information in the National Patient Registry regarding the cosmetic products our GNS patients were using."

"Unfortunately, none of the hospitals thought to include those questions in the basic family interview."

"Before we send the whole country into a frenzy with a theory that may be nothing more than a good bedtime story, let's reinterview the GNS families here in Alabama regarding skin care and other cosmetic products."

"You're talking about a few hundred patients, and time is something we don't have a lot of. We're going to need some help."

She sent an easy nod in his direction. "You're an industrious young man, Wright. I'm sure you'll be able to muster all the assistance you'll need."

With a dubious grin, he answered, "I'll put a questionnaire together for the families and run it past you before we get started."

"Sounds good. Our next meeting's in Atlanta in a few days. It would be nice if we had some preliminary information on this stuff to present."

"Shouldn't be a problem."

He jumped to his feet and headed for the door.

Grandeson closed the lid to her laptop. Her mind was doing backflips, wondering if there could be any possibility Wright was onto something. There were hundreds of brilliant minds in the country working tirelessly to solve the enigma that was GNS. All of them were feeling the mounting pressure from countless national and state medical organizations and elected officials to come up with an answer. You couldn't turn on the television or pick up a newspaper without being inundated with the latest GNS horror stories. Mary was no different than millions of other people in the country—the usual joy of the holiday season was conspicuously missing from her life.

Her eyes drifted to the far wall. She thought about her pregnant sister in Oklahoma she had been calling twice a day since the first case of GNS was reported. She was five months pregnant and, so far, perfectly healthy. Staring at a framed photograph of her sister and her on a ski vacation, she wondered if Wright could possibly be correct, which would mean the solution to GNS had been staring her in the face right from day one.

38

By the time Jack and Madison reached Isabella's room, Marc had already powered up the ultrasound machine and applied a generous layer of jelly to her lower abdomen.

"I'm all set," he said, selecting one of the probes that hung from the side of the machine. "It might help if I knew what I was I looking for."

"I want to see her ovaries," Madison said, looking over her shoulder at Jack. "What side did you say her pain was on?"

"Her right."

She looked back at Marc. "Start on the left."

"She's very thin. We should get a pretty good view," he said, using a practiced touch to tilt the probe in various directions and angles across her abdomen. "There," he said, gesturing at the screen. "There's the left ovary. Size and appearance seem fine. Looks like a normal ovary to me."

"I agree," Madison said. "Let's have a look at the uterus and then the right ovary."

Marc eased the probe toward the right. "The uterus appears normal."

To Jack's untrained eye, the blending of the gray, black and white shades and shadows looked more like a complex weather map than the female reproductive organs.

It took Marc only a few seconds to locate the right ovary. He was still making the final adjustments to sharpen the image when Madison jumped forward. "There it is," she said, pointing to the central portion of the screen. "It's not the biggest ovarian tumor I've ever seen, but it's real and it's right there."

Marc held the probe perfectly still. "I'd say it's about two centimeters."

"Three," she stated with certainty "Make sure you get some good pictures."

"Have I ever let you down before?" he responded with a broad smile.

Feeling invisible, Jack asked, "What are you guys talking about?"

"Isabella has a tumor on her ovary," Madison explained. "Some of these tumors produce large amounts of hormones, which are the exact same hormones that normal pregnant women produce. So, it would seem likely from a hormonal standpoint that there's no difference between Isabella and every woman in the country with GNS."

Marc's grin widened. "So, if we measure the hormone levels in Isabella's blood . . ."

"We might be able figure out exactly which one made her and the other women susceptible to GNS. Let's get a gynecologist down here right now. I want this tumor out as soon as possible."

"Anybody in particular or whoever's on call?" Marc asked, reaching for his phone.

"See if Schiller's available. If he doesn't answer, leave a message for him to call me on my cell."

Jack tapped his chin a few times, and then, with a note of caution in his voice, said, "I'd agree this is an important discovery, but I'm not sure it means we've hit the mother lode." Marc and Madison stopped what they were doing and then shifted their collective gaze to Jack. "Well, even if your hormone theory's correct, it just means that GNS is associated with a high level of some hormone. It doesn't mean it's the cause."

"I don't think you're getting this," Madison said. "If we remove this tumor and Isabella recovers, it will mean that the other women with GNS don't need Vitracide or any other dangerous drug Hollis Sinclair might suggest. They'll get better on their own once their hormone levels are back to normal."

"But that wouldn't happen until their pregnancies come to an end . . . in one way or another."

"Obviously," Madison said.

"But . . . for those women who haven't reached their twenty-sixth week . . . well, aren't those babies too small to survive?"

"I know where you're going with this, Jack. I don't think now's the best time for us to enter into a moral debate on the pros and cons of termination. Every physician in the country who's trying to cure this disease believes we're going to start seeing a lot more deaths in the days to come."

"I understand that, but don't you think we should at least think about the—"

"When we encounter the moral bridges, well . . . we'll just have to jump off them then. Right now all I care about is getting this tumor out of Isabella."

Jack took a steady look at Madison. It was clear to him she had nothing more to say regarding his concerns. It was at that moment that her cell phone rang.

"Hi, Jeff. Thanks for calling back. I was hoping you had a few minutes to come over to the ICU. I'm taking care of a pretty sick fourteen-year-old with GNS. We just discovered she has an ovarian tumor, which I'd like to have removed as soon as possible." A few seconds passed and she said, "That's great. No, I consider this urgent. I'll wait for you." She quickly tapped in another number. She covered the mouthpiece and looked over at Jack and Marc. "Schiller's on his way. I'm going to call Helen Morales and fill her in."

Jack wondered if in her excitement, Madison had overlooked one obvious reality: If removing Isabella's tumor didn't work, Hollis Sinclair's theory that Vitracide therapy, even with its dangerous side effects, was the only way to cure GNS would dramatically gain credibility.

39

Dr. Jeff Schiller turned sideways and used his hip to shove open the doors to operating room seven. It had been just over three hours since he had consulted on Isabella's case. Moving toward the center of the room, he waited for his scrub nurse, Beth, to drop a sterile towel on his freshly scrubbed arms and hands. A common sense thinker who rarely took no for an answer, Schiller seemed old school for a physician who was only five years out of his residency.

The second nurse in the room was already in the process of applying an iodine jelly to Isabella's abdomen. When she was finished, Schiller and his chief resident, Sam Erving, draped the surgical field with four sterile towels, followed by a large drape that covered Isabella's entire torso. Beth pushed her small metal table containing all of the sterile instruments closer to the surgical field. Just as

Schiller was about to call for the scalpel, the doors to the operating theater swung open.

He looked up. "Are you sure you don't want to scrub in?" he asked Madison. "We're just getting started."

"I'm fine just watching. I did enough gynecological surgery as a resident to last me a couple of lifetimes."

Schiller opened his outstretched hand and Beth handed him the scalpel. Normally, he would have allowed Sam to do the case with him assisting, but because of the special nature of the illness, he decided to do it himself.

"Let's go," he told all present, making a careful incision across Isabella's lower abdomen. After four years, Schiller and Sam had done hundreds of cases together. Each knew the other's moves as well as two seasoned trapeze performers would. The result was invariably an effortless operation that unfolded in perfect synchrony.

Madison moved to the head of the table. Standing next to the nurse anesthetist, perched on a metal stool, she had an excellent view of the procedure. Five minutes after the skin incision, Schiller opened the final layer of the abdominal wall giving them access to the organs of the abdominal cavity. After setting the exposure with a large retractor, he reached an exploring hand deep into Isabella's pelvis.

"Apart from the obvious tumor," he began, "the other ovary's normal. So is the uterus." Another minute passed. "I don't feel any enlarged lymph nodes and there's no fluid in the abdomen, which is a good sign." Schiller allowed a lungful of air to slip out. Finished with his exploration, he pulled his hand out of Isabella's abdomen and stepped back for a few seconds. "Okay, let's get this thing out of here."

The two worked for the next few minutes dividing all of the arteries, veins and attachments of the ovary. When everything had been divided, Schiller gently rocked the tumor out of the abdomen and placed it into a stainless steel bowl held over the operative field by the scrub tech.

"Send it for both frozen section and permanent per protocol," he said to her.

Schiller looked up over the anesthesia screen at Madison. "That should do it. We're going to close. Assuming this works, when do you think you'll see signs of recovery?"

His question made her stomach roll. "I don't have the first damn clue," she told him.

40

As soon as Southeastern's administrative team realized the GNS outbreak was a major threat to public health, they set up a command crisis center in their executive boardroom. The IT department moved quickly to fit the room with a dozen computer stations and a sophisticated teleconference system.

Jack was seated at one of the stations reviewing the latest patient information posted on the National GNS Data Record when his phone rang.

"I just got off the phone with Helen Morales," Madison said in a shaky voice. "She asked us to meet her at her office in half an hour."

"What's going on?" he asked, checking his watch.

"It seems Helen called the surgeon general to brief her on Isabella Rosas's surgery. Dr. Brickell then called the president to update him. He told her he wants to talk to us personally about her condition."

"When?"

"Tonight."

"We should probably take the call right here, that way we'll have all the information at our fingertips and we—"

"He wants to talk to us in person, Jack."

"I beg your pardon?"

"The president of the United States wants to have a face-to-face with us tonight."

"He's coming here?"

"No. At Homestead Air Reserve Base."

"Why Homestead?"

"Because he called us from Air Force One and that's where they'll be landing in just over an hour."

41

As Madison and Jack approached the black Denali that had been sent by the president's team to take them to Homestead, a young man in a dark suit and a Marine Corps haircut emerged from the car. Jack thought to himself he didn't look much older than most of his medical students.

"My name is Robert Carson. I'm a special assistant to President Kellar. He sends his greetings and asked me to thank you in advance for meeting with him on such short notice." He opened the door. "Dr. Morales is already in the car. On our way to Homestead, I'll be briefing you on the security measures and protocol for all Air Force One guests."

According to information Madison had received from Helen, the president had been in Louisiana all day touring the hospitals that were caring for GNS patients. His original itinerary called for him to return directly to Washington at the end of the day, but after his conversation with Dr. Renatta Brickell, he decided to make a stop in South Florida.

Once they arrived at Homestead, Carson escorted Madison, Jack and Helen to a cordoned-off security area where they answered a series of questions and went through a metal detector. A young woman carrying a tablet escorted them on board the four-thousand-square-foot aircraft. She introduced herself as Caitlin Nance.

"Dr. Brickell accompanied President Kellar on his trip to Louisiana and is already aboard. She'll be sitting in on your meeting with the president."

Caitlin showed Jack and Madison to their seats. She then escorted Helen back to sit with Dr. Brickell. Jack shifted in his seat, trying to settle in. The plush leather chair was anything but standard airline issue. His awe at his surroundings equaled his nervousness about meeting the president of the United States.

A few moments passed and Caitlin returned.

"We'll be departing in about fifteen minutes," she told them, scrolling down the tablet, reviewing the president's agenda. "President Kellar has a very busy schedule all the way to Andrews. You'll be meeting with him in about an hour. He fully understands the inconvenience this is causing you, and he has asked me to express how much he appreciates you meeting with him this evening. As soon as we land, you will be escorted to another plane that will take you back to West Palm Beach. If there's anything you need, please let me know."

After she walked away, Jack looked over at Madison with surprise on his face.

"I thought we were just meeting with the president on the plane," he said. "You didn't say anything about flying to Washington."

"I guess the president forgot to call me to go over the exact details of his plan," she responded in a sarcastic voice. "What's the difference, anyway? What would you have said if you did know? Oh, I'm sorry, Mr. President, I'd love to discuss a matter of grave national importance with you but I'm not in the mood to fly to Washington tonight?"

With his lips pressed together, Jack glared at her. "I'd answer that but you'd probably accuse me of being a disingenuous liar."

With a tolerant smile, Madison shook her head a few times.

"Okay, Jack. Ever since we discussed this whole UF mess, you've been dying to bring it up again. We have an hour to kill so I guess now's as good a time as any. So, why don't you just go for it?"

"What's the point? You've already made up your mind."

She shrugged. "Whatever you want, but don't say I didn't offer."

Sensing his golden opportunity evaporating, Jack said, "Do you remember Marietta Rhodes from the neurology department at UF?"

"I don't think so."

"She's the administrative coordinator. She's kind of the go-to person for all the students and residents on the neurology service. She was there when you and I were. She's the unofficial eyes and ears of the neurology department. Nothing happens without her knowing about it."

"And the reason this would be of interest to me is?"

"I called her yesterday. Students very rarely failed the neurology rotations, so she had quite a good recollection of what happened to you. I remembered that after I gave a student his or her final exam, I had to fill out a written evaluation but I never assigned a grade. All of the old reports have been scanned into the computer. I was hoping Marietta could locate the one I filled out on you."

"I assume you're now going to tell me that she was able by some miracle to find it, and it proved that you gave me a glowing evaluation."

"Actually, the report I filled out on you was missing from your file," Jack said. "Do you remember Dr. Gaitley?"

"Of course. He was the pompous jerk in charge of all student rotations. He personally summoned me to his throne room to inform me I had failed neurology and that I would have to repeat the rotation. He seemed to enjoy telling me. He had all the warmth and compassion of Jack the Ripper. The man was a complete and total jackass."

"Marietta told me that a year or so after you and I had left, he was fired. He was accused of committing a number of ethical violations including a host of academically dishonest acts. According to Marietta, his dismissal resulted in a scandal that was quite an embarrassment to the medical school." Jack paused, waiting for a response, but Madison looked at him plain-faced, clinging to her silence. Undaunted, he went on, "Evidently Gaitley was going through a really ugly divorce of his own at the same time you were."

"So?"

"You mentioned to me the other day you were married to David Casas, the neurosurgeon."

"I still don't understand what all this has to do with—"

"Gaitley was the one in charge of assigning the students' final grades. He decided who passed and who didn't. According to Marietta, Gaitley and your ex-husband had the same divorce lawyer and got pretty chummy."

With narrowed eyes, Madison said, "Are you proposing that there was some kind of a conspiracy against me?"

"I'm not proposing anything. I'm simply giving you some facts. But you don't have to be a genius to connect the dots here. The physician in charge of assigning grades is fired for academic dishonesty. He turns out to be buddy-buddy with your ex-husband and my evaluation of your examination mysteriously disappears from your file." Jack shrugged his shoulders. "This isn't exactly the unsolved enigma of the century."

"But why would my ex do that?" she asked.

"To get even," he said flatly, taking a couple of swigs from his bottle of water. After blotting the corners of his mouth with a napkin, he added, "I'll be happy to give you Marietta's number if you'd like to speak with her personally about it. I'm sure she'd be happy to talk to you."

"I'm sure that won't be necessary."

"You can think I'm an . . . what was it you called me again? Oh, yes—an asshole. It's not a big deal. I just thought you'd like to know what really happened."

After a giant stretch of his arms, he reached into the seat-back pocket, pulled out a magazine and began flipping through the pages as if nothing had happened. Madison stared down at her hands. More than pleased with the way the conversation had gone, Jack had to admit he couldn't have scripted things better. He realized it wasn't exactly the courthouse at Appomattox with the lady wearing gray and he in blue, but he did feel vindicated.

"You think I owe you an apology, don't you?" Madison asked.

"Not really. I'm sure if things were the other way around, I would have felt the same way."

"Sure, Jack," she said, with a skeptical grin.

Although he was gloating on the inside, and as much as he wanted to, he saw no gain in breaking into a fist-pounding victory dance. Instead, he said nothing. Air Force One's engines pitched louder. Jack looked out the window, watching as the massive jet began to creep forward.

42

Bedford, Indiana

Ever since Maggie Recino could remember, she hated being alone. For reasons she didn't understand, her phobia became worse when she learned she was pregnant. Making matters even more difficult, a week after she found out she was expecting, her husband, Eric, a lance corporal in the Marine Corps was deployed to the Middle East. That was seven months ago and Maggie still had no reliable information when he'd be returning. Not long after his departure, she moved in with her mother in the two-story duplex where she'd been raised.

After a day filled with what seemed to be one long nap after another, Maggie pushed herself out of her mother's lumpy recliner and strolled into the kitchen to get something to eat. Usually, they ate dinner together, but two days earlier her mother had left on a business trip. Maggie opened the refrigerator, scanned the shelves and then blew out a protracted breath. Hardly in the mood to create anything magical, she focused on yesterday's leftovers. Finally, she removed a large plate containing three slices of pizza, the remains of her dinner from the night before.

Her Chesapeake Bay retriever, Burty, ran over, sat by her feet and whined as if he hadn't been fed since Thanksgiving.

"C'mon, Boy. You ate your dinner. Let me eat mine."

Just as Maggie was setting the microwave, she suddenly became unsteady on her feet. She had had the same woozy feeling twice in the past couple of days but it was worse this time. Leaving the pizza on the counter, she took a few cautious steps over to the table and sat down. Burty followed her and put his head on her lap. She folded her arms on the table and then rested her forehead on them. A few minutes passed but her light-headedness became worse. Her dizziness grew in intensity, leaving her nauseous. With food now being the last thing on her mind, she managed to push herself to her feet and find her way back to the living room.

Unsteady and breathless from the short walk, she flopped down on a denim couch. In front of the couch, two jar candles sat atop a wooden coffee table. The pumpkin-scented candles had become her only relief from the daily nausea her obstetrician promised her would subside four months earlier. She shoved one of the throw pillows under her head and closed her eyes. Hoping that the dizziness would pass, she held her head steady. She checked the time. It was five minutes past seven.

At quarter past seven, she was still no better. Her trepidation mounting, she decided to call her mother. She searched the coffee table for her cell phone but it wasn't there. Overcome with fear, she plunged her hand between the pillows and then behind her, desperately searching for her phone. When she came up with nothing, she stopped, covered her head with her hands and flogged her memory. A few moments later, she remembered she had put the phone on the bookcase before going into the kitchen.

After steadying herself on the armrest for a few seconds, she gathered all of her strength and pushed herself to a sitting position. Looking up, Maggie could see her phone protruding over the edge of the shelf next to the television. She let out a long breath, stood up and then took the few steps over to the floor-to-ceiling bookcase. When she went to grab the phone, her coordination faltered and she knocked it to the back part of the shelf and beyond her grasp.

"Great," she muttered.

In spite of feeling wobbly, she struggled to extend her reach. Finally, her fingertips touched the edge of the phone, but she was still unable to grab it. She looked down. By standing on the lowest shelf, she hoped to gain the extra couple of inches she needed. Cautiously stepping up, she grabbed onto the television shelf with her left hand to stabilize herself. Just as she reached back to snatch the phone, she was consumed with an intense wave of vertigo.

The room spun like an out-of-control carousel. Pushing her face against the bookcase, she held on to the shelf with a death grip. Her equilibrium faltering, Maggie felt herself tipping backward. At the same moment the television skidded forward, grazing the side of her face before slamming to the tile floor below.

With the bookcase fully tipping and trailing her to the ground, Maggie somehow gathered the wherewithal to sharply twist her body to the side and push off. She cleared the path of the tumbling bookcase by a matter of inches. Her left shoulder struck the armrest of the couch at the same moment the bookcase smashed to the floor.

For the next few seconds all Maggie did was take one labored breath after another. She said a silent prayer that she was conscious. She also gave thanks that her sister had picked her son up earlier and was watching him for the evening. She opened her eyes but her vision was blurred and the normal sharp images of the living room were a latticework of melding grays and blacks. Burty had already jumped off the couch, barking incessantly while turning tight circles in front of her.

Bedford was a small town where neighbors knew each other well and embraced a common sense of responsibility for one another. Burty's nonstop barking had not gone unnoticed by the next-door neighbor, Tim Oneida. He knew Connie was out of town and that Maggie was alone in the house. Being a naturally overprotective father and husband, Tim walked over to Connie's house and rang the doorbell. When there was no response, he went to the other side of the porch and peered into the living room through a bay window.

Seeing the shambles of the room and Maggie motionless on the floor, he whirled around and grabbed a metal chair. Holding it by the back, he launched the legs through the window, instantly shattering the glass. It took him three more full power swipes before he could clear all the jagged fragments from the window frame and climb through the window. He was already dialing 911 when he arrived at Maggie's side.

43

For the first half of his twelve-hour shift, Dr. Lewis Cole had been working feverishly to care for the predictable onslaught of Saturday night patients. In addition to the usual variety of illnesses and injuries, he was spending a lot of time reassuring one pregnant woman after another suffering from a mild headache or a runny nose that she was not the latest victim of GNS.

The ER staff checked the surgeon general's advisories every eight hours. To date, not a single case of GNS had been reported in the entire state, which made Indiana one of only ten states where there was no documented outbreak. After sewing up a jagged laceration on a sixty-year-old man who was trying to figure out the nuances of his new power band saw, Cole strolled out of the treatment room. After a peek out into the waiting room, he made his way to the nursing station.

"The paramedics brought in Maggie Recino about fif-teen minutes ago," came a voice from behind him. "She's in room four."

Cole twisted in his chair and saw Patsy Ames, the nurse manager hovering over him like a Blackhawk heli-copter. A woman with no airs or graces, she was twenty years his senior. Every time she sensed Cole was becoming too consumed with himself, she reminded him that she'd been the one to read to him from *Charlie and the Choc-olate Factory* the day he broke his wrist on the playground and needed it casted.

"Connie's daughter?" he asked.

"Yeah. She fell backward off a wall unit."

Maggie had been born at Bedford Community. She had had her appendix out there when she was seven and had given birth to her son one floor up from where she was now lying. Her first and only job since graduating from Butler University was as the director of volunteer services at the hospital. Her mother, Connie, was a hospital admin-istrator in charge of business development.

"Is she okay? I thought only kids did that."

"The next-door neighbor found her and called 911. Her vital signs en route were normal but she's still a little out of it."

"Why didn't you come get me?"

"Because you were kind of tied up and we're experi-enced enough to triage a patient and decide if we need a physician stat or not."

He held up his hand in surrender. "Sorry."

"We sent her for a CT of her head just to be on the safe

side. She just got back to her room a couple of minutes ago. The radiologist already called and said it was fine—no bleeding and no skull fractures."

Cole pushed back in his chair and then stood up. "Isn't Maggie pregnant?"

"She's in her seventh month. Her tummy's fine and she's had no vaginal bleeding. We have her hooked up to a fetal monitor. Her blood work should be back in a few minutes."

"I don't care how smart they think they are. They still should have gotten me," he muttered to himself, as he turned and started down the hall toward Maggie's room.

"I'm sorry, Doctor. I didn't quite hear that."

"Nothing. It was nothing," he said, wondering why he again allowed himself to fall victim to Patsy's superhuman hearing. He made the short walk down the hall and went into Maggie's room.

"Hey, young lady. I heard you had a little fall at home. How are you feeling?"

"Probably more embarrassed than anything else."

"No cramps in your tummy or bleeding?"

"Nope."

"Do you remember what happened?" he inquired.

"Kind of."

"Tell me about it."

"I've been feeling a little dizzy lately. It got worse tonight and then my vision got blurry. I had bad migraines with my first pregnancy. I just assumed it was the same kind of thing but without the horrible pain."

"Is your vision still blurry?"

"A little."

Cole walked over and examined her head and neck. As usual, Patsy was right. There was no bruising or swelling. She had no pain to any area he palpated. He had seen hundreds of head injuries in his career ranging from the most minor to the most grave. Even when it was only a mild concussion, there should be some visible evidence of an injury to the head.

"Are you sure you didn't hit your head?" he asked.

"I'm positive."

"Tell me more about this dizziness you've been having,"

"It started on Saturday."

"Today's Saturday. Do you mean it began today or you've had it for the last week?"

"I guess it's been about three days, not a week."

"Patsy said you were alone when you fell."

"Uh-huh. My mother's on vacation and my son's with my sister tonight."

"I thought your mom was in Chicago attending the meeting on operating room safety."

"Uh . . . that's right. I forgot. I guess I thought she was on vacation."

Becoming increasingly more concerned with Maggie's confused responses to his questions, Cole stopped his exam and studied her face. In spite of the normal CT and absence of physical signs of a head injury, it was still possible she had a concussion, but he was unconvinced.

"Have you had any muscle cramping?"

"In my legs a little. I didn't have that when I was pregnant with Matt."

He removed his stethoscope. "How's your mom?" he asked again on purpose.

"She's fine. I should have called her to meet me here."

Taking note of her answer, Cole quickly shifted his exam to her eyes. They appeared normal. He then moved straight to his neurologic assessment. Before he tested her ankle and knee reflexes, he examined her thighs. It was barely perceptible but there was a fine tremor of the muscles. He swallowed against a tightening throat and took a step back. His fingers quivered from the bolus of adrenaline filling his bloodstream.

"How long have your legs been twitching like that?"

Her eyes were closed and she didn't respond. Cole renewed his question but she again failed to respond. He quickly checked her vital signs. According to the cardiac monitor, her blood pressure and pulse were normal. She was breathing without difficulty and the level of oxygen in her blood was fine.

His sense of urgency climbing, Cole walked over to the other side of the room and picked up the phone.

"Have one of the nurses come down and sit with Maggie," he told Patsy in a calm voice. "No, Patsy. Right now."

He walked back to the bed. A few seconds later one of the nurses hurried into the room.

"Keep an eye on her, please. I'll be right back."

Cole quietly closed the door behind him and made his way back to the control desk.

"What's going on?" Patsy asked.

Cole said nothing at first. Instead, he studied a bulletin board, which contained dozens of advisories, lab bulletins and memoranda. When he found the posting from Illinois Memorial in Chicago he was looking for, he removed it from the board and picked up the phone.

"I'm worried about Maggie," he said, dialing the number.

"What do you mean?"

He covered the receiver and then touched his index fingers to his lips.

"Illinois Memorial transport team. This is Chris speaking."

"Good evening. This is Dr. Cole. I'm calling from Bedford Community Hospital in Indiana. I'd like to arrange an emergency transfer. I believe the patient may have GNS." Patsy sat down next to him. Her stare was intense and her lips widely parted. "Yes, I'll hold."

"The nearest reported case of GNS is over a hundred miles from here," she said in just above a whisper.

"Up until now," he said, again cupping the mouthpiece with his palm. "Get on the phone and alert the other hospitals in the county that this may be the beginning of a local outbreak." He again raised a restraining hand to her. "Yes, this is Dr. Cole. Thank you for taking my call. I'm seeing a twenty-seven-year old in her seventh month whom I believe has early GNS. She has a several-day history of intermittent confusion. On physical examination, she has a fine tremor of her thigh muscles. She has no rash or fever." He paused for a few moments to take a breath and to listen to Dr. Gaylord Smithey's response. "Yes, I realize there have been no cases in Indiana, but I'd still like to transfer this young lady up to your facility as soon as possible. She's stable for transport." He nodded his head while he listened. "Thank you, Dr. Smithey. We'll expect the helicopter within the next hour or so."

Cole hung up the phone and came to his feet.

"Are you going to call Connie?"

"If you can track her down for me, I'll speak with her. I'll tell her to meet us in the emergency room in Chicago."

"Us?" Patsy asked with raised eyebrows.

"I'm going with her. The ER physician said I could accompany her. Once she's tucked in, I'll rent a car and drive back." Cole started back down the hall. "Would you give Dr. Almont a call and tell him I'll need him to cover the rest of my shift?"

"Sure, but this still doesn't make any sense. Emergency rooms are being flooded with cases. They're not seeing one isolated case here and there."

"I think Maggie has GNS," Cole insisted. "But I'm happy to let the folks in Chicago sort things out."

Maggie was awake when Cole walked back into her exam room. In spite of her confusion, he expected she'd understand everything he was about to tell her. He pulled up a chair and took her hand in his. Taking his time to explain his concerns to her, Cole emphasized that his desire to send her to Illinois Regional was only out of an abundance of caution. Cole couldn't be sure how much Maggie understood. In front of his eyes and in a matter of minutes, she was worsening. He could sense that she was struggling to keep her eyes open.

Lewis Cole was no different from any other physician. Making a difficult diagnosis always evoked a sense of pride and accomplishment. But tonight was an exception. Every optimistic cell in his body hoped he was dead wrong, and that he'd be getting a call from the doctors at Illinois Regional in the days to come that Maggie Recino was doing fine and that she didn't have GNS. But his pragmatic side, the one that had been engrained in him through medical school and residency, was telling him something entirely different.

44

At the president's request, the conference room aboard Air Force One was always kept at sixty-eight degrees. Set upon a plush alabaster carpet, eight beige leather arm-chairs were positioned with geometric precision around a rectangular conference table. One wall of the room contained a series of windows that were typical of any commercial airliner, while the opposite one was lined with a row of thick-cushioned window-bench-type seating. Holiday instrumentals played softly in the background. As he was being escorted to his seat, Jack detected the telltale aroma of a recently smoked cigar, an indulgence the president was well-known for.

Kellar, dressed in his personalized Air Force One crew jacket and khaki pants, warmly greeted each of them. Before formally beginning the meeting, he introduced Jack, Madison and Helen to the only other person in the room, Mitchell Kincaide, his principal advisor on health care issues.

Once they were all seated, Kellar glanced down over the top of his glasses at a few loose pages of paper in front of him.

"I want to begin by assuring each of you that you have your country's and my heartfelt thanks for your tireless efforts in trying to cure this disease." He paused briefly before going on. "I'd like to ask the surgeon general to bring me up to speed on the most recent developments."

"Of course, Mr. President," Brickell began. "We are treating patients in forty states. Ninety medical centers are participating. Our official case count won't be finalized until tomorrow at six a.m. but it's likely to exceed three thousand. To date, there have been no cases reported outside of the continental United States. It's the general impression of the physicians caring for these women that their conditions are gradually deteriorating. Fortunately, the mortality rate from the disease is still low but we have to assume it's going to climb."

"Thank you, Renatta," the president said, interlacing his fingers behind his neck.

"The specific reason I requested to meet with all of you this evening was to discuss the young lady at Southeastern State with GNS who isn't pregnant. Are we absolutely convinced she has GNS?"

"There's no doubt, sir," Helen answered.

"I understand she's already been operated on."

"The procedure took place a few hours ago. We removed a tumor from her ovary."

"How did she come through the surgery?"

"Very well."

"That's good to hear. What's the young lady's first name?"

"Isabella."

"I'm sure everyone appreciates that the care of this young lady raises some very difficult and . . . sensitive questions." Lifting his chin and cutting his eyes toward Helen, he asked, "Am I correct in assuming if Isabella should recover, it would be fairly strong evidence that termination of the pregnancy either by C-section, induction . . . or other means, would result in a cure of GNS?"

"That's what we believe, Mr. President," Madison said.

Glancing overhead, he asked, "Would we then recommend all women who are beyond their twenty-sixth week undergo a C-section or induction of labor?"

"That would seem to make the most sense," she said.

"What about those women who are less than twenty-six weeks pregnant?"

The president's eyes shifted to Jack, who had the presence of mind to gather his thoughts before responding to the booby-trapped question. He swallowed against a throat that had suddenly become as dry as a swath of burlap.

"If we prove termination cures GNS, and we can't find an alternative effective treatment for mother and baby, I expect it would become a viable option for consideration."

"A viable option for consideration," the president said with an easy grin. "You should have been a politician, Dr. Wyatt. Do you feel we are any closer to that alternative cure?"

"I'm sorry, sir. I don't."

"The reason I ask is that I saw Dr. Sinclair's impromptu press conference. He's certainly not shy in front of the cameras. I asked a member of the surgeon general's office to speak with him personally. He seems convinced GNS is a viral illness and there's an FDA-approved drug that can cure it." Kellar paused, looked around the table and asked, "Do any of you agree?"

Helen Morales answered, "Dr. Sinclair's an excellent physician and doesn't generally shoot from the hip. He's done extensive research and has presented some interesting evidence, which lends merit, but not proof, to his viral theory."

"What I'm asking is if any of you believe there's a significant chance his theory's correct and that . . . that this wonder drug will cure GNS?"

"It's possible," Madison said. "But what concerns all of us is that Vitracide is extremely toxic to both mother and fetus. I think we're all in agreement that we don't have nearly enough hard evidence to recommend its use."

Kellar shifted in his chair, directing his next question at Helen Morales. "Hard evidence," he repeated, seemingly in distant thought. "How many people at Southeastern State are aware of Isabella's . . . special situation?"

"That's difficult to say with certainty but there have been many people involved in her care."

"Have the details of her surgery been posted in the National GNS Data Record as yet?"

"We decided not to post any further details until we had something definite to report," Helen responded.

"I think that was a wise decision," he said, standing up and moving to the back of his chair. He faced the group. "I'm not breaching national security when I share with you that over the past two days I've met with several highly concerned religious groups and other organizations on both sides of the aisle of the abortion issue. I'm sure it comes as no surprise that there are those who vehemently oppose any governmental agency advocating termination under any circumstances." He paused for a moment, placing his hands on the chair. "And that would remain true even if there's convincing medical evidence it would result in a cure for the mother.

"As the president, I have grave concerns regarding the impact the details of Isabella's condition could have on the nation. Even if she should recover, I'm not sure it would be advisable to make sweeping medical recommendations based on her case alone. If we should advocate termination and it turns out there was an alternative way to cure the disease . . . well, the outcry will be heard around the world."

Kellar pressed his palms together and continued, "Let me assure all of you that from a political standpoint, Dr. Sinclair's treatment plan is far more appealing than anything I've heard here tonight. He has communicated to my staff that he believes if we don't begin therapy soon, we'll lose our window of opportunity and that it's quite likely we'll start seeing hundreds more deaths of both mothers and babies." Jack was hanging on every word Kellar was saying. He had a strong suspicion where he was leading them. "Therefore, until I authorize otherwise, I am directing that all medical information regarding this young woman's care remain sealed and strictly confidential." Speaking in a voice that could leave no doubts, he added, "I consider the details of her medical condition to be a matter of national security." He returned to his seat and looked out over the group. "I welcome your comments."

"With all due respect, Mr. President," Madison began with a measure of hesitancy in her voice. "I'm not sure as physicians we can guarantee—"

"Dr. Shaw," Kellar began, "as I'm sure you're aware, approximately six million women a year become pregnant in this country. About four million of those pregnancies result in a live birth. Even as we speak, thousands upon thousands of obstetricians' offices are being flooded with frantic calls from families wondering if they should terminate their first trimester pregnancies as a precaution." He pushed forward in his chair and placed his hands flat on the table. "I'm asking you not to discuss any of this information with anyone until we're absolutely convinced we can't cure this disease by some means other than termination."

Helen Morales said, "Let me assure you, sir, that the administration and medical staff at Southeastern State will do everything in their power to comply fully with your request."

"It's not my intent to place anybody in a difficult position but until we can get a better understanding of Dr. Sinclair's claims, I feel as if there's no other way. A cure for this dreaded disease without resorting to termination would be the preferred scenario by far."

For the next thirty minutes, the president asked Jack and Madison a number of pointed questions. Jack felt he was legitimately interested in the specifics of the GNS cases, but that he had already addressed the main reason he had requested the meeting.

The president was beyond cordial in thanking each of them for disrupting their busy schedules to speak with him. Jack and Madison returned to their seats. It was another fifteen minutes before either of them uttered a word.

45

Twenty minutes after they had arrived at Andrews, Jack and Madison were airborne on their way back to West Palm Beach. The much smaller military jet had few of the comforts of Air Force One but it didn't matter. Both of them were overwhelmed by their encounter with the president and hardly in the mood to discuss it any further.

Madison finished the last sip of her sparkling water and then asked, "How long ago was your divorce?"

"I don't recall mentioning I've ever been divorced." She looked at him as if he were trying to persuade her the world was flat. He shrugged and said, "Nine months ago."

"Any children?"

"I have a five-year-old daughter."

"What's her name?"

"Annis."

"Pretty. Do you see her often?"

"Four times."

"A week or a month?" she asked.

"Since the divorce. My ex-wife's French. She had an excellent attorney who persuaded the judge to allow her to move back to Paris. So, since our divorce, I've made two trips to France, and twice, Nicole's brought Annis to New York."

"Which one of you wanted the divorce?"

"I'd say we both did."

"That's crap. It's always one person who wants out more than the other. Let me guess. You were never home and when you were, you had your head glued to your computer screen writing a paper or another chapter for the latest textbook in neurology. Your wife was going through life alone, you were insensitive to her needs and you had long forgotten how to enjoy your marriage."

"That . . . and Nicole was sleeping with her boss."

Madison chuckled but quickly covered her mouth. "I'm sorry, I shouldn't laugh. It was just the way you said it. How did you find out?"

With a slight head shake, he asked, "Are you sure you want to hear this?"

"Pretty sure."

"We used to eat out a lot, but every Thursday we would stay home and order pizza. Well, I had just finished my third slice and was working on my second glass of Chianti when Nicole took my glass from me and set it down. I thought she was going to tell me how much she adored me but, instead, she used the tender moment to inform me she had never really loved me the way a married person should. Before I could get a rational explanation, she confessed she'd been horribly lonely for a long time and that she was in love with someone else." He spun the ice cubes in the bottom of his empty glass before going on. "She then told me the best thing for the both of us would be a divorce. The whole thing was very well prepared and took all of two minutes."

"You really had no clue how unhappy she was?"

"Nope. I guess she viewed being married to me as a little bit worse than residing in the seventh circle of Hell."

"Did you know him?"

"Her boss?"

"Yeah."

"No, and, not that it's important, but him was a her."

"Actually, that makes things a lot easier. You had what my laser club calls a no-brainer divorce."

"What's your laser club?"

"A group of my friends, mostly doctors, one of whom is a plastic surgeon, get together every couple of months for dinner at somebody's house. We spend the evening bitching, drinking margaritas and lasering off anything that might make us look older."

"And the no-brainer divorce?"

"Simple. Once you had the information about your wife, you had to get a divorce. You didn't have to waste six months beating yourself up wondering why your marriage failed or how you could have saved it."

"Why did you get divorced?" Jack asked.

With a bemused grin, she said, "I guess I finally figured out he just wasn't worth fighting for."

"Any kids?"

"Only him. Our breakup was one of the great legal olympiads in modern history. The worst part was that a couple of months into it, we talked seriously about reconciliation. By an incredible act of stupidity, I got pregnant. Two months later, I lost the baby. I always blamed it on the stress."

"What did you do?"

"After a few months of self-loathing, I went into a complete emotional free fall. I wound up taking some time off and getting a lot of help." She sighed and added, "It was a struggle but I finally put my life back together."

"I . . . I'm sorry. I wasn't really trying to . . ."

"No need to apologize, Jack. People recover. It was a long time ago and I'm fine now. It doesn't matter what happens to you or who's to blame. If you can't figure out how to get comfortable in your own skin . . . well, life winds up being intolerable."

Jack was surprised how candid Madison was being with him. It was the human side of her he hadn't seen a particle of until this moment. Nothing further was mentioned about either of their divorces. Instead, they covered a host of much less depressing topics. He enjoyed speaking with her and it made the rest of the flight seem like it only lasted a few minutes.

It was just after eleven when their driver pulled up to

the hospital. Instead of heading back to his hotel, Jack decided to stop by the ICU to check on Tess and Isabella. Finally seeming like a mere mortal, Madison told him she was too exhausted to join him and would meet him first thing in the morning in the ICU.

46

Because of the late hour, the number of reporters in front of the hospital had thinned out considerably. Entering the hospital through the main entrance didn't pose a problem. Jack was a few feet from the ICU when he saw Bud Kazminski coming toward him. Since Bud had first ambushed him in the lobby of his hotel, Jack had made it a point to speak with him at least once a day to update him on his daughter Sherry's condition.

"Evening, Doc," he said.

"How's she doing?"

"About the same. Walk with me," he said, pointing to a bank of vending machines in a small alcove at the end of the hall. "David and I met with Dr. Sinclair earlier. He recommended to us that Sherry undergo a brain biopsy. He said the results could very likely lead to a cure." They reached the machines. Jack said nothing while Kaz studied the selections. "How about something to eat? I'm buying."

"Nothing for me, thanks."

He slid a dollar bill into the machine, tapped two buttons and retrieved his honey-glazed peanuts. Before he opened the bag, he turned and asked, "This brain biopsy thing strikes me as a little extreme. What do you think?"

It was obvious to Jack why Sinclair was recommending a brain biopsy. If he were right about GNS being a viral illness, the biopsy might be the only way to definitively prove it. As much as Jack had come to dislike Sinclair on both a personal and professional level, the idea of a brain biopsy had actually crossed Jack's mind two days earlier. Politics and emotion aside, from a pure medical standpoint, a brain biopsy was a reasonable test to consider.

"It's a little hard for me to advise you on Dr. Sinclair's recommendation. We're dealing with a disease medical science has never seen before. A biopsy could conceivably lead to the diagnosis, but it could also show absolutely nothing. There's just no way of telling."

"What really worries me is the risk of anesthesia," Kazminski said.

"There's simply no way of knowing what the risks of surgery and anesthesia would be." Jack waited a few seconds and then added, "I guess I haven't been much help."

With a quick shake of his head and a glint of his acerbic smile, Kazminski said, "Actually, you've been a big help. I'm going to give David a call and recommend that he agree to the biopsy."

"When does Dr. Sinclair want to do it?"

"He told me if we agreed, the neurosurgeon could schedule it for tomorrow," he answered. "Listen, Doc. When we get the results of the biopsy, do you think we could talk again?"

"Of course."

"Thanks."

He popped a handful of the peanuts into his mouth, nodded at Jack and then started down the hall. His limp was worse. Jack couldn't quite figure out why, but there was something about Bud Kazminski he very much admired. Jack was convinced that in spite of his bumbling exterior, he was a man of substance, uncommon insight and one who obviously loved his daughter very much.

47

When Jack entered Tess's room, Marc was setting up the portable ultrasound machine. A wide-eyed, third-year medical student stood next to him studying his every move.

"How's she doing?" Jack asked.

Marc shook his head. "Not great. She's still in a deep coma and she spiked another temp about two hours ago."

"Still no idea what's causing it?"

"Not a clue. We've checked everything."

"What do you think?" Jack asked him.

"I'd say she's getting worse by the hour. I don't know how much longer she can go before she needs medications to keep her blood pressure up. And her breathing's becoming more rapid and shallow," he added. "Putting her on a respirator can't be too far away." Marc checked the settings and selected a probe. "Unfortunately, we're finding the same thing in almost all of the other patients."

"Did Tess have the MRI?" Jack asked, studying the monitors.

He nodded. "Earlier this evening. I called the radiologist who read it. He told me for the first time he's seeing subtle evidence of brain swelling."

A number of possibilities, none of them good, flashed into Jack's mind. Swelling was a sign the brain tissue was deteriorating. The disease was progressing even faster than he had anticipated. He assumed that whatever was happening to the patients at Southeastern was being played out in every hospital in the country. Jack had never been good at concealing his emotions. He assumed the look on his face betrayed his mounting desperation.

"What's next?" he asked Marc.

"Apart from keeping a careful eye on things, we have no specific plans. Hopefully the ultrasound will show the baby's still doing okay."

Having no new ideas or suggestions, he said, "I'll check in with you in the morning." Finding his way to a small consultation room, Jack sat down for a few minutes to gather his thoughts. Through the open door, he stared without purpose into the ICU. When he was as ready as he was going to be, he reached for the phone and dialed Mike's number. "Did I wake you?"

"No. I've been waiting for your call. I figured you'd check on Tess before going back to the hotel. What do you think about the fever?"

"Almost all of the GNS patients have a fever. I'm assuming it's just part of the whole picture."

"Do you think she's getting worse?"

Jack was anticipating the question. "I think she's a little worse . . . but still stable."

"Stable?" There was a lengthy pause, and then in a voice painted with despair he said, "I guess there are a lot of questions I could ask, but at the moment, I'm too afraid."

Understanding the immense weight of the emotional pain Mike was shouldering, Jack said, "I realize we haven't made much progress as yet, but I'm hopeful that will change in the next few days." As soon as the words were out of his mouth, Jack realized he sounded vaguely and unjustifiably optimistic.

"I spoke with Dr. Sinclair," Mike said. "He claims he's within days of finding the cure for GNS. He wants to meet with me as soon as possible to discuss his treatment plan. What do you think?"

"I would encourage you to talk with him, but I also think we should discuss any treatment proposals before you agree to proceed."

"Okay."

"You sound exhausted. Get some sleep. I'll see you over at the hospital in the morning."

Jack realized that Mike's growing sense of doom was probably no different than Bud Kazminski's or any of the other family member's across the country gravely worried about their loved one with GNS. Jack was consumed with concerns on every level, but at the moment, his greatest fear was that within a few days, Mike Ryan and thousands of others would find themselves faced with making the hardest choice of their lives.

48

NUMBER OF CASES: 3,125
NUMBER OF DEATHS: 19

Jack was hardly surprised when he received a call from
Helen Morales's assistant requesting his presence at a ten
o'clock meeting in her office. He checked his watch. He
still had time to go the ICU and check on Tess's condition before the meeting. After reviewing her record and
examining her, he concluded she was the same as when
he'd last seen her eight hours earlier.

At ten A.M., Jack, Madison and Sinclair were assembled in Helen's office.

"I wanted to get together so that Madison might update

us on Isabella's condition since surgery, and perhaps give us some more details about her theory."

"I'm all ears," Sinclair said. In spite of his obviously sarcastic comment, Madison spent the next few minutes briefing him on the tumor they had discovered in Isabella's ovary and every aspect of her care. She stressed the significance of the finding, especially with respect to a possible cure for GNS. When she was finished, he stared at her as if she were trying to sell him the tollbooth concession at the Golden Gate Bridge.

"Is . . . is that it?" he asked.

"I beg your pardon," Madison said.

"I asked if that was everything you wanted to tell me."

"Yes, Hollis. That's everything."

Jack was hardly surprised at Sinclair's rude response. From the moment he learned Helen wanted all of them to discuss Isabella, he was less than optimistic Sinclair would embrace Madison's theory.

"There are no secrets here," Sinclair said. "I've already heard about this case in detail. And as interesting as it may be from a medical oddity standpoint, I'm afraid it's equally irrelevant. Whatever the factors are that make these women susceptible to GNS are totally immaterial. I don't deny that an elevated inhibin level may be an associated finding of the disease, but it's not the cause."

"So, it's still your belief that GNS is a viral illness," Madison said.

"Why shouldn't it be? Nothing you've said here this morning gives me any reason to alter my opinion. Especially now that all of the patients have a fever. As sure as the sun will set this evening, these women are suffering from a new strain of parvovirus. If somebody has frostbite you treat the injury, not the blizzard that caused it. In order to eradicate GNS, you have to find and treat its cause, which is a virus, not an elevated hormone level." He stopped for a moment to blow out a tired breath. Then, in a controlled voice he stated, "It's inevitable we're going to see the death rate accelerate. If there's any hope of curing these mothers and babies, we have to begin a program of Vitracide therapy immediately." He stood up and pushed his hands deep into the pockets of his white coat. "You may have removed this girl's tumor, but you're not going to cure her."

"I guess that still remains to be determined," Madison said.

"Even if she does recover, that's still not hard evidence the pregnant women with GNS will also recover if their pregnancy is terminated. I think the vast majority of families will opt to treat the disease per my treatment plan and not disturb the pregnancy." Sinclair turned to Helen. "I have several pressing matters to attend to. If there's nothing further . . ."

The disappointment in Helen's eyes was unmistakable, but Jack said nothing. He realized attempting to discuss other possible causes of GNS besides a virus with Sinclair was a waste of time.

"I understand how busy you are, Hollis," Helen said. "I appreciate you finding the time to speak with me."

Sinclair stood up, shook his head a few times and then waltzed out of the room.

Jack had seen all forms of professional faux pas and rude behavior, but they all paled in comparison to the gross disrespect Sinclair had just shown Helen.

"Is there anything else we can do?" Madison asked her.

"I'm running out of wiggle room. It would certainly help if you and Jack could discover how to cure this damn thing before Hollis Sinclair checkmates me."

49

NUMBER OF CASES: 4,323
NUMBER OF DEATHS: 19

Madison and Jack hovered over Isabella's bed like two nervous medical students awaiting the results of their first anatomy exam. A few minutes earlier, Jack had checked on Tess. Her condition was still critical. He had spoken to Mike and they had agreed to meet for lunch. For good reason, Jack was expecting another difficult conversation.

"Has there been any improvement in her neurologic status?" Madison asked Dr. Josh Marcos, who had been at her bedside for the past eight hours. Sporting a three-day crop of bristly whiskers, Marcos's eyes were colored crimson from sleep deprivation.

"None," he answered. "In fact, she's probably a little worse."

"Maybe it's still too early to see any improvement," she suggested. She then looked at Jack, and in a voice struggling to cling to any shred of optimism, asked, "What do you think?"

"It's difficult to say. Neurologic injuries can have a slow recovery process. Even if the factor that's causing GNS has been completely removed with the tumor, it's still hard to know when we might see signs of improvement. We also have to consider that whatever neurologic damage has occurred . . . well, it might be permanent."

"So, what do we do from here?" she asked.

"Nothing, I'm afraid," Jack answered. "All we can do is support her vital functions, closely monitor her neurologic status and . . ."

Just at that moment the door opened. When Jack saw it was Sinclair, he did his best to force a cordial smile.

"How's your patient doing?" he inquired, making his way over to the bed.

"She's about the same." Madison answered.

"Really? I heard she's worse. I understand her inhibin level's zero. If my memory serves me correctly, you predicted we'd see signs of recovery by this time."

"It hasn't even been two days yet, Hollis. It's still too early to dismiss the possibility she'll recover."

Sinclair rolled his eyes, moved up to the bed and then

reached down and ever so slightly elevated Isabella's chin.

"I see she still has the rash. What about fever?"

"She's still has a fever," Madison answered.

"Boy, it looks like you got that tumor out just in the nick of time," Hollis said, with a sardonic smirk as he shook his head and started toward the door.

50

After his visit to the ICU, Hollis Sinclair was convinced the chances of Isabella Rosas's recovering from GNS were a pipe dream at best. He bounded up the three flights of stairs to the office of Dr. Liam Kenney in the department of pathology.

Kenney, a specialist in neurologic pathology, was a pallid man with bony fingers and sharp angular shoulders. Sinclair found him hunched over his microscope, humming a Broadway tune.

"Good morning, Liam."

Kenney lifted his head from the microscope's eyepiece, sat straight up and then reached up to his balding head, where his glasses were perched, and slid them down.

"Kind of early for a neurologist, isn't it?" he asked Sinclair.

"I'm here every morning at seven. How's the family?"

"Everybody's fine."

"Good. By the way, I understand you're coming up in front of the tenure committee again at our next meeting."

"That's right."

"Well, I've always found you to be a highly competent pathologist. You should have been granted tenure the first time around. You've built your reputation on being a team player. I don't have to tell you how political these things can get, but I'm sure with the right people in your corner, there shouldn't be a problem this time."

"Thank you, Hollis," he said. "I was extremely disappointed the committee failed to recognize my contributions to this university."

"As I mentioned, these things can get pretty political."

"I suppose," Liam said with uncertain eyes.

"I was wondering if you had any preliminary news on Sherry Rosenfelt's brain biopsy."

"Actually, I still have a few more slides to go over before I complete my report."

"I'm well aware of the official process, Liam. I'm asking you for any preliminary thoughts you might have. I'm not going to hold you to anything. I understand nothing's official until you dictate your final report."

Liam eased back in his chair. "I can appreciate how anxious you are, Hollis, but maybe it would be best—"

"C'mon. We've known each other a long time. Anything we discuss is completely off the record and confidential. I would really appreciate your help."

"Of course, Hollis. What would you like to know?"

"Is there any evidence on the biopsies to confirm a viral illness?"

"Her brain tissue shows gliosis and a few other non-specific findings, which are all signs of inflammation."

"A viral illness?"

With a wrinkled brow, he answered, "It certainly could be."

"You realize that these women have been running a high fever. When you consider their other symptoms, especially the rash, we have overwhelming evidence that GNS is a viral disease, and one, I might add, that's spreading out of control. I'm convinced I have the cure for this devastating illness, but I need the support of strong-willed men who have the courage of their convictions to commit."

"I understand, Hollis, and I admire your passion."

"I look forward to reading your final report. When did you say it would be ready again?"

"Hopefully, later today."

"I truly appreciate your help," Sinclair said, extending his hand. "I suspect within a week's time, there will be thousands of grateful family members who will share my feelings."

For a few moments after Sinclair was gone, Liam stared across his office with a vacant expression. He had just been summarily checkmated by his esteemed colleague and there was little he could do about it. The last thing he needed at this stage of his career was to make a political enemy of every influential member of South-eastern's medical staff. Unable to see much wiggle room, Liam resigned himself to the fact that his biopsy report would state that Sherry Rosenbluth's brain tissue was infected by a virus.

51

Metropolitan Clinic
Birmingham, Alabama

Every Thursday morning, Dr. Mary Grandeson made formal teaching rounds with her residents and medical students. She had just finished answering the last of the group's questions when Wright Zarella stepped up with a self-satisfied grin. Humility in the face of accomplishment was not a social grace he possessed.

She looked at him and shook her head a couple of times. "Before you explode, I suggest you tell me what's burning in your mind."

"I got a call about a half an hour ago from the New Hampshire Department of Health and Human Service. New Hampshire has a very sophisticated electronic health data bank. They are meticulous to a fault in their information gathering regarding all forms of public health disorders."

"I'm sure New Hampshire appreciates your praise. What did you find out?"

"About eight weeks ago two pregnant women were treated for strange neurologic symptoms."

"What type of symptoms?"

"Muscle twitching of the arms and legs, fatigue and seizures."

"Dancing eye syndrome?"

"No."

"So, what happened?"

"They both fully recovered after a few days, so the illness didn't attract an enormous amount of attention. But no cause was ever found. The cases caught the attention of the epidemiologist who put them in the state registry. When he read my blast e-mail, he responded right away and briefed me in detail on the cases. He also put me in touch with the women."

"And?"

"Well, it seems both of them began using a new skin moisturizer a week or so before they got sick. The manufacturer's a new boutique company headquartered in Dover, New Hampshire. Nanotechnology was used in the product's creation. The company decided to confine the distribution of the moisturizer to New Hampshire as kind of a test market."

"And there have been no further cases?"

"None to my knowledge, but remember we're talking

about a fairly small distribution with respect to both area and population."

"There are no cases of GNS in New Hampshire. Do we have enough information from our patients here in Alabama to cross-reference this data?"

"Only partially, but none of our patients used the same product the women in New Hampshire used, which obviously makes sense."

With her posture stiffened, Grandeson drew a deep breath. "Leave me everything you have on this. I'm going to ask Kendra and Roger to pursue it."

"Kendra and Roger are two years behind me. I was the one who found out about this," he said, dropping his hands to his side. "Don't you think I should be the one to. . . "

She smiled. "The surgeon general and I have much more important work for you."

"I beg your pardon."

"I sent Dr. Brickell the article you gave me the other day. Last night, she called me back and we had a nice long chat about it. She was very intrigued and thinks the researchers in Germany may be onto something. She called Dr. Kurt Dressin, who's the researcher heading up the project. He trained in Chicago."

"This is all very interesting, but I'm not sure . . ."

Mary paused long enough to button the middle button of her white coat. "We'd like you to spend a few days in Magdeburg."

"You want me to go to Germany? Are you serious?"

"Don't I sound serious?"

"But, why?"

"Because that's where the medical school and the research unit are. Dr. Dressin personally extended the invitation."

"What exactly am I supposed to do over there?"

"Observe, ask a lot of questions and bring home as much information as you can. This group is obviously a lot more advanced than any research team in the U.S."

"I agree, but I'm just not sure going to Germany is necessary."

"The surgeon general and the president disagree. They think it's a good idea to send the individual who may have stumbled across the cause of GNS. If you feel like taking up your objections with them, be my guest."

He cupped his chin. "The president of . . ."

"Yes, Wright, of the United States."

Wright's face filled with surrender. He blew out every molecule of air in his lungs and then shrugged his shoulders. "When do I leave?" he asked.

52

Pleased with his meeting with the pathologist, Hollis returned to his office. He was just beginning to review the information he had requested on the national supply of Vitracide when his assistant buzzed him on the intercom.

"Dr. Sinclair. I have a call from a Dr. Cole in Indiana. I forwarded the call to the crisis center but they suggested you take it. The doctor said it was very important."

Sinclair stole a peek at his watch. He only had a minute or two before he was to attend a phone conference with six physicians across the country—all of whom strongly supported his viral theory.

"Put him through," Sinclair told her.

"Dr. Sinclair. My name is Cole. I'm an emergency physician in Bedford, Indiana."

Neither the name of the hospital, nor the physician was familiar to Sinclair. He rolled his eyes. He was tired of answering inane questions from every hick physician in the country taking care of a pregnant woman.

"How can I help you?" he asked.

"I recently transferred a patient by the name of Recino to Illinois Memorial. This patient's of particular interest because she's the only documented case of GNS within a two hundred mile radius of Bedford. In spite of taking a detailed medical history, I just discovered that Ms. Recino omitted an important piece of information."

"Really?" Sinclair said, wondering when Cole would get to the point.

"It seems Maggie and her mother spent the early part of her pregnancy in Fort Lauderdale. She received her initial prenatal care from a Dr. Charles Lipshank. I thought you might want to speak with him and get her obstetrical records."

"That's an excellent suggestion Dr. Cole," he answered, half-listening as he picked up a letter on his desk. He had already decided that Dr. Cole's information had no practical value. "Of course. I'll make sure we thoroughly review Dr. Lipshank's records."

"I've already called Illinois Memorial about the matter. They said they would enter the revised information into the National GNS Data Record."

"We certainly appreciate you calling," Sinclair said while reading the first paragraph of the letter. "We'll be in touch with you if the information leads us somewhere.

Thank you, again." With several other issues crowding his mind, Sinclair called his assistant. "I'm ready to join the conference call now." By the time his call ended thirty minutes later, his conversation with Dr. Cole of Bedford, Indiana, was a faint memory at best.

53

NUMBER OF CASES: 4,812
NUMBER OF DEATHS: 20

Agent Maxime Barbier stepped off the airplane into a deeply overcast morning. The flight from Quebec City to Port-Menier, the island's principle city, had taken just over two hours. Barbier was a ten-year veteran of the Royal Canadian Mounted Police. He was regarded by most as one of the most outstanding agents, especially in the area of missing persons. After obtaining a computer science degree from McGill University, he served a four-year stint in the military, volunteering for the elite Special Operations Forces Command. His beanpole appearance and mild methods disguised a man highly trained in many forms of combat weaponry and the martial arts.

He began researching the ex-biological weapons scientist Alik Vosky five minutes after the director of the CSIS personally handed him the Russian's dossier. The director made it a point to inform him he'd been handpicked to head up the operation. He was instructed to put all of his other cases on the back burner until Vosky was located. In a pledge Barbier had never heard the director make, he promised him any and all resources he might require to bring Vosky in.

He rolled up the collar of his coat and made his way to the car rental agency.

Fortunately for Barbier, Vosky wasn't the most sophisticated individual he'd ever encountered when it came to changing identities. To get the job in Winnipeg at the pharmaceutical company, Vosky had assumed the name of Eli Steinhoff. Because he was still using it, it hadn't taken Barbier very long to discover the Russian had rented a small house on Anticosti Island.

After filling his lungs with the moist salt air, he stuck his hands deep into the pockets of his coat. He took another look around and then got into his rental.

After a short drive that took him through the center of the city he pulled up in front of a Queen Anne house with a wide porch and gable that were crying out for a couple coats of fresh paint. The driveway was empty. He stepped out of the car. The heavy clouds had faded and were now nothing more than a delicate haze. Barbier walked up the front path of the house and then climbed the three steps to the front door. Shading his eyes with his hand, he attempted to peer through a small glass pane. Even squinting, he couldn't see a thing. Unable to locate a doorbell, he knocked several times on the arched door.

"Nobody lives there," came a gravelly voice from behind him.

Barbier turned around. A stocky man with a sparse gray beard dressed in stained overalls and a baseball cap was standing on the sidewalk. He walked back down the steps and approached him. He was a stone-faced man of short stature. His unsteady hand reached for the cigarette that drooped from the corner of his mouth. Barbier guessed he was at least eighty years old.

"Do you live around here?" he asked, showing the man his RCMP identification.

"As a matter of fact I do. My name's Martin Daigle."

"I'm looking for a man by the name of Eli Steinhoff. Do you know him?"

"Yeah. He rents the guest house in the back," Daigle said, pointing down the driveway.

"How well do you know him?"

"I speak to him from time to time."

"Would you mind answering a few questions about him?"

Daigle took a second look at Barbier's identification. The corners of his mouth curled into a slight grin.

"Do I have a choice?"

"Let's just say your country would appreciate your help." The old man smiled proudly. "Did Mr. Steinhoff ever mention anything about his prior jobs, political views, family . . . anything of that nature?"

Daigle shook his head slowly. "The few conversations we had were pretty short and boring."

"Did he have any regular visitors?"

"None that I've ever seen. He was kind of a loner. He told me once all of his friends and relatives lived in Europe somewhere."

"When was the last time you spoke with him?"

"A couple of days ago. He said he had urgent business outside the country. He told me he wouldn't be back for a week or so." Daigle shrugged and then pawed at his stubbly gray whiskers.

"Are you the . . . the caretaker of the property?"

"No. I'm the landlord."

"You didn't mention that."

"You didn't ask."

"What kind of tenant is he?"

"He pays his rent in cash and always on time. I got the feeling he had plenty of money."

"Really? What made you think that?"

"His clothes were pretty nice and he drove an expensive car. My father always taught me never to count another man's money, so I guess I could be wrong . . . but I don't think so. I'll tell you one thing, though. He's a pretty strange fellow."

"What makes you say that?"

"Sometimes, he'd barricade himself in that house for days. And for the last week or so the lights have been on all night. He has about ten different newspapers from the U.S. delivered every day."

Barbier again glanced down the driveway. "I'd really like to have a look inside," he said, slipping his hand into the pocket of his coat and handing Daigle a search warrant.

"This is official business, right?"

"Absolutely," he answered the old man's irrelevant question.

"I guess it'll be okay then," he said.

"After you," Barbier said, gesturing toward the house.

With a slight limp, the man escorted him down the dirt driveway. When they reached the entrance to the single-story house, he pulled out a key ring. After a few seconds of fumbling, he located the correct key.

Daigle unlocked the door and pulled it toward him. He reached in and flipped on the lights. They both stood in the doorway, staring into the living room.

The room was small and had been painted a drab shade of gray. A light but even layer of porous dust covered a set of shabby green drapes. In the center of the room there was a long table. Three desktop computers each with its own monitor occupied the majority of the space. Barbier stopped briefly at the table and quickly examined the computers. They were all shut down and he decided against trying to boot any of them up. He crossed the teak floor. He felt it give just a little with each step.

The door to the first bedroom was closed, but it was poorly hung and a crescent of light streamed from beneath it. He reached for the handle, pushed open the door and turned on the light. Taking a few steps forward, he stopped in the middle of the room. If Barbier were exploring a gallery of a modern art, he would have called it one of the most intriguing exhibits he'd ever seen.

Vosky had left without dismantling his scientific workshop. There were still countless papers affixed to bulletin boards and piles of books and scientific journals were festooned across the floor. In disbelief, Barbier walked over to the far wall and began scrutinizing the documents. He had never excelled in foreign languages but he knew enough from his training to recognize Russian when he saw it. Vosky's handwriting was impeccable, but each line of writing had a slight upward bend to it. Some of the pages were filled with mathematical formulas and equations. Others contained complex graphs, algorithms and long narrative paragraphs.

After spending time in front of each of the four walls, Barbier walked over to the kidney-shaped desk. It, too, was piled high with scientific books and journals with dozens of bookmarks sticking out from between the pages. He opened each of the five drawers in turn. They were all empty except the middle drawer, which contained a single manila folder. Opening it, he found a couple dozen newspaper clippings that had been cut out with meticulous precision. The articles were from various newspapers across the United States and Canada, but all of them dealt with the same topic—the GNS crisis. At the back of the stack, there was a separate group of articles fastened together by a large paper clip. Barbier removed the paper clip and slowly began thumbing through the articles. To his surprise, they were all from newspapers published in various cities in the U.S. In many of the margins, Vosky had made notes and each time a doctor's name appeared in the text, he had underlined it in green ink.

54

Barbier walked out of Vosky's bedroom and headed for the front door. He suspected it would take the forensic division of the RCMP days to analyze all the material. He stopped when he saw Martin Daigle standing in the middle of the living room looking past him into Vosky's room.

"There'll be some other agents arriving in the next few hours. I'd appreciate it if you would assist them."

"Of course. What is all that stuff in there?"

"I don't know but it's way beyond anything I'd understand," he answered, escorting Daigle out of the house and back to his car. Barbier did take the time to remind Mr. Daigle that he had assisted him in a highly confidential matter that involved the national security of Canada. He handed him one of his cards.

"Please call me if Mr. Steinhoff should return unexpectedly."

Daigle glanced at the card. "I'm a patriotic man, sir. You can count on me."

With his inward grin, Barbier climbed back into his car and reached for his cell phone. He tapped in the number to the director's office so that he could make the arrangements to get a team out to Vosky's house to gather up the contents and get them back to RCMP headquarters.

"It's Barbier. Would you please see if the director is available to speak with me?"

"Please hold." The director was a compulsive and highly organized man but was rarely available when Barbier called. He was, however, generally good about returning his phone calls in a reasonable amount of time. Barbier knew he couldn't leave the island until he had heard from him. He figured his best bet was to go into town and get something to eat. Barbier started the engine and pulled away from the curb expecting to hear from his assistant that the director would call him back as soon as possible. He had just pulled away from the curb when she came back on the line.

"The director will speak with you now. Please hold."

55

> NUMBER OF CASES: 6,123
> NUMBER OF DEATHS: 24

Dr. Renatta Brickell had always been a stickler for punctuality. At precisely nine A.M. she called the third meeting of the Presidential Task Force on GNS to order. There were a few new faces at the table but the remainder of the group was the same. At the invitation of the surgeon general, one of the new physicians in attendance was Hollis Sinclair.

To begin the meeting, Dr. Mary Grandeson from Birmingham brought the group up to date on her investigation into the possibility that GNS was being caused by a toxic skin product. Wright was still in Germany. She had received more than one phone call from him informing her that he was duly impressed with the German group's cutting-edge research. He couldn't give her a definite answer, but felt the possibility GNS was being caused by a nanotoxin found in a cosmetic product was real. Knowing how desperate everybody in the group was for encouraging information, Grandeson shared the conversation with them. She finished her comments by assuring the task force her group would diligently continue their work on nanotoxins.

When Grandeson concluded, Brickell made a special point to thank her before continuing with the meeting's agenda.

"I'm sure we all know Hollis Sinclair, who is presently serving as the acting chief of neurology at Southeastern State. As you are aware, he strongly questions the CDC's feeling that GNS is not a viral illness. I thought it was important to invite him to join us today so that we all might hear his theories firsthand." She smiled at him and took her seat.

"Thank you, Dr. Brickell. To expand on what the surgeon general just mentioned, I'm far more suspicious GNS is being caused by a virus than Dr. Cox and his colleagues at the CDC." He then turned to Mary Grandeson. "And, as compelling and as extraordinary as your work is, Mary, I don't believe you'll be able to show that this illness is the result of a toxic nanoparticle or an e-waste product. As many of you already know, I'm convinced GNS is being caused by a new strain of parvovirus.

With your indulgence, I've prepared a short presentation that will explain how I arrived at that conclusion."

Sinclair spent the next fifteen minutes presenting what Jack would call a well-organized argument for his theory. Because the president had lifted the gag order on Isabella Rosas the night before, Sinclair wasted no time informing the group that she was no better and expecting her to recover was a pipe dream at best.

After he concluded, Renatta Brickell was the first to ask a question.

"Hollis, I think I speak for many of us in the room when I express my concern that you've not been able to identify or grow this new parvovirus in the laboratory from any specimen taken from a GNS patient."

"I understand your concern, but we believe in time we will able to grow the virus in the laboratory. The problem is it will probably take weeks, maybe months, which naturally begs the question: Do we have the luxury of waiting that long? From where I sit, the answer's no. I believe we have enough solid medical evidence to prove GNS is a parvovirus infection." He looked over at Jack as if he expected him to make a comment on the assertion, but Jack was not so inclined to do so. Sinclair continued, "I'm quite comfortable recommending that a national program of Vitracide therapy be initiated immediately. I would remind everyone that not only are we diagnosing hundreds of new cases every day, but the women we're presently treating are getting sicker and sicker by the hour." He shook his head slowly and then in a grave voice added, "Treating these women and their babies with Vitracide is the only hope we have of saving them. To wait any longer would be a medical error of catastrophic consequences."

Douglas Fraiser, an epidemiologist from New York, raised his hand. "I completely agree with Dr. Sinclair. I would like to make a motion that this committee inform President Kellar we strongly endorse the use of Vitracide."

"Dr. Fraiser, I can assure you the president is keenly interested in any recommendation this committee might make, but please remember we serve in an advisory capacity only. We don't make policy."

"I would be interested in hearing Dr. Sinclair's thoughts on treating the mother and fetus together," Madison said.

All eyes in the room fell on Sinclair.

"From a medical standpoint, I believe both mother and fetus are infected and need to be treated. On the other hand, I'm not naïve to the complex moral and religious issues involved. I believe we should educate the families and make it clear to them that they have options. Those options should be handled on an individual basis by the families in consultation with their physicians and spiritual advisors."

"I'd like to say something," came a voice from the far end of the table.

Dr. Carol Quinton from Stanford University raised her hand. Quinton was highly respected and had achieved a praiseworthy list of academic accomplishments during her thirty-year career. She was a woman of short stature who generally spoke in a hushed tone.

Before addressing the group, she stood up. "It's well known the majority of errors we make as physicians are those of commission, not omission. In other words, when we screw up, it's usually because we did something ill-advised as opposed to failing to act. Dr. Sinclair makes a convincing argument that GNS should be treated with Vitracide, but before we agree to a wholesale endorsement of this plan, I urge you to strongly consider the price our patients will pay if we're wrong. For all we know, a week from now, most of these women could fully recover without any intervention on our part and go on to give birth to perfectly healthy babies." She shook her head slowly. "Let's not shoot from the hip because we're all frustrated. I'm quite familiar with Vitracide. It's an effective drug but it's also nasty as hell. It can destroy normal heart tissue after only a few doses." A guarded look came to her face before she continued. "We shouldn't kid ourselves: If we do decide to use it, there are going to be some bad results—including deaths to both mother and baby."

After the buzzing in the room subsided, Brickell thanked Dr. Quinton for her insightful comments. For the next half an hour, there was considerable debate on both sides. Almost everyone in attendance offered an opinion on the use of Vitracide. Jack didn't tabulate the votes exactly, but his impression was there were more in favor of recommending the drug's use than those who were opposed.

"The president's well aware that at this time of the year everybody would prefer to be at home with their families and not traveling. He's asked me to convey his profound gratitude to all of you for attending these meetings."

Brickell stood by the door to personally thank each

of the physicians as they exited. When the last one had left the room, she returned to the table and sat down.

"That was an interesting meeting," she told Julian Christakis.

"Sinclair seems pretty convinced he's got the answer to GNS."

"Maybe," she responded, reaching for her cell phone. "But I couldn't tell if that's gifted medical intellect or unbridled ego doing the talking. I'm going to call the president."

"Maybe we should let some time pass so we can get a better feel for—"

"I think time is something we're running out of. You may not have noticed, but Hollis Sinclair was quite perturbed with my failure to provide him with a blanket endorsement of his plan."

"Just how important is it that Hollis Sinclair is perturbed?"

She grinned at Julian's naïveté.

"Hollis Sinclair's a man consumed with an enormous sense of purpose. Before the sun comes up tomorrow, the president's going to know every detail of what transpired here today. I can't predict how he'll react, but if he gets bombarded with calls from Hollis Sinclair's allies and we haven't briefed him, well . . . we both might be looking for a job."

"It's hard for me to believe it's—"

She raised her finger to her lips to silence him. "This is Dr. Renatta Brickell. I'd like to speak with the president, please."

56

DECEMBER SEVENTEENTH

NUMBER OF CASES: 6,823
NUMBER OF DEATHS: 26

After yawning and then stretching his arms high over his head, Jack closed his laptop and got up from the desk. He was just about to step out on the balcony to watch the last few minutes of the sunrise when his cell phone rang. It was Marc.

"There's been an interesting development," he told Jack. "Every couple of days I check the National GNS Data Record for late entries. If you recall, there was a single case reported in a small town in Indiana. The patient's name was Maggie Recino. They transferred her up to Chicago. Initially Ms. Recino's travel history was reported as negative, but later her mother informed Dr. Cole in Indiana that she was staying in Fort Lauderdale when she learned she was pregnant."

"For how long?"

"About a month. I called Cole. He really didn't have anything to add, but he did mention he'd called Dr. Sinclair and shared the information about Fort Lauderdale with him."

"When was that?"

"Two days ago."

"Dr. Sinclair didn't say anything to me," Jack said. "Maybe he mentioned it to Madison or Dr. Morales."

"I can't speak for Dr. Morales, but I checked with Madison. She said she didn't know anything about it."

Jack noticed Marc was careful not to make any judgmental comments about Sinclair's failure to share the information with them.

"And we're sure there haven't been any further cases from the same area in Indiana?"

"Zero."

"If that's true, it doesn't take a genius to connect the dots," Jack said. "Obviously, something happened to Ms. Recino when she was in South Florida that allowed her to contract GNS. It might be interesting to have a look at her Fort Lauderdale obstetrical records."

"I already put them in the Patient Data Record. You can access them there."

"Do we know why she was in Fort Lauderdale?"

"No idea. Her husband's in the military and was out

of the country. Her mother's in Chicago with her. I'm assuming her reasons were personal. I was planning on giving her a call later this morning to get a more detailed history."

"Where are you going to be later?" Jack asked.

"The ICU. I should be there all morning. Madison wants to repeat all the fetal ultrasounds."

"I'll see you there."

Jack returned to his laptop and brought up Maggie Recino's file. Her Fort Lauderdale obstetrical record contained only one office visit, which looked to be a fairly routine initial prenatal appointment. As Jack reviewed the form Maggie had filled out detailing her past medical history, a vague idea played in his mind. But as hard as he tried, he couldn't bring it into focus. Finally, his frustration escalating, he shut down the computer.

After a ten-minute shower, he got dressed, gathered up his personal items and headed for the door. It wasn't until he was halfway to the elevators that the vague idea that had eluded him thirty minutes earlier finally crystalized. He stopped and turned around, staring back in the direction of his room.

"Idiot," he muttered to himself, removing his cell phone from its case and tapping in Madison's number. She answered on the second ring.

"Can you and Marc meet me in the crisis center?"

"Sure. We're about halfway through rounds, and then we're supposed to meet with the radiologists," she answered. "Is a couple of hours okay?"

"That should be fine. I want to check out a few things in the National Data Record before we meet. I'll see you in the crisis center."

"You sound a little . . . weird. What's going on?"

"We'll talk about it when I see you."

With a sudden burst of adrenaline coursing through his veins, Jack turned around and sprinted toward the elevator.

57

Jack barely noticed when Marc and Madison came through the door of the crisis center. He had spent the last hour poring over the latest information posted on the Data Record.

"Okay, we're here," she said, sitting down directly across from him. "What's going on?"

"As of nine o'clock this morning, there are about a hundred and thirty women hospitalized in South Florida with GNS. I've spent the last hour looking at their obstetric records."

"I thought we covered that ground already," Madison informed him.

"I'm looking specifically at each of their vaccination records."

"All the way back to childhood?" Marc asked.

"Actually, I'm only interested in whether they received

the most recent flu vaccine." Jack paused long enough to study their dubious expressions. "The new vaccine became available nationally about ten weeks ago. According to our records, two hundred sixty-five of the GNS patients definitely received the vaccine; the other thirteen we have no records on." He closed the lid to the laptop, folded his arms in front of his chest and added, "I can't find a single patient who definitely did not receive the flu vaccine."

Marc said, "Maybe it's just a coincidence. There are thousands of women with GNS. Looking at two hundred and seventy-eight of them . . . well, it might not prove a thing."

"I couldn't agree with you more," Jack was quick to say. "That's why we're going to expand the search. All the information's right here in front of us. We can start by checking the hospitals in Orlando, Tampa and Jacksonville. That would increase our patient population base to almost three hundred, which should be enough to at least suggest a trend."

With a less than convinced expression, Madison asked, "When are we going to do that?"

"There's no time like the present."

For the next half hour the three of them combined their efforts to comb through the patients' vaccine records. When they were finished they projected their results on the large screen.

"The information's about the same for all seven hospitals," Jack said. "Two hundred and sixty-five women who were definitely vaccinated. There are thirteen with no record one way or the other." He looked up and smiled. "What's interesting is that there's not a single patient whose record clearly states she did not receive the flu shot." He paused for a few seconds and then asked, "What do you think?"

"There are only two possibilities," Marc answered. "It's either an incredible coincidence or there's a definite connection between the vaccine and GNS."

"What next?" Madison asked.

"We check with the families of the thirteen patients to find out for sure if they received the vaccine or not."

"I hate to point out the obvious," she said, "but the flu vaccine is strongly recommended in pregnancy. There's no medical controversy about it."

"Your point?"

"Maybe all this isn't as earth-shattering a revelation as you think. Maybe it's no surprise that almost all of them got the flu shot."

Jack raised his index finger. "Most patients follow their doctor's recommendations. But there are those that don't, especially when it comes to vaccinations. Maybe they had a prior bad reaction, or maybe they read somewhere or talked to somebody who advised against it. There's a ton of anti-vaccine stuff out there. I have patients, friends including physicians who wanted nothing to do with the flu vaccine."

"I'm one of them," Marc confessed, with a casual shrug.

"Okay, for argument's sake, let's assume you're right and the flu vaccine is somehow tied into GNS. How do you explain all the pregnant women who had the vaccination and never got GNS? I ask the question because for every one vaccinated woman, there have to be thousands more pregnant women who were vaccinated, but never got sick. What about them? What made them so fortunate to be immune?"

"My best guess is that all the women with GNS have some other factor or condition in common that made them susceptible. When we figure out what that factor is, we'll have the final piece to the puzzle."

"When the Salk vaccine was first introduced, there was a bad batch and a lot of people got very sick," Marc said. "It doesn't sound like you're suggesting GNS is a tainted vaccine problem."

"I'm not. I believe the problem lies with the women themselves. My guess is there's something about the vaccine that changes their basic metabolism or immunological system. Whatever that change is makes the victim predisposed to getting GNS."

"But you have absolutely no idea what that factor is," Madison said.

"None whatsoever."

"So, where do we go from here?"

"I assume none of us knows too much about who manufactures the flu vaccine or how it gets distributed. So, somebody needs to become an expert on the topic ASAP."

As if it had been choreographed in advance, Jack and Madison eyes fell on Marc at the same moment. He returned their knowing stares with a sneer.

"The trickle-down theory at its best," he complained.

"I'll get some of the residents and med students to help me."

"I'd start with the CDC," Jack advised. "We need to know the name of every pharmaceutical company that manufactures the flu vaccine and their specific areas of distribution. I would also check with the FDA to get a list of all reported adverse and allergic reactions to the vaccine. And we need all of this information as soon as possible."

"No problem," Marc said. "I do my best work with a sword of Damocles hanging over my head."

"I'm afraid the sword's hanging over all of our heads," Jack said. "At best, we only have a few days to figure this thing out before Vitracide therapy starts on a national level."

"Supposing you're right about this vaccine thing, what do we do about it?" Madison asked.

"I'm not sure." With a subtle grin, he added, "Maybe that's one of those bridges you jump off when you get to it that you're always telling me about."

Jack was certain of one thing. He knew if his theory panned out, he'd have to share it with other doctors for their scrutiny and input. He realized as soon as he did, Hollis Sinclair and the naysayers who supported his parvovirus theory would label him a heretic. For the moment, he forced himself to push the problem of Sinclair from his mind. Every particle of his being was sure he was onto something, and the last thing he needed was to allow the politics of the situation to distract him.

58

It was seven P.M., and Jack had just finished a three-mile jog on the beach. On his way back to the hotel, he glanced overhead at a formation of gray catacombed clouds that had just moved in from the west. Feeling as if the temperature had dropped ten degrees, he crossed his arms across his chest. A few moments later his cell phone rang.

"You sound like you're still running," Marc said.

"I just finished a couple minutes ago," he answered with clipped words wedged between heavy breaths. "What's going on?"

"I have some interesting information on the flu vaccine."

Jack slowed his pace. It was getting windier with each passing minute, but he decided to sit down on a bench instead of going back inside the hotel.

"What did you find out?"

"There are seven companies that manufacture the vaccine. Six of them are distributed in the United States. We wound up spending most of the day on the phone calling clinics and obstetricians' offices trying to get a general idea of which vaccine each woman received. We were able to get specific information on one hundred eighty-one of them."

"Was it an even distribution of all six companies?"

"Not even close. All of the women with GNS received a vaccine manufactured by one of two companies; either Aptiprev or Ontryx. They're both European companies."

"Are they distributing in Europe, because to my knowledge there are no cases there?"

"Not yet. The U.S. demand was too high."

"You're absolutely sure none of the women received the vaccine from any of the other four manufacturers?"

"No way. I'm positive."

"Were you able to check with the FDA if there have been any problems with either of those two companies?"

"It took a while but I finally got through to them. They have no record of any significant side effects."

Jack puffed out a few quick breaths.

"We need specific information from the two companies regarding the national distribution of their vaccines. We have to know if it's available in all areas of the country where we're seeing cases of GNS. We also have to find out exactly how their vaccines are produced. They must be doing something different than the other manufacturers."

"I assumed you'd want that information so we're already working on it."

"Is Madison up to speed on all this?" Jack asked.

"That was going to be my next phone call."

"And Dr. Morales?"

"I assumed either you or Madison would want to let her know."

"Thanks," Jack told him. "I'll discuss it with Madison." His feeling was that as a visiting professor, it would be more appropriate if the call came from Madison. "What do you think about getting some more help and expanding our inquiries to other hospitals across the country?"

"You must be reading my mind. I already have some new volunteers. I know it's a little late but we're having our first meeting in about an hour in the crisis center."

After going over everything they had discussed again, Jack told Marc he'd speak to him later. He then headed up to his room to grab a shower before calling Madison. He assumed as soon as she brought Helen up to speed on the latest developments, she'd want a sit-down with Sinclair. She hadn't said it in so many words, but Jack suspected she didn't embrace his parvovirus theory. Jack clung to one hope: that for every hour Helen Morales could keep Sinclair from convincing the hospital board to support Vitracide therapy, he and Madison would be that much closer to finding the real cause of GNS.

59

Alik Vosky looked up and down the hall one final time before opening the door to Southeastern State Hospital's environmental services department. He walked down a faintly lit corridor unit he reached a lengthy row of double lockers. Trying each of the lockers in turn, he found himself somewhere between pleased and surprised to find so many of them open. Well before he reached the final locker, he found a standard-issue powder blue golf shirt with the hospital's logo on it and a tool belt. It further delighted him to find Max Shudderman's identification badge clipped to the pocket. After a quick look around, Vosky changed his shirt and left the locker room.

It was no secret that every hospital involved in the care of GNS patients had a designated crisis center. By asking an unassuming elderly volunteer, it didn't take him long to find out where Southeastern State's was located.

Under the guise of fixing a faulty thermostat, he opened the door and walked in. As he assumed before leaving his hotel, the late hour would increase the likelihood of being left undisturbed while he gained access to the National Patient Data Record. With his computer skills, he had no concerns that in short order he'd be able to penetrate the Data Record's security system.

He chose the computer closest to the thermostat in case someone saw him. He wasn't at work on the keyboard for more than a minute or two when he heard voices outside the room. After an annoyed half sigh, he stood up and took the few steps over to the wall. He reached for a small Phillips-head screwdriver from the tool belt and removed the outer case of the thermostat.

While Vosky pretended to be working, Marc and several of the residents and medical students sat down around the table. He didn't acknowledge any of the group, and they treated him as if he were invisible. He was, however in an excellent position to hear everything they were saying. He hoped they wouldn't be there long, allowing him another opportunity to hack into the Data Record.

"I know it's late," Marc told the group, raising his hands in the air, "but Dr. Wyatt really needs the flu vaccine information as soon as possible. If we all work together on this thing we can be out of here in an hour."

For the next forty minutes, Vosky listened to everything that was said. The information he gathered regarding Dr. Jack Wyatt and his flu vaccine theory was, in his mind, beyond fortuitous—it was fate. He decided against trying to wait out the research group any longer and reattached the outer case of the thermostat. Vosky made his way out of the crisis center.

The pain in the back of his head and neck, which he'd first noted before he left his hotel, reached a crescendo. He rubbed his neck slowly, refusing to allow something as subjective as pain to interfere with his thought processes. Everything was clear to him now. He had been completely wrong about Hollis Sinclair. He was an amateur and posed no risk, but Dr. Jack Wyatt was different. Vosky didn't understand how, but Wyatt had somehow managed to stumble upon the key element of his work. Ultimately, the question was purely an academic one because the manner in which Wyatt had discovered the truth behind GNS was irrelevant. The only thing that mattered was to assure the spread of GNS would continue without interruption.

He thought about a professor he had idolized while obtaining his doctorate. The old man's life's lessons had a strange but logical way of intersecting with certain tenets of scientific research. One of Vosky's favorites was that sometimes the best solution to a highly complex problem was so simple—it was a gift.

An easy grin came to his face. There was no question in his mind what he had to do. As much as he hated to admit it, he had been a fool. Hollis Sinclair was nothing more than a clever decoy. For all his showboating, he wasn't larger than life; he was a buffoon. If given all the time in the world, he'd never figure out how to stop GNS.

Vosky's task was simple. It was an easy matter of simply changing his focus from Hollis Sinclair to Dr. Jack Wyatt. The small variation in his plan would ensure GNS would continue to spread through the United States like a brush fire in a gusty wind.

60

> NUMBER OF CASES: 7,389
> NUMBER OF DEATHS: 29

As Jack had predicted, Helen called him to ask him to sit in on a meeting she had arranged with Madison and Hollis Sinclair. He accepted her invitation, and even though the vaccination theory had been his brainchild, he decided it would be better to allow Madison and Helen to be the principals in the meeting. Jack's gut feeling was the plea they would make to Sinclair would fall on deaf ears, but he allowed an ember of optimism to flicker.

The meeting began at ten as scheduled. Before Helen could thank everyone and talk about the basic reason for the meeting, Sinclair spoke up. "I'm very busy, Madison.

What's so important that I had to drop everything to meet with you?"

"I apologize for disrupting your schedule but we have some new information we'd like you to share with you."

Sinclair heaved an impatient breath and then looked at his watch. "Go ahead."

"I would ask you to listen with an open mind."

"If you'll promise to get to the point, I'll promise to listen with an open mind."

"Our information is still preliminary, but we've studied the charts of over five hundred women in Florida and found all of them received the flu vaccine from one of two companies. What's of particular interest is that they all received it about six weeks prior to becoming ill."

Sinclair said nothing, glancing back and forth every few seconds at all three of them. Finally, in an incredulous voice he asked, "That's it? You dragged me away from what I was doing to tell me that? As I recall, the flu vaccine is recommended for pregnant women. I would guess to date, millions of doses have been administered. And what difference does it make which company manufactured it?"

"Because there are six companies that manufacture a vaccine. It's too much of a coincidence that five-hundred-plus women with GNS all received the vaccine from one of the two companies."

Leaning back in his chair, Hollis raised a finger and inquired, "How many pregnant women received the vaccine from either of these two companies who are perfectly fine?" When Madison didn't answer, he said with a smirk, "That's what I thought."

"We believe the vaccine may be an important factor in facilitating the disease," Jack said. "We're not saying it's the direct cause."

"A factor facilitating the disease? For God's sake, man, we're looking for a cure not a facilitating factor." With undeniable disbelief on his face, he continued, "First it was an elevated hormone level that you were going to cure by removing an ovarian tumor. The last I checked Isabella Rosas is worse now than she was before the operation. Now it's the flu vaccine?" He laughed and threw his hands up. "What are you going to tell me next—all women with GNS use the same brand of mouthwash?"

"We think that both the elevated inhibin level and the flu vaccine are factors necessary for GNS to take hold," Madison answered.

"I'll restate my question. How do you explain how thousands of pregnant women, all of whom have elevated inhibin levels and all of whom have received the flu vaccine, don't have GNS?"

"We don't know that yet," Madison said.

He came to his feet with a dismissive sneer. "As soon as you do figure it out, let me know. In the meantime, I would remind you that our patients' families aren't interested in wild theories about shots and hormones. They are interested in a treatment that will cure their loved ones. This isn't a high school science fair; this is real medicine. The only thing you two have accomplished is to plunge further into the depths of irrelevance and absurdity."

"We disagree," Madison said in a clear and calm voice.

"Really? I've laid out in detail why I think GNS is caused by a virus. What's your evidence that it's not?"

"We just don't feel it fits clinically," Madison said.

"That's it?" he demanded, looking at each of them in turn. "Speaking as a perinatologist with no training in neurology or infectious diseases, you have a feeling?" His eyes switched to Helen. "I can't believe they have you believing this ridiculous bedtime story about the flu vaccine."

Helen said, "Jack and Madison are just asking you to hold off beginning Vitracide treatment until they can look into these findings a little further."

"Nothing that was said here this morning would give me the slightest reason to delay treatment." He took a few steps toward the door before stopping and turning around. "Since the day you arrived, Dr. Wyatt, you've been uncooperative and openly dismissive of my professional efforts. Based on your personal relationship with Michael Ryan, I've chosen to overlook your rude and unprofessional behavior. But now we're on the cusp of curing this disease and saving not only Tess Ryan's life but thousands of others. I understand you're under great personal pressure and I'm sorry you weren't the one who discovered the cause of this disease, but isn't it time to set your ego aside and do the right thing?" Sinclair didn't wait for a response. With a tired shake of his head, he strolled out of Helen's office.

Feeling no need to explain himself to a man such as Sinclair, Jack did nothing to stall the retreat. Jack had never been one to throw a quick punch, but at the moment he was hard-pressed to think of a better solution to Sinclair's arrogance than taking matters into the alley.

"I guess none of us is surprised at Hollis's reaction," Helen said. "I'm not sure he's as difficult as he tries to be. He's just so convinced he's right."

"It's obvious he's not going to cooperate with us, so our only choice is just to keep working," Madison said.

"I'm afraid it's not quite that simple. Hollis has put the full-court press on everybody he's ever met in the hospital or at a cocktail party. We're not the only ones he's told that Jack's presence is disruptive to the care of the patients. He's made several requests that his guest professorship be terminated. He's also complained that your argumentative and inflexible approach is impeding measures to cure GNS."

"As the dean, isn't there anything you can do?" she inquired.

"Unfortunately, this isn't a monarchy. I, too, have people to answer to. For reasons beyond comprehension, Hollis Sinclair has the sympathetic ear of a lot of influential people. He's already gone over my head. I have the tire tracks to prove it."

"Just because he's a persuasive man with the gift of gab doesn't mean he's right about GNS," Madison said.

"There's enormous pressure in every state of this country to find a way to treat GNS. Politicians, public health officials and hospital boards are getting thin on patience.

In addition to the families of the GNS victims, they're being squeezed by every social organization and religious organization under the sun to come up with a cure. We already have numerous reports of a cottage industry of scam artists selling a host of products guaranteed to prevent or cure GNS." She covered her mouth for a few moments and added, "People are desperate for an answer right now, and unfortunately, Hollis Sinclair is the only one claiming to have it."

Jack looked squarely at a woman he had grown to admire. "I'm here at your invitation, Helen. If you feel my presence at Southeastern State has become a . . ."

"I have no such concerns, Jack. I'm still the dean of this medical school, and until I say otherwise, your invitation is good." She turned to Madison. "If you could keep your head down a little, it would help. I'll do the best I can to keep Dr. Sinclair calm, but you and Jack need to come up with something pretty damn quick—even if it's only the promise of a cure. My phone's ringing off the hook and I'm running out of ways to keep the enemy from storming the gate."

61

After spending most of the morning in the ICU, Jack went to the doctors' dining room to meet Madison for lunch. Earlier, they had visited Isabella Rosas and finally agreed the removal of her ovarian tumor had done nothing to improve her condition.

"Did Mike call?" Madison asked, taking the seat across from him.

"A couple of hours ago. I'm going to meet with him tonight at his house."

"I'm happy to come along if you think it would help."

Jack thought about Madison's offer for a few moments. "Thanks. I think that's probably a good idea."

They were just starting to get up to go through the food service line when Madison's phone rang.

"We're in the doctors' dining room." Madison nodded a few times. "No, that's fine. We'll wait right here for you." Replacing her phone in the pocket of her white coat, she said, "That was Helen Morales. She wants to talk with us. There appears to be another new development. She'll be here in a couple of minutes."

Helen Morales waved as she approached Jack and Madison's table. From the somber look on her face, he assumed that more bad news was on the way. She sat down, interlacing her fingers as she placed her hands on the table.

"I just got off the phone with the surgeon general. She called me as a courtesy to let me know she met with the president and his key health care advisors earlier today. The president has decided to make a national address tonight. In his speech, he will talk about the option of using Vitracide."

"I can't believe it," Madison said averting her gaze. "How can the president of the United States come out in support of such a potentially dangerous and unproven treatment?"

"I'm not sure you're going to see an across-the-board endorsement. The president's in a tough spot. Try and remember the mood of the country is somewhere between irate and terrified. A lot of people believe the medical community and government haven't been forthcoming or effective in the way they're dealing with GNS. Emergency rooms are packed, obstetricians are working till midnight and state and federal health agencies can't begin to handle the volume of calls they're receiving." Helen shook her head slowly. "You can't blame the president. He's got to do something to get the country out of this tailspin. From a political standpoint, it's the smart move."

Madison frowned. "Politically smart. That's great."

"I assume Southeastern State will make Vitracide available for those families who elect to go that route?" Jack asked.

"I don't think we'll have a choice," Helen responded.

"So, I guess the key question is how long will it take Sinclair to get his treatment protocol up and running?" Jack asked.

"Once he has the tacit approval of the federal government, which I think the president's address will provide, he'll be ready to start treating within a few days."

"That doesn't leave us much time," Jack said.

"What are you two going to do?" Helen asked.

"I don't think Madison and I are ready to cut and run just yet," he said with the slightest of shrugs. "We'll just keep working. Hopefully, we can gather enough information in the next few days to convince our colleagues and the public that the last thing in the world they want to do is authorize the use of Vitracide."

62

Jack pulled into Mike's driveway at a few minutes after seven. When Tess had discovered the two-story Spanish-style house, she knew it was a treasure. As soon as they purchased it, she began a major renovation. Her efforts became a labor of love, and one year later she finished the home she'd been building in her mind since she was a freshman in college.

Walking up to the house, Jack took a second look at the lighted crystal sleigh with Santa sitting in it. It was the same one Tess had been displaying since the first Christmas she and Mike had spent in the house. Mike opened the door and escorted them through the foyer and into his library. The room was paneled in mahogany wood, with the far wall a floor-to-ceiling bookcase with a rolling library ladder on brass rails. A series of marble tables displayed Mike's collection of military-styled chess sets from numerous historical eras. Tess's hand in things was clearly present in the elaborate Christmas decorations that filled the room. The tree was in the far corner, adorned with shimmering ornaments and an arrow-shaped sign pointing to Santa's workshop.

"Would anybody like something to drink?" Mike asked, pointing to the couch. They both declined with a wave of the hand. Once they were all seated, he said, "I spent all afternoon with Tess. I never saw her move once and her face is lifeless."

"She's not improving," Jack said, "but I'd say she's holding her own."

"Dr. Sinclair disagrees," Mike said flatly.

"That doesn't mean he's right," Madison said.

"He called me earlier. He told me the hospital's close to authorizing his Vitracide program. He wants me to consent to treatment as soon as possible." He set his glass of red wine down on a coffee table. "Would you agree with him that the young girl who was operated on is not going to recover?"

"I'd say the possibility's remote," Jack answered.

"If you decide to go ahead with treatment, what's your plan regarding the baby?" Madison asked in a cautionary tone. "Did Dr. Sinclair make a recommendation?"

"He said the decision was mine. Right now, I'm leaning toward a C-section."

"Tess is only in her twenty-eighth week. The baby will be extremely premature."

"I guess being very premature is better . . . better than the alternative."

Mike stood up and walked over to one of his Civil War chessboards and mindlessly moved a few of the pieces around. "A few days ago, you said if the girl didn't get better after the operation and Tess didn't improve, you would agree to go with Sinclair's recommendations. But I'm getting the feeling you still think I should wait."

"I do."

"If I wait and do nothing, what are my guarantees we won't lose them both? The thought of losing the baby is painful enough, but the thought of Tess dying is beyond anything I can possibly imagine. I just don't know what losing . . ." His voice was choked and his eyes became glazed by a veil of tears. With his hands folded in his lap, he added, "Most men are brothers by circumstance. I was fortunate enough to choose you. There's no man I admire more than you, Jack, but you're going to have to explain to me why you're right and Sinclair's wrong."

"I can't do that. And I don't have any guarantees that I'm right. The only thing I can tell you is that my gut's telling me Vitracide is not the answer." After a weighted sigh, he added, "This is not a decision you have to make right now. We still have a couple of days. If another option becomes available . . . well, we can talk about it then and you can decide if you want to reevaluate your decision."

"Okay," he said in a monotone, staring down at the floor. "Okay."

Mike spent the next few minutes talking to Madison about the baby's condition. Jack only listened, but he studied his closest friend carefully. Mike's voice and manner were like a beleaguered marathoner too cramped and spent to take another stride. From the beginning Jack had considered the consequences for Mike if he lost Tess but the true impact hadn't crystalized for him until now. The price his friend would pay in untold suffering from losing the love of his life was, at least for the moment, more than Jack could fathom.

63

Thirty minutes before President Stephen Kellar was to make his national address, Renatta Brickell was escorted into his office by one of his assistants. He sat behind his desk, his eyes intently focused on the pages of his speech. A few moments later, he looked up and saw her. He glanced around the Oval Office at the harried group of aides and technicians.

"May I have a few minutes, please?" he asked them as he stood up and escorted Renatta to the couch. "My address is only twenty minutes long. I thought I should speak a bit longer but Carmondy and the rest were opposed to the idea. What do you think?"

"I think the length is fine, sir. It covers all the key points without belaboring or skimming over any of them."

He flipped through the pages, making little eye contact with her.

"I know you've looked over the text but I'd like to read a part of it aloud to you." He reached for a glass and took two quick sips of water. "From the beginning, my administration has viewed the safety of both the mothers and the fetuses as paramount in importance. We have invited the leading scientific and religious minds in the country and individuals from all walks of life to attend meetings and fact-finding sessions. Every one of those participants has searched his or her soul in evaluating this difficult moral dilemma. Ultimately, this decision has to be left to the families, their consulting physicians and spiritual advisors." He looked up. "What do you think?"

"It's well phrased, Mr. President."

Just then, one of his aides entered the room.

"Ten minutes, sir."

"Thank you." He turned to Renatta. "Is there anything else you can think of?"

"No, Mr. President. I wouldn't change or add a word. It's an excellent speech."

Kellar stood up and walked back to his desk. The cameras and lighting equipment had been in place for hours. He picked up the phone and told his administrative aide to send everybody back in.

"Any last-minute thoughts?" he inquired, his face just slightly flushed.

Renatta was taken back. President Stephen Kellar's calm but stalwart confidence was conspicuously absent.

"Sir, in a few minutes the people of this country are going to know how seriously their president is reacting to this catastrophic outbreak. They'll know as a result of your efforts, thousands of scientists, doctors and other health care professionals are doing everything humanly possible to stop the spread of this disease."

"I wish I shared your unbridled optimism," he said with a wrinkled brow.

Renatta again wished Kellar luck and then exited the Oval Office to watch his address with other key members of his team. She wasn't an expert on the political process; she was a doctor. But at the moment she was convinced that President Stephen Kellar was five short minutes away from making the most important address of his career.

64

After watching the president's speech at Mike's house, Jack and Madison headed back to the hospital.

"What do you have planned for the rest of the evening?" he asked her.

"I haven't eaten anything since breakfast. The possibility of dinner has crossed my mind a few times."

"I'll tell you what. I'll buy you all the pizza you can eat if afterward you get the team together for a meeting in the crisis center."

"Now there's a classy dinner invitation."

"If I thought we had the luxury of a three-hour gourmet dinner, I would have suggested it."

"How many toppings on the pizza?" she asked.

"No limit. It's your heart attack."

"I'll accept your offer on one final condition."

"Shoot."

"During dinner, the topic of GNS and everything and everybody related to it is off limits."

"Agreed."

"Good. We have a deal," she said reaching for her phone. "There's a pretty decent pizza place a few blocks from the hospital. I'll call Marc. We'll have time to eat while he gets the team together."

65

A little over an hour later, Jack and Madison met Marc in the crisis center. Seated around the conference table were two obstetric residents, a pharmacist, three medical students and one of the intensive care physicians. The room was cool and the table was covered with an assortment of coffee mugs, legal pads and at least a half dozen medical texts. In the middle, a mound of computer printouts stood on the verge of toppling over.

"I apologize for the hour," Jack began. "But with the new evidence we've uncovered regarding the flu vaccine and the limited time we have, I wanted to see if there's anything further we can pull from the National Patient Data Record to identify any other common factors amongst these patients." He turned to Marc. "I know this is the last thing any of us wants to do, but let's go back to the beginning and review our basic patient profile."

"Our prototypic patient," Marc began, "is a woman in her second or third trimester of pregnancy. As a result of what we learned from Isabella Rosas, an elevated inhibin level seems to be essential in order to contract the disease. We are all painfully familiar with the symptoms, so I won't restate them. The final relevant factor is that the vast majority of these women have been pregnant before."

"Which means that a prior pregnancy changed something in their metabolic or immunologic makeup that made them susceptible to GNS," Jack stated.

"I agree," Marc said. "The question is, how?"

"Have you considered chimerism?" came a partially muted voice from the far end of the table.

Every head turned at the same time.

"I beg your pardon," Jack said, looking at the young lady with short blond hair, nervously tapping a pencil against her notepad. A yellow medical student identification badge was clipped to the pocket of her white coat. Jack had seen her a few times at the team meetings and on rounds, but this was the first time he'd heard her say anything, which was hardly unexpected for a third-year medical student. But what made Carolyn Olesanger unique was that prior to enrolling in the Southeastern State University medical school she had earned both a masters and Ph.D. from Rutgers University.

Dutch Richardson, a senior pharmacist weighed in, "For those of us who have absolutely no idea of what you're talking about, perhaps you could explain."

Carolyn looked at Madison for approval, which she

received in the form of a single nod and a hand gesture to proceed with impunity.

"Ninety-plus percent of the population has one DNA cell line. Chimeras are individuals, largely women, who possess two distinct DNA cell lines. The term comes from Greek mythology. A chimera was a mythical creature that had the head of a lion and the tail of a goat. Pregnancy is by far the most common way women become chimeras."

"How?" Richardson asked.

"Normally the fetus and the mother have two separate circulations, but sometimes a very small amount of the baby's blood cells pass through the placenta to the mother. These blood cells can then become a permanent part of the mother's DNA. They are most commonly found in the thyroid gland and lymph nodes."

Jack and Madison swapped an intrigued glance.

"Your background is in . . ." Madison asked

"I have a Ph.D. in molecular genetics."

"I'm not sure I understand the significance of all this," Jack said. "Supposing our patients are chimeras. From what I recall, being a chimera is . . . is a medical oddity, not a disease."

"That's probably not entirely true," Carolyn said in a voice increasing in confidence. "Over the past few years there's been a firestorm of controversy over the relationship between chimerism and disease. There is a large group of medical researchers who believe chimerism predisposes individuals to certain diseases. The way this occurs hasn't been totally worked out but it has been documented that chimeras have a higher incidence of autoimmune diseases such as lupus and rheumatoid arthritis."

One of the residents spoke up. "You mentioned that being pregnant was one way a woman could be become a chimera. What are the others?"

"People who have received a blood transfusion for any reason can be converted to chimeras. Another way is to be a bone marrow or organ transplantation recipient. It's also been shown that in vitro fertilization and artificial insemination can do it." Carolyn paused and looked around the room before going on. "Twins can be chimeras if some of their red cells exchange during fetal life. There are only a few places in the country doing serious research on the subject. There's still a lot of controversy, but if there's one area of agreement, it is that the total number of women chimeras in the population has been grossly underestimated."

Jack was intrigued by what he was hearing, but he was far from convinced the information on chimerism was the key that would unlock the mysteries of GNS. But with Sinclair breathing down his neck and Tess slipping further away with each passing hour, he was ready to grasp at any straw that might lead him to the cause of the most enigmatic disease he'd ever come across.

Jack said, "Let's take another look at the patients who are pregnant for the first time."

Marc tapped in the command and waited a few seconds for the information to appear on his screen. "There are only four at Southeastern State who are pregnant for

the first time," he said. "The first one is Grace O'Malley.
She was admitted five days ago. The only thing of interest
in her history is that she had her tonsils out at age six.
She bled for several days and required an emergency
operation to stop the bleeding."

"Did she receive a blood transfusion?" Madison asked.

Marc looked up and with a surprised grin and said,
"Yes. According to her mother, she did."

"Who's next?"

"Laura-Anne Elby. Let's see . . . she was also admitted five days ago. She had leukemia as a teenager. She
was treated in Atlanta at Scottish Rite Hospital. It took
three years, but she fully recovered."

"Does it mention whether she had a bone marrow
transplant?" Carolyn asked.

"No, but it's certainly possible," Madison said. "It
shouldn't be too hard to find out. I'm sure her family must
know."

Marc looked over at Clayton Morton, the chief resident in obstetrics. "Clay, why don't you give the ICU a
call and see if any of Laura's family is up there? I'm sure
they'll know if she had a transplant."

"No problem," he said, coming to his feet.

"Keisha Adams is next," Marc said. "She was one of
the first patients we admitted." He scrolled down through
her basic medical information. There was nothing of
particular interest. When he reached the summary of her
past medical history, his chin dropped. He projected the
page onto the large screen. "In 2003, she underwent a
kidney transplant."

Jack's eyes narrowed as his mind began to race. He could feel his stomach clench. "I know who the fourth patient is. Her name's Sherry Rosenfelt."

"The one who had the brain biopsy," Madison stated.

"Yeah. I've gotten to know her father pretty well. I've been over her medical history so many times I could recite it by heart. She's always been healthy."

"Then how did she become a chimera?" Marc asked.

"I don't have the first clue," Jack responded, shifting his gaze to the other end of the table to address Carolyn directly. "How difficult is it to test someone for chimerism?"

"The testing has become fairly straightforward. There a several methods but the easiest is a DNA analysis of a blood or skin sample."

"What's the turnaround time?"

"I think most labs can give you an answer within forty-eight hours. There's a pretty experienced one in Fort Lauderdale."

Jack pushed his chair away from the table. "Let's get Dr. Morales involved. With a little arm twisting, maybe we can get the lab to give us results in twenty-four hours."

"How many of the women should we test?" Madison asked.

"To start, every one hospitalized at Southeastern State," he answered flatly.

Marc's cell phone rang. He nodded a few times and then slowly replaced the phone on his belt and cleared his throat.

"That was Clay. He just spoke to Laura-Anne Elby's

mother. She told him that after fourteen months of leukemia treatment in Atlanta, Laura was sent to Seattle for a bone marrow transplant."

The meeting continued another half hour before Jack ended it by assigning everybody in the room a specific project to investigate the possible link between chimerism and GNS.

"That may have been the most productive meeting we've had so far," Madison told Jack after everyone had left the room. He agreed with a quick nod, but his mind was only half there. He slipped his laptop back into the same scuffed black leather case his ex had given him for Christmas four years earlier.

"How hard would it be to get a copy of Sherry Rosenfelt's slides from her brain biopsy?"

With a wary expression, Madison angled her head to one side. "I assume you have more than an academic interest for asking me that."

"I was toying with the idea of getting another opinion."

"The last time I checked, the slides had already been reviewed by two other pathologists who concurred with the findings."

"Yeah, but all three of those pathologists are on staff at Southeastern State. Maybe it would be a good idea to speak with somebody who isn't."

"It shouldn't be a big deal to get a copy of the slides, but tomorrow's Sunday. Even if we overnight them to somebody on Monday, by the time he or she reviews them and gets back to us, it will be the middle of the week." She shrugged. "I think we'll be out of time."

"I was thinking more of hand-delivering them . . . to expedite matters."

"How come every time you and I have a conversation, I find myself lost?"

"How do you feel about driving up to Orlando tomorrow?"

"At the risk of repeating myself, I've never met a pathologist who worked on Sunday."

"I know one who does," Jack responded, not mentioning he had already made a phone call.

Madison shook her head and started toward the door. "I'll tell you what. I'll meet you in the pathology department at eight. I'll arrange for the technician on call to be there and give us a copy of Sherry's slides."

"Great. Was that a yes or a no about coming with me?"

"I'll come on one condition."

"You're just full of conditions tonight. Name it."

"I drive."

Unable to silence his groan, he said, "I wouldn't have it any other way."

66

> NUMBER OF NEW CASES: 7,850
> NUMBER OF DEATHS: 31

It was twenty minutes to ten when Madison and Jack pulled into the visitors' parking lot of Orlando Memorial Hospital. They went directly to the patient welcome center, where an elderly woman wearing a pin recognizing her two thousand hours of volunteer service to the hospital directed them to the third-floor office of Dr. Lucien Androise, the chief of pathology. Before accepting the position, Androise had spent fifteen years at Case Western Reserve University. Over the years, Jack had worked with him on at least a dozen cases. They had an excellent professional relationship and there wasn't a pathologist alive he respected more than Lucien.

Jack and Madison followed the main corridor to its end outside Lucien's office. The door was ajar, and Jack saw his old colleague, a squat man with fatty ears and stubby fingers hunched over a microscope. Jack rapped on the door of couple of times. Lucien looked up, smiled broadly and waved them in.

After exchanging a warm greeting, Jack introduced Madison.

"My pleasure to meet you," he said, shaking her hand. He redirected his attention back to Jack. "Let's see what you two have."

Jack handed him the leather case containing the slides. Lucien invited them to have a seat at the Formica-topped counter. Spaced equally apart were four state-of-the-art microscopes. They were of the teaching variety, manufactured with two eyepieces; one for the pathologist and one for the student.

"I can't thank you enough for agreeing to review the case," Jack said.

"It's my pleasure. We're taking care of a lot of women with GNS, but we haven't performed any biopsies as yet."

"To my knowledge, Southeastern State's the only hospital that has," Jack said.

Lucien ran his finger down the slides until he reached the one he wanted to look at first.

"So, did you pluck anybody's tail feathers at Southeastern State by sneaking away with these slides and coming up here?"

"We may have ruffled a few," Jack answered. "Officially, the request for your opinion comes from Arnold Kazminski, the father of the young lady whose brain tissue you're about to look at. So, from a medical ethics standpoint, we're on solid ground. I can't say the same is true regarding the wisdom of the decision from a political standpoint. But, even if we come under fire when we get back, it shouldn't amount to much more than a flesh wound."

"You've always been the consummate diplomat, Jack."

After arranging the two dozen slides in his preferred order, Lucien slid the first one on the viewing platform. He removed his five-dollar flea market reading glasses and looked in the eyepiece of the microscope.

"As I mentioned on the phone, I'm interested to know if you see anything at all that's definitely diagnostic of a viral infection," Jack said.

Lucien took several minutes studying a large sampling of the slides before he invited Jack and Madison to have a look.

"There's a component of inflammation here that could possibly be the result of a viral infection," he said.

Jack lifted his eyes from the microscope. "You're saying possibly. The pathologists at Southeastern State were more on the definitely side."

Androise interlaced his fingers behind his neck. "In my opinion, the findings on these slides are not specific. I can't exclude a viral infection but it's by no means the only possibility." He raised his hands and turned his palms toward the ceiling. "You asked for another opinion.

All I can say is I don't feel nearly as strongly as the South-eastern State pathologists do that this young lady's brain tissue is infected with a virus." With an easy shrug of his shoulders, he reached for one of the few slides he hadn't as yet looked at and positioned it on the microscope.

Jack glanced over at Madison. Her face was painted with a stony expression.

"I certainly appreciate you coming in on Sunday to have a look at—"

"Wait a sec," Lucien said abruptly. He rotated the lenses to a higher magnification. "This is interesting. On this slide, there are some very subtle features of . . ." Lucien said nothing for the next minute or so, but then glanced up from the microscope with a puzzled look on his face. "Let me have a closer look at these and I'll give you a call."

"What are you . . ."

"I'd rather not say anything right now."

With narrowed eyes Jack asked, "I don't mean to sound pushy but we're on a pretty tight schedule, Lucien—do you have any idea when we might hear from you?"

"I understand. I'm only talking about a day or two. I don't suppose you brought any of the original biopsy material. I might want to do some different stains on them."

"I thought you might ask for that," Jack said, removing a small container of formaldehyde and handing it to Lucien.

"Great," he said, sliding his glasses back in place and coming to his feet.

With a knowing smile, Jack extended his hand. "Thanks again for having a look at the slides."

"I'm happy to help . . . but I'm not sure I've done anything more than further muddy the waters."

"I doubt that's the case," Jack assured him. "I look forward to your call. One last favor: Would you mind keeping our little visit here today confidential?"

"What visit?" he asked Jack before turning to Madison and extending his hand. "It was such a pleasure meeting you."

Jack followed Madison out of Lucien's office and down the main corridor. He was more than familiar with Lucien's coy and cautious manner. Jack had a feeling his old friend was onto something.

"Do you feel like making a stop on the way back?" Jack asked Madison as they waited for the elevator.

"What kind of a stop?"

"My mother lives on Hutchinson Island. I owe her a visit."

"Jack, I hate to sound like a jerk but do you really think with the time constraints we're under this is the best time for a family—"

"You might find her interesting to talk to. She recently retired from the University of Georgia as the chief of pediatric cardiology. She spent her entire career doing research. Her department became pretty renowned for their work on congenital heart disease."

"Really? Do you know if she worked with Charlotte Duffy?"

"I would say they were inseparable. She is Charlotte Duffy."

"I beg your pardon?"

"You've obviously heard of her."

"Are you kidding? I'm a perinatologist. Of course I've heard of her."

"Does that mean you wouldn't mind stopping by?"

"I'd love to meet her."

Jack removed his cell phone and tapped in a text message. A minute later his phone chimed twice. He looked down at the message.

"Okay, she's expecting us."

67

Madison's Mini kicked up a spray of gravel as it pulled into the driveway of Charlotte Duffy's oceanfront home. A few yards away, standing on the freshly cut lawn, Jack saw his mother waving at him. She was wearing orange-tinted sunglasses and a straw sun hat. He pushed open the door, stepped out and gave her a hug. She was only a few inches shorter than he was and had a lean face with long curving eyelashes.

"This is Madison Shaw. She's working with me on the GNS cases."

"It's wonderful to meet you," Charlotte said, taking both of her hands in hers and kissing her once on each cheek.

"Madison's a perinatologist at Southeastern State."

"I know, dear. You told me that last night on the phone, and the night before." Jack pretended to look toward the house. He prayed his face wasn't as red as he suspected it was. He watched Madison press her lips together, struggling to hold back a grin. His mother turned back to Madison. "I'm so pleased to have this opportunity to chat with you. I knew Jack would figure out some way of getting you up here."

"It's certainly a great pleasure for me to meet you. I'm very familiar with all of your groundbreaking cardiac research."

"Thank you, my dear, but I'm afraid all of that has become of historical interest only now." She took Madison by her arm and started down the driveway. "I'd much rather hear about you."

Jack absently tugged at his ear a couple of times while the two of them walked off leaving him standing there. For as long as he could remember, his mother had a unique penchant for embarrassing him, mostly by being painfully blunt. He looked past the house at the deserted beach, wondering if either of them remembered he was there.

Finally, after an exasperated sigh, he followed them to the side entrance that led into the kitchen, which Charlotte had decorated to be a mirror image of the rustic one in her Vermont summer home. She was an accomplished chef, and all forms of cookware dangled from an oval-shaped iron rack that hung over a rose-colored granite center island. It had been Jack's impression for many years that his mother's unpretentious choice of décor seemed to match her personality.

"May I get either of you something to drink?" she asked.

"Do you have any beer?" Jack asked.

"Don't be ridiculous. But I do have a lovely Chablis."

"My absolute second choice."

"Madison?" she asked.

"Just water for me, thank you."

With a glower, Charlotte said, "Jack, you're starting to remind me more and more of your father. God rest his soul."

"I'm sorry," Madison said. "Jack didn't mention that his father had passed away."

"That's because he's still alive," he said emphatically.

"Jack's right, I'm afraid. He's been living in London for the past twenty years." She sighed and then continued, "I keep checking the obituaries, but so far there hasn't been any good news."

"It's been a long time, Mom. You really need to let this go. Dad's really not that bad."

"Whatever you say, dear."

"I think this would be a good time to move on," he answered, arching his back and then stretching his neck muscles.

Charlotte led them into the great room with its ornate crown moldings and a rich hardwood floor. A bay window offered a sweeping view of the Atlantic. Next to it stood an eight-foot tree decorated with poinsettias, which was the only type of Christmas tree Jack could remember his mother displaying.

Charlotte ushered them over to the sofa and then left them to get the drinks.

Madison leaned back, smiled and silently applauded.

In just above a whisper, she said, "She's great, Jack. Talk about meeting somebody with no airs or graces."

"A true national treasure. No question about it."

Charlotte returned with their drinks on a silver tray, and for the next hour and a half there was no shortage of conversation. She asked Madison a litany of questions about her life. She answered openly and honestly and the conversation between them rolled on. Barely allowing Jack to wedge a word in from time to time.

It was almost three o'clock when Jack caught Madison's attention and tapped the crystal of his watch.

"We should get going, Mom."

"I was hoping you would stay for dinner."

"We're up against a pretty tight schedule. We really should be getting back."

"I'll agree to this abbreviated visit on one condition," she said sternly. "You have to promise to bring this lovely young lady back again very soon."

"I'll look forward to that," Madison said, shaking Charlotte's hand. She then excused herself for a few minutes.

"She's a very impressive young woman, Jack."

He held up his hands. "I know what you're trying to do and you can forget it. We're just working together. Our relationship is purely professional."

She touched his cheek. "I'll tell you what, dear. You can pretend you're not infatuated with Madison, and I'll pretend you're not trying to fool me about it."

He looked down the hall. "I really don't think now is the best time to—"

"If you don't mind me saying so, you looked stressed and completely exhausted."

With a furrowed brow, he said, "That's probably because my best friend's wife is on the verge of dying and I can't seem to help her. Mike's terrified and every time I look at his face I feel like I've failed him.

"Did he tell you that?"

"He doesn't have to."

"What have you done about it?"

"Other than beating my brains out twenty hours a day trying to figure out what's causing GNS and how to treat it—nothing."

"I understand you haven't made the kind of progress you had hoped to, but tell me what you have learned about the disease."

"Our sum total of knowledge is that the affected women have all recently received the flu vaccine and the vast majority have already been pregnant at least once. We're in the process of testing them, but we suspect they're all chimeras, but I have no idea of the significance of that . . . if any."

"You said chimeras."

"It's a genetic situation where—"

With a knowing smile, she whispered, "I'm quite aware of what chimerism is."

"Sorry," he said, realizing his mistake of underestimating his mother's vast knowledge. "I keep looking at these women over and over again, and I feel like I have five miles of medical data, but the whole thing is one inch thick."

"Maybe you're studying the wrong group of women."

"I beg your pardon."

"You're a gifted physician, Jack, but your entire life you've suffered from tunnel vision. You're too pragmatic and structured in everything you do. Sometimes medical research is about letting your mind go. You can't always be a slave to conventional thinking."

"What are you trying to tell me, Mother?"

She gently patted his cheek. "Sometimes, to understand a disease you have to look at the people who don't have it instead of the ones that do."

"Thanks," he responded in an unconvinced tone, "but I'm not sure you fully understand the . . ."

"The full breadth of the problem?" she asked with a quirked eyebrow.

"I didn't mean to imply . . ."

Before Jack could finish his thought, Madison strolled back into the room. Charlotte took her by the arm. With Jack trailing behind, she escorted her back to the car.

"It was an absolute pleasure meeting you, Madison. I look forward to your next visit."

"I'll look forward to that as well. Your home is beautiful. It was wonderful spending time with you."

Charlotte walked over to Jack, gave him a hug and then a quick peck on the cheek.

"Call me later, dear."

Jack again waved to his mother as Madison backed down the driveway. Nobody knew better than he how insightful she was. She was never one to shoot from the hip, make idle comments or offer gratuitous advice.

"What are you thinking about?" Madison asked. "Your lips are moving. My father does the same thing when he's lost in thought."

"Just something my mother said. It's probably not important."

During the drive back, they covered ground they'd already been over countless times. It came as no shock to either of them that they came up with no startling revelations or new directions to move in. In the morass and chaos that GNS had become, Jack was losing hope he'd figure out how to help these women before it was too late.

68

Maxime Barbier's first order of business upon returning to the Royal Canadian Mounted Police headquarters in Toronto was to meet with his supervisor, Clive Minify, to discuss the status of the Alik Vosky investigation.

When he walked into the small conference room, Clive was seated at the table waiting for him. Over the years the two of them had met on countless occasions, but to the best of Maxime's recollection, he couldn't think of a single time that Clive had arrived first. He was a stocky man who had a flare for the unconventional. He never allowed his expectations to exceed his reach. It was a source of amazement to many in the Mounted Police how he had ascended to a level of such authority.

Maxime wasted no time hanging up his coat and sitting down. Before Clive spoke, he removed the meerschaum pipe from his mouth. Maxime rarely saw him without it, although he'd never seen him raise a match to the bowl.

"We've expanded our staff to have a look at all the material you sent in from Vosky's house. In addition to our usual people, we brought in a couple of pharmacological and biochemical experts." Maxime was already well aware of what Clive was telling him. He had more than one friend in the forensic lab who was providing him with regular updates on their progress. "They've come across a lot of complex pharmaceutical and obstetric information. Vosky seems to have created dozens of sophisticated laboratory procedures. The files are not only in Russian, but they're also in some complex encrypted code Vosky invented. I have some of the brightest minds in Canada working on this thing. The only thing they can agree upon so far is that Vosky's a scientific genius. What they're wrestling with is trying to figure out if he's a cold, calculating mastermind who's responsible for the GNS crisis in the U.S. or some raving madman who needs to be permanently confined to a locked ward. I realize they haven't had the material that long, but you'd think with the brain trust we've got working on this thing, they'd at least be able to tell us something." Clive moved his pipe from one side of his mouth to the other. "What are your plans for the next few days?"

"Well, it seems like a certainty that Vosky won't be returning to Anticosti Island for a while. I've got some ideas where he might be."

"Any you feel like sharing?"

"Let me work on them a little first."

"Fine. Are you still planning on flying out today?"

"Yeah."

Clive stood up and started toward the door. Maxime escorted him the rest of the way. "I know you work alone and that you tend to be a little quirky when it comes to following the rules, but try to make an exception just this once and keep me informed. I'm getting a lot of pressure from the top on this one."

"Of course, sir."

Clive opened the door, but before walking out of the office, he put his hand on Maxime's shoulder. "I'll give you as many people as you need, but you have to bring this son of a bitch in, and I mean soon."

"I understand, sir."

Maxime released a lungful of air and then made his way down the corridor to his office. Instead of sitting down at his desk, he walked over to the window and stared out at the bottlenecked traffic below. He assumed within the next few minutes Clive Minify would soon be on the phone giving the prime minister the bad news that the RCMP still hadn't located Alik Vosky. Making matters worse, they couldn't give him the go-ahead to assure the president of the United States that GNS was not the act of an insane bioterrorist.

69

Instead of returning to his hotel after the drive home from his mother's house, Jack went to the hospital to check on Tess. He had just entered the lobby when he heard his name being paged overhead. With the melodious sound of a holiday instrumental playing in the background, he walked over to the information desk, reached for the physician phone and dialed the operator. While he waited, he noticed a stack of morning newspapers. He shuddered when he read the headline about the death of another woman suffering from GNS. He shook his head and closed his eyes. A few moments later, the operator connected the call.

"This is Dr. Wyatt."

"I'm sorry, Dr. Wyatt. I know we've been asked not to page any of the doctors with outside calls during the crisis, but this gentleman was so persistent. He claims he's a physician with information on GNS and that it's imperative he speaks with you, and only you."

"That's fine. Put him through, please."

"Thank you, Doctor."

After two rings, Jack heard the call connected. "Hello, this is Jack Wyatt."

"Dr. Wyatt, my name is Konrad Bilka. I'm a neurologist on the faculty of the Charles University School of Medicine in the Czech Republic. I've been in Florida for the past four weeks lecturing at Florida Atlantic University as part of a faculty exchange program."

"How can I help you, Dr. Bilka?"

"I've been following with great interest the GNS outbreak. I think I may have some information that would be of particular interest to you. Do you think we might be able to meet?"

Jack noted that although his Eastern European accent was unmistakable, his command of English was good.

"I'd be pleased to hear your ideas. Would you like to meet me here at the medical school?"

"I have many notes, scientific articles and other information. If you can find the time, it might be easier to meet at my hotel."

"Of course. Where are you staying?" Jack asked.

"At the Sealodge in Boca Raton. I'm in room 704."

"When would be a good time for you?" Jack inquired, making a mental note of the hotel and room number.

"Would you be able to make it tomorrow morning at ten?"

"Ten tomorrow will be fine."

"Thank you, Dr. Wyatt. I am sure you won't regret taking the time to have a look at my work."

"I look forward to talking with you tomorrow."

Four miles away in room 704 at the Sealodge Inn, Alik Vosky tossed his phone on the bed. He had entered the United States and checked into his hotel using a forged passport. With a self-satisfied grin, he crossed the room and sat down at the desk. In less than a day, he would have Dr. Jack Wyatt, the man who was far too close to undermining everything he had worked for, exactly where he wanted him—alone in his hotel room. He opened the center drawer of the desk and removed the serrated hunting knife he had purchased immediately after he'd arrived.

Vosky tested the knife's edge against his index finger, and then licked away the trickle of blood. He was calm, devoid of any anxiety or uncertainty. The risk involved was small and didn't concern him in the slightest. By the time Jack Wyatt's body was found, he'd be a thousand miles away using yet another name, and the police would be looking for a man who didn't exist.

70

It was six P.M. when Jack and Madison sat down across from each other in the crisis center. They had called a meeting of the entire group but none of the team had arrived as yet. When Jack heard the door open, he looked up expecting to see Marc. To his surprise it was Helen Morales. With hunched shoulders, she made her way over to the conference table and took the chair next to Madison.

"The hospital board met a couple of hours ago." Madison slowly lowered the lid of her laptop while Jack absently rubbed his hands together. "Hollis Sinclair did an excellent job convincing the members they should endorse the Vitracide program. They listened to his plea and voted seven to one in favor."

"I thought the board doesn't make medical recommendations," Madison said.

"As a rule, they don't. Let's just say they see a difference between their seal of approval and an outright medical recommendation. In practical terms, I'm not sure there is one."

"How does this 'seal of approval,'" Madison asked, making air quotes with both hands, "affect the timetable?"

"We've just received our first shipment of Vitracide and Sinclair has submitted a completed protocol for its use. So, I'm guessing we should be ready in a day or two."

"We are pursuing some promising leads," Jack offered. "Is there anything we can do to buy a little more time?"

"I'm afraid not. The board expects the medical staff to be unified in the decision to endorse Vitracide. I'm sure you both realize what this means in terms of the work you and your team have been doing." She stood up and started toward the door. "I'll keep you both advised."

"I guess that's it, then," Madison said.

Jack reluctantly agreed. He realized they weren't on the verge of finding a cure for GNS but he felt they were making some real progress. It wasn't for a lack of determination or effort on his team's part they had come up short. There was no blame to assign. Time had simply run out, which had been Jack's greatest fear right from the beginning.

After another fifteen minutes had passed the last members of the research group had taken their seats at the table.

"I'm afraid I have some bad news," Madison began. "Just prior to this meeting, Dr. Wyatt and I were informed the hospital has decided to go ahead with the Vitracide program. We anticipate treatment will begin within the next few days. So, for now the work we've been doing is on hold. We thank all of you for your participation. Everybody in the room went way beyond what was asked of them."

"Does this mean we're totally shutting down?" Marc asked.

"The hospital feels, and Dr. Wyatt and I agree, that we should all be unified behind the Vitracide program. If the treatment plan doesn't . . . meet expectations . . . well, we can revisit the prospect of starting up our work again."

One of the obstetric residents raised her hand. "My understanding is that the Vitracide protocol calls for ten days of treatment. Based on the increasing number of deaths were seeing, we may be too late to pick up where we left off in ten days."

Jack knew she was right. With Sinclair in the wheelhouse, no matter how bad things were going, he wouldn't admit defeat until the last second of the tenth day.

Jack stood up. "Your point is a valid one, but Dr. Shaw and I still feel the best thing for all of us to do is adopt an optimistic outlook and hope Vitracide turns out to be an effective treatment. If that's not the case, we're not closing the door on further investigation."

For the next few minutes, the group remained, discussing their now futile efforts to find a cure for GNS. Finally, the last despondent team member made their way out of the room. Marc lingered.

"I guess it doesn't matter anymore but we finished the analysis of the chimera testing. As it turns out, their distribution in GNS patients is different than the healthy chimera in the population."

"In what way?" Madison asked.

"Usually, the chimera cells can be found in several areas of the body. The liver, lymph nodes and the thyroid gland, just to name a few. But it seems in our GNS patients almost all of them are in the thyroid gland." He shrugged. "I'm not sure it means anything."

"I guess if Vitracide fails and we ever get up and running again, we can look into it," Jack said.

After Marc left, Jack and Madison stayed to gather up the volumes of computer printouts and notes strewn across the conference table.

"What are you going to do?" she asked.

"Right now or in ten days?"

"I meant now, Jack."

"I'm going to get some dinner."

"Mind if I join you?"

"Really. You must be desperate for company." Madison folded her arms and glared at him with narrowed eyes. "Sorry," he said. "Bad joke. You name the place."

"As long as it has a full bar, I couldn't care less."

"Finally, something we can agree upon."

Madison suggested a local sports bar, and they drove together. It took some effort, but Jack was able to empty his mind of all matters related to GNS, hospital politics and Dr. Hollis Sinclair. Their conversation was free flowing and easy and it was hard for Jack to deny he was becoming more captivated by her. But she was still a mystery to him. Even so, he had become more attracted to her than any woman he'd met since his divorce. He never felt his instincts regarding matters of the heart were particularly astute, but in the matter of Madison Shaw, he suspected she felt the same way. Jack had just finished paying the check when his cell phone rang. It was Mike.

"Of course I understand," Jack said nodding his head. "I told you, if I were in your position, I'd do the same thing." Trying to cast the indelible image of Tess Ryan lying in the ICU from his mind, he continued to listen patiently. "I think that's a good idea; let's talk in the morning." With despair painted on his face, Jack slid his cell phone back into its case.

"Mike?" she asked.

"Yeah."

"That didn't sound good. What's going on?"

"Tess is scheduled for a C-section tomorrow," he said with a disconcerted sigh. "I guess Sinclair's moving faster than we thought."

"What time?"

"Noon."

Jack followed Madison past the bar and toward the exit. Two men, both dressed in dark sports coats, approached and stopped in front of them.

"Dr. Wyatt?" the taller one asked, reaching into his coat pocket and removing his identification.

"Yes."

"My name is Craig Westenson. I'm a special agent with the FBI. This is Inspector Maxime Barbier with the Royal Canadian Mounted Police. I wonder if we might have a word with you. It won't take long, sir."

Jack and Madison looked at each other briefly.

"I'll meet you outside," she told him.

"It's been a long day. Go home and relax. I'll grab a cab."

Jack walked Madison to the front of the restaurant.

"Watch your six," she told him.

"I beg your pardon?" he said with a blank look.

"Obviously you don't come from a military family. My father was career Air Force. I'll speak to you in the morning."

Jack returned to the bar. Westenson and Barbier were sitting at a booth. He slid in across from them.

"Thank you for taking the time to speak with us," Westenson said. "What I'd like to discuss with you might strike you as a difficult to believe, but I assure you the United States government wouldn't be making these inquiries unless we felt there was substance to our concerns."

Jack saw no uncertainty in either of their faces. He already had more than a clue in his mind of what they wanted to talk to him about. He clasped his hands, set them flush on the table and asked, "How can I help you, gentlemen?"

"We have a request, Doctor," Westenson answered. He then took a few minutes to explain the details of why he and Barbier had sought him out. Jack listened carefully and asked no questions. When Westenson was finished, Jack emptied his lungs of a full breath, steepled his fingers and set his hands on the table.

"I think I have some information that may interest you," he told them.

71

Twenty minutes after his meeting with Special Agent Westenson and Inspector Barbier, Jack was on his way home. Even though he told Mike he'd call him in the morning, he thought about placing a call now to check on him. He was just about to make that call when his phone tang.

"What the devil was all that cloak-and-dagger stuff about?" Madison asked him.

"Nothing, just routine."

"C'mon, Jack. The FBI and Canadian police hunt you down to speak with you, and you tell me it's nothing but routine stuff. Are you kidding? I thought you were done trying to con me."

"I'm not trying to con anybody. I was instructed not to discuss the details."

"That's fine. You can skip the details and just give me the highlights."

There was no doubt in Jack's mind Madison would persist until he gave her some morsel of information.

"Suffice it to say," he began with caution, "that the government's concerned the scientific community may be operating under a rather large misconception in its efforts to cure GNS."

"That's what I assumed. So, how does all that affect us?"

"Good question. As soon as I have an answer, I'll let you know," he said. "I was thinking of giving Mike a call. Do you mind if I get back to you in the morning?"

Jack was pleased Madison didn't protest. A few raindrops began tapping against the cab's windshield. At the same time, an ambulance, with the hi-lo wail of its siren, sped past him. Jack tried in vain to gather his thoughts before calling Mike. He knew that unless something dramatic regarding GNS happened, his best friend wouldn't change his decision to have Tess undergo a C-section and begin Vitracide therapy.

Finally, he placed the call. Their conversation was brief. It was obvious Mike had made up his mind regarding Tess's treatment, and Jack knew it would be impossible to convince him otherwise.

Amongst the many things Jack admired about Mike was his sixth sense when it came to evaluating a complex problem. Even as a kid, Mike rarely made the wrong decision. Deep in thought, Jack absently bit his lower lip. As hard as he tried, he couldn't shake the nagging fear that, in spite of his flawless track record, Mike may have made the first truly bad choice of his life.

72

As soon as Jack arrived back in his hotel room, he got on his computer. He wanted to get some further information on what Marc had told him regarding the distribution of the chimera cells in the women with GNS. He hadn't been at work for more than a few minutes when he realized he was exhausted. He was just about to wrap things up and climb into bed when his phone rang. He checked the caller ID. It was Lucien from Orlando Memorial calling.

"Hi, Jack. I'm sorry to call you so late, but do you have a few minutes to talk about the biopsy slides?"

"Of course," he answered, instantly feeling as alert as if he had just awakened from a solid eight-hour sleep.

"I made a new set of slides using alternative staining techniques, and I have to tell you that a number of the slides bear a very subtle resemblance to the brain tissue of patients with some of the rarer forms of autoimmune diseases."

Jack was instantly reminded of his team meeting when the possibility that the women suffering from GNS were all chimeras was first raised. He specifically remembered Carolyn, the medical student, informing the group that women with chimerism have a greater chance of having one of the autoimmune diseases.

In a guarded tone he said, "I'm sure you're aware that all of the GNS patients have had a complete set of blood tests to see if they have an autoimmune disease. They've all come up negative."

"I wasn't aware of that, but it doesn't surprise me. The slides I prepared are not diagnostic of any specific disease in the autoimmune family. All I can say is they have a vague resemblance to the brain tissue of patients with diseases like lupus. If GNS does turn out to be an auto-immune illness, it's going to be a new one that's never been described or seen before, which would account for why all of your blood tests have come up negative."

"Almost all of the women who died were autopsied. I've read the reports. None of them even hinted at the possibility of an autoimmune disease."

"I'm not surprised," Lucien said. "The special techniques and stains we used to look at the young woman's brain biopsy would never be part of a routine autopsy. Plus, the pathologists who did the autopsies were dealing with dead tissue while we studied specimens from viable brain." He shook his head a few times. "There's no way our findings would have been observed at any of the autopsies done on the GNS victims."

Like most physicians, Jack was well aware that one of the most poorly understood groups of diseases known to medical science were the autoimmune ones. Normally, the body makes antibodies to fight off harmful bacteria and viruses. In patients with autoimmune diseases, this important process goes completely haywire. The individual's antibodies, for unknown reasons, are defective and instead of fighting off infection, they attack and severely damage normal tissue. In spite of an enormous amount of sophisticated research, medical science had never figured out why the body attacks its own normal tissues. No cure had ever been found. Various treatments such as chemotherapy and steroids had been tried but the results had been far from encouraging.

Jack stood up and started in a slow pace around his room.

"Do you have a theory why the pathologists at Southeastern didn't make the same observation you did?"

"I don't know. What I'm seeing is the furthest thing from obvious, or maybe they weren't looking for it," Lucien offered. Jack knew what he was thinking and saw no reason to ask him to explain his comment. "The other reason could be that the findings I'm talking about are extremely thin. It's not unreasonable to theorize that they could have gone unnoticed, or noticed and rejected as a possibility."

"I know you're a superb pathologist, Lucien, and

please take this with the spirit it's intended. Did you consider asking another pathologist to have a look at the slides?"

Lucien chuckled. "As a matter of fact, I did. I called Jacob Shoemaker in Tampa for a second opinion. He's considered a national authority on autoimmune diseases. I assumed you wanted to keep this matter highly confidential, so I didn't tell him the slides were from a GNS patient. He called me an hour or so ago and agreed with my findings."

"Well, that's certainly a fascinating observation you two have made."

"Hopefully this will lead somewhere. It's been a pretty lousy Christmas for a lot of people. Let me know if I can be of any further help."

"Thanks, Lucien. I owe you one."

Jack stopped pacing and sat on the end of his bed. He was already quite knowledgeable on the neurologic problems one sees in the autoimmune diseases. Lucien was right about one thing: If GNS was a new autoimmune disease, it certainly didn't resemble any of the others and may not be detectable with the standard diagnostic tests available.

After a few minutes, he went out on his balcony. Looking across the Intracoastal Waterway and out to the Atlantic, he went over every detail of his conversation with Lucien. Even though he had promised Helen to stop all of his team's efforts to discover the cause of GNS, Jack reached for his phone and called Marc.

"Are you still in the hospital?"

"Yeah," Marc answered with a sigh. "We've been slammed with six new admissions. I'll be here for a while."

"Do you think you can find some time to check something out for me in the Patient Data Record?"

"Sure . . . but I thought we were no longer . . ."

"This is unofficial . . . and confidential."

"I understand. What do you need me to do?"

"I want to repeat the autoimmune testing on all of the GNS patients just to make sure we haven't missed something."

"No problem I'll take care of it right away," he told Jack. "I assume you heard that Tess Ryan is scheduled for a C-section tomorrow."

"I heard. I'll see you in the morning."

Jack tossed his phone on the bed. He then walked over to the desk, turned his computer on again and brought up his preferred medical information website. The website was a convenient resource for finding all the most recent scientific publications on any disease or medical topic. It was the same website he had used to educate himself on chimerism.

Jack would have gone to the hospital himself and done the research he'd asked Marc to do, but he had far more important plans for the next several hours. He continued to face countless uncertainties, but there was one thing that was unshakably true—by sunup he'd know everything that medical science knew about autoimmune diseases.

73

> NUMBER OF CASES: 8,265
> NUMBER OF DEATHS: 38

Alik Vosky stood in front of the window, staring out at a large high-rise complex to the north. After a minute or so, he walked over to the refrigerator and removed a mini bottle of vodka. He didn't consider himself a drinking man, but today was an exception, even if it was only nine forty-five in the morning. He found a glass, poured the vodka over a few cubes of ice and downed it in one long gulp.

Setting the glass down, he reached into his pocket to make sure the mace pepper spray gun he'd purchased was facing with the handle pointing up.

He hadn't slept very well the night before, his mind cluttered with anticipation regarding his meeting with Jack Wyatt. He had written out in precise detail how the events of their twenty-minute rendezvous would play out. A few minutes earlier he checked the desk drawer to make sure the duct tape and hunting knife were also where he'd have easy access to them. Once he had Dr. Wyatt restrained with the duct tape, he would take five minutes to explain why his death was an absolute necessity. They were both scientists; surely Wyatt would understand.

Vosky sat down on the love seat and waited for Wyatt's arrival. He considered pouring himself another drink, but then dismissed the notion as ill advised. As he expected, at exactly ten o'clock, there were three quick knocks at his door. He came to his feet, crossed the room and opened the door.

"Dr. Wyatt. Thank you so much for coming," he said with a broad smile, extending his hand. "Please come in. I have all my notes and research set up on the table." Before closing the door, Vosky took a moment to place the Do Not Disturb sign on the handle.

"I'm honored you asked me to have a look at your work. I truly appreciate the opportunity."

Vosky motioned to the opposite side of the suite. "As I mentioned on the phone, I don't think you'll be disappointed. I understand you think the entire outbreak is related in some way to the flu vaccine."

"That's our theory."

"Well, in that case, it seems as if we've both arrived at the same conclusion," Vosky stated, a little surprised

Wyatt hadn't asked him how he knew about his flu vaccine theory. As far as he knew, the theory had not been made public. "I've read about Dr. Sinclair's virus theory, and I have to tell you, I believe he's wrong. Please, have a seat on the couch, I'll get my notes and I'll explain to you why."

"If you don't mind, I injured my back a few days ago. I'd prefer to stand."

"I'm sorry to hear that. I hope you're feeling better soon." Vosky returned from the table and handed him a stack of papers. "So tell me, Dr. Wyatt. How did you arrive at your conclusion that the flu vaccine is the direct cause of GNS?"

"We were lucky."

"You're being too modest," he said as a mysterious smile spread across his face. "It took me years to figure out what you did in just a week or so."

"I'm not quite sure I understand. How could you have been working on this for years? The first cases of GNS were only diagnosed a couple of weeks ago."

"That's true. But based on research I conducted three years ago in Russia, I was able to create the disease in mice. You see, Dr. Wyatt, I engineered the entire thing."

"I apologize, Doctor, but I'm not sure I understand what you're saying."

"Of course not. How could you? I genetically engineered GNS but I had no way of causing the epidemic in pregnant women until I figured out how to use the flu vaccine as the method of infection and transmission." His smile broadened. "Don't look surprised, Dr. Wyatt. I assure you, everything I say is true." He pointed to the table. "It's all there in my notes. Unfortunately, I doubt there's a handful of scientists in the United States with the intellectual capacity to understand them." Vosky casually sighed. "Everything was progressing just as planned until you got involved. As much as I respect you and admire your work, I'm sure you can appreciate why I can't possibly allow you to continue your research. If you should somehow stumble across a means to stop the spread of GNS . . . well, it would drastically upset my plans."

Vosky casually slid his hand into his pocket. Finding the mace pepper gun, he began to slide it out. He only looked down for a split second, but it was then that he felt a crushing grip on his wrist. Before he could offer any resistance, the man he believed to be Dr. Jack Wyatt jerked his hand out of his pocket. In one motion, he stepped under Vosky's arm, twisted his wrist and took up a position behind him. In the process, he locked Vosky's arm in an inescapable bar hold. A jolt of upward pressure on his wrist was all that it took to send the mace pepper gun sailing from his grip. Vosky cried out in pain, feeling as if the tendons in his wrist and elbow were being snapped and sheared off. His scream was still hanging in the air when the door to the hotel room crashed open. Four men dressed in plainclothes raced across the room. Five seconds later, Vosky was completely subdued.

"Dr. Vosky. I'm not Dr. Wyatt. My name is Westenson. I'm a special agent with the FBI," he informed him as two of the other agents finished handcuffing him. "We're going to get you the help you need, but right now we have to place you under arrest."

When Vosky was securely in custody, he was read his rights and led away. One of the agents present was Maxime Barbier of the Royal Canadian Mounted Police. He had remained behind the other men and had not physically participated in the arrest.

Westenson reached into the inner pocket of his sports coat to check his recording device.

"Thank you," Barbier said.

"We should be the ones thanking you. You figured out Vosky would eventually show up in Florida," Westenson said. "When were you planning on heading back to Canada?"

"In a couple of days. I want to make sure there are no loose ends regarding extradition."

"Do you think he'll ever stand trial in Canada?"

"I doubt it. I spoke with the lead psychiatrist on the case last night. His team's conclusion is that Vosky fits the pattern of a classic paranoid schizophrenic. Obviously, they reached that conclusion without interviewing and examining him. So, I'm sure the first order of business will be to get him into a psychiatric facility for an evaluation and to begin treatment. I don't know what will happen after that."

"Based on what occurred here this morning, I would have to assume in his delusional state he would have killed Dr. Wyatt."

By this time a team of forensic technicians had entered

the room. Having signed out to his partner, Westenson motioned to Barbier and they left.

"I think the FBI owes Dr. Wyatt a personal thanks for his cooperation," Westenson said. "Without him informing us about the phone call he received from Vosky, this could have ended in a disaster. I think I'll take a ride over to the hospital later to thank him."

"I'd like to go with you if you don't mind."

"Of course," Westenson said, as they started down the hall. "I don't know about you, but this kind of work always makes me hungry. How about getting something to eat? The FBI is treating."

With a grin, Barbier extended his hand. The doors to the elevator opened and they stepped on.

74

It was ten thirty when Jack walked into the hospital coffee shop. He had been awake for the past four hours, but he had stayed in his hotel room finishing up his reading on autoimmune diseases and chimerism. His mind was so consumed with other things, he hadn't even given any thought to the information he had shared with the FBI about the phone call he'd received from Vosky posing as a physician and the meeting he was supposed to attend.

There was only one person in line in front of him who seemed to take forever deciding what she wanted. Finally, Jack was able to order two cappuccinos. He picked them up at the end of the counter and carried them out to the lobby. When he saw Mike approaching, he did everything in his power to push an encouraging smile to his face.

"How are you feeling?" he asked him, handing him one of the containers.

"Scared," he answered directly. "If anybody had asked me a few weeks ago if I would ever be in a position to second-guess my—"

"What happened to Tess is nobody's fault and—"

"That's not what I meant. I was the one who encouraged Helen Morales to invite you here." Mike's face flushed. "I've made a decision that could result in the death of my wife and unborn baby. That's hardly an easy thing to do. Going with Sinclair's advice over yours was the toughest choice I've ever made in my life. But whatever happens, don't ever think, even for a second, that I don't know you did everything possible to help Tess."

Jack took a couple of sips of his cappuccino before responding, "I can't begin to imagine what you've been going through. There's an awful lot I don't know, but what I do know is that you're got a lot more important things to concern yourself with than my feelings." Mike opened his mouth to speak but Jack raised his hand. "We're both way past owing each other explanations or apologies for anything." He pointed toward the elevators. "C'mon, let's go upstairs."

75

Crossing the lobby, Jack spotted Bud Kazminski coming toward him. He looked exhausted and even more disheveled than usual. With no improvement in his limp, he hobbled up and greeted Jack with a fatigued expression and a hangdog shake of the hand.

"Go up without me. I'll meet you up there. We have plenty of time before the operating room calls for Tess," he told Mike, who continued toward the elevators.

Kaz said, "I don't know if you heard: Mia Kleinfield died a few hours ago. She was admitted the day before Sherry. They managed to save the baby. She was a nurse on the dialysis unit. Everybody's taking it pretty hard." Kaz looked away for a few seconds and then added, "Sinclair already called my son-in-law this morning. He's pushing David pretty hard to start treatment tomorrow.

To build his case, he's telling everybody Mike Ryan had already agreed, which kind of makes your best friend the poster boy for Vitracide. Anyway, David called me and we had a long talk about it. I think we're going to give Sinclair the go-ahead."

"A lot of physicians across the country agree with Dr. Sinclair that antiviral medication's the way to go."

"I'm sure they do—but, obviously, you're not one of them," Kaz said, with a dubious half smile. "Is it Sinclair you don't trust or are you just opposed to using Vitracide because you don't think it will work and it's nasty as hell?" He held up his hand and after a protracted sigh, added, "You don't have to answer that. You know, Doc, I've spent the better part of my adult life interviewing all kinds of people. The hard part isn't dragging information out of them—it's trying to figure out how much of it's the truth." Jack didn't comment on Kaz's observation. He got the feeling he was fishing, trying to find out what Jack thought of Sinclair. "I'd love to know what you really think about our decision to treat Sherry with Vitracide."

"I think I told you."

"The other thing I've learned as a reporter is to recognize hedging when I hear it." With a mixture of gloom and hopelessness on his face, Kaz sluggishly raised his eyes. "I've loved three women in my life, Dr. Wyatt: my wife and my two daughters. Sherry and I have always been close but Lisa hasn't spoken to me in years. I guess in her eyes, I made some mistakes she can't forgive me for. She and Sherry have stayed close. Lisa visits almost every day, but only after her husband makes sure I'm not around. Do you know what it's like to have twin daughters and only one of them cares to speak with you?"

Jack felt his breath catch. "I don't recall you mentioning Sherry was a twin. Are they identical?"

"Yeah."

"Are you sure?" Jack asked in a voice rising in intensity.

"Of course I'm sure. Why? What difference does it make?"

"Does Lisa have any children?"

"Two, and one on the way."

"How far along is she?"

"About seven months," Kaz answered.

"But she doesn't have GNS."

"Of course not. I think I would have told you that."

"Has Lisa been healthy her whole life?"

"Neither of the girls has ever been seriously ill."

Jack renewed his question. "No major illnesses or surgeries?"

"One of them had their tonsils out as a kid," Kaz answered as he let out a slow breath. "I'm pretty sure it was Lisa. She was about six at the time. I remember her eating ice cream nonstop for three days."

"I should get going," he said. "I'll stop in and see Sherry in a couple of hours."

Jack shoved his hands in the front pockets of his

chinos and walked slowly toward the elevators. Before meeting Mike, he decided to stop in the medical library.

Being a twin: At least now he knew why Sherry was a chimera. He assumed Lisa was as well. But what had him reeling was a simple question. Why had Sherry contracted GNS and Lisa hadn't?

76

Dr. Lyman Douglas had cared for Tess Ryan through two miscarriages and her present pregnancy. She and Mike had the resources that would have allowed her to be cared for anywhere in the country, but it was Lyman Douglas she insisted upon. She knew he wasn't the busiest doctor in town but she revered him for his calm, caring manner and meticulous approach to her care.

Tess Ryan's C-section was scheduled for noon but since the entire operating team was present and ready to begin, Douglas instructed the nurse manager to have Tess brought to the operating room early.

Fifteen minutes later, accompanied by Mike, Tess was wheeled into the preoperative holding unit. Douglas was there to meet them.

"Are you ready?" he asked Mike.

"I was kind of hoping Jack would be here. I've been

calling him but he's not picking up. I'm a little surprised."

Douglas glanced down at his watch. "We're only about thirty minutes early. We can wait if you want."

Mike shuffled his feet for a few seconds. "We might as well go now. I'm sure he's on his way."

"Okay," Douglas said. He then motioned at the patient care assistant who moved forward, kicked the break release and slowly began to bring Tess out into the main corridor.

Before they started down the hallway into the operating room, Mike raised his hand. "Can you hold it a sec?" he asked.

Leaning over the railing, Mike eased the sheet a little higher up on Tess's chest. He then leaned over and kissed her twice on the forehead. A couple of his tears dropped on her cheek. He gingerly dried them aside with his finger. He then interlocked his pinky with hers for a few seconds—a habit born from their high school days. Lowering his head, he whispered, "I love you, Tess." He then took a step back, looked at Douglas and nodded.

"Just have a seat in the waiting room," Douglas said. "I'll be out to talk with you as soon as we're done. You can still come into the operating room and watch if you'd like. It's not too late."

"I don't think so. I'll be in the waiting room."

He then watched as the stretcher carrying the woman he cherished disappeared through the doors that led to operating room number two.

77

The moment the ICU doors swung open and Jack walked in, he spotted Marc at the nursing station with his head glued to one of the computer monitors. His conversation with Kaz was still on his mind. For some reason, the words of advice his mother had offered him popped into his head. He envisioned her knowing eyes as she suggested that sometimes studying patients without a disease can provide important information in finding its cure.

Instead of walking over to talk with Marc, he reached for his phone. He leaned against the desk and scrolled through his phone book until he found Kaz's number. He checked the time. He still had plenty of time before Tess was scheduled for her C-Section.

"Kaz, it's Dr. Wyatt. I'd like to speak with your daughter. Do you have her phone number?"

"It's not necessary to call her."

"It's quite necessary. I'm not sure you understand," he explained in a voice, thinning with patience. "What I want to speak with her about directly relates to helping Sherry."

"I'm not sure you understand. What I'm saying is you don't need to call her because she's upstairs in the ICU visiting Sherry. That's why I'm still down here in the lobby waiting for her to leave."

"Thanks. I'll speak with you later." Jack replaced his phone, turned and started toward the other wing of the ICU.

"Where are you going?" Marc asked.

"I'll be back in a few minutes."

Jack walked past the nursing station and then down the corridor that led to Sherry's room. Between lengthy strides, he couldn't help but wonder if stumbling upon the fact that Sherry had an identical twin might turn out to be the twist of fate he'd been praying for. He was a few feet from Sherry's room when he saw David step out in the hall followed by a woman.

"Excuse me," Jack said to David. "I'm Dr. Wyatt, I'm one of the doctors looking after Sherry."

"David Rosenfelt," he answered, extending his hand to Jack. "I'm Sherry's husband. This is Lisa, her sister. My father-in-law has told me a lot about you. We're both very appreciative of everything you've done for Sherry."

"Thank you," Jack said. He turned to Lisa. "A few minutes ago, I spoke with your father. He mentioned to me you were here. Would you mind if I asked you a few questions about your health?"

"Not at all."

"Have you had any difficulties with your pregnancy?"

"No. Everything's gone very well," she answered without hesitation.

"How far along are you?"

"I'm just finishing my sixth month."

"I assume you've had obstetrical care the entire time."

"Yes, of course."

"Did you take the flu shot?"

"About two months ago. Sherry and I use the same OB. As a matter of fact, we both had the shot the same day. It was in his office."

"Would you say your overall health is good?"

"I'd say it's excellent."

"Besides having your tonsils out, have you ever had any other surgery?"

She frowned. "As usual, my father's a tad confused about the facts. It was Sherry who had her tonsils out, not me."

"Are you presently taking any medications?" Jack inquired.

"I take a thyroid pill once a day."

"When were you diagnosed with low thyroid?"

"Actually, I take it because I don't have a thyroid gland," she answered.

Jack looked at her neck with a quizzical expression. There was no scar indicating her thyroid gland had been removed.

"Were you born without a thyroid gland?"

"No. I had a very overactive thyroid as a teenager. I

remember my mother taking me to see all kinds of doctors. My father was too busy. They tried a bunch of medications but none of them worked. Finally, one of the doctors gave me some kind of radioactive pills to destroy all of my thyroid gland. It worked. I've been fine ever since . . . except for having to take a thyroid pill once a day."

"You probably had Graves' disease," Jack said, feeling the muscles and tendons in his neck tighten like a hangman's noose.

"Yeah. I think that's what they called it. I guess I should have mentioned it when you asked me about my prior health, but it was so many years ago . . . well, I've kind of forgotten about it."

"Is there anything else at all about your general health that you haven't mentioned?"

"No. I don't think so."

Jack extended his hand to Lisa, "I appreciate you taking the time to talk with me."

Starting back toward Tess's room, Jack practically broke into a sprint. He grabbed his cell phone and tapped in Madison's number. His stomach was in a flutter. She answered on the first ring. Trying not to rush his words, he said, "I need you to do something for me right now."

78

With his conversation with Lisa still playing in his mind, Jack hurried across the ICU until he reached Tess's room. When he slid the glass door open, he was surprised to see her bed was gone and Mike was nowhere in sight.

"They went down to the operating room about twenty minutes ago," the nurse said.

Jack looked at his watch. "I thought the C-section wasn't scheduled until noon."

"Dr. Douglas called and moved it up. If you're looking for Mr. Ryan, I'm sure he's in the OR waiting room."

Jack started for the door. "I was supposed to meet Dr. Shaw here. Would you please ask her to meet me in the OR waiting room when she gets here?"

"Of course, Dr. Wyatt."

Fortunately, the operating rooms were on the same floor as the ICU. Two minutes later, Jack approached the waiting room. Through a large glass window, he spotted Mike sitting in an upholstered chair. His eyes were cast downward, blankly staring at the floor. Just at that moment, Madison appeared.

"They just put her to sleep but they haven't started as yet," she told Jack. "I told Douglas not to make an incision until he hears from me. He wasn't happy about it and I don't think he's going to wait very long."

Jack and Madison walked into the waiting room together. When they were a few steps away from where Mike was sitting, he looked up.

"Where the hell have you been?" he asked Jack, coming to his feet.

"I had to speak with a patient's family. How come you didn't tell me the surgery had been rescheduled?"

"I called you twice. Check your voice mail."

"I need you to authorize Madison to tell Dr. Douglas to cancel the C-section."

"What are you talking about? Have you lost your mind? We talked about all this last night and decided the best thing—"

Jack waved his hand. "I know we did, but something's changed. I think we may have found a way to cure Tess. It's going to sound unconventional, but I'm convinced it's the only thing that has a real chance of working."

"I'm . . . I'm not sure—"

"I'm asking you to trust me, Mike. Please tell Madison she can contact Dr. Douglas and put Tess's C-section on hold."

Mike took a hard look first at Jack and then at Madison. He raised his hands and covered his face for a few seconds before dropping them back to his side.

"Okay. Tell them I'd like to hold off on the C-section for right now."

Jack turned to Madison. "Please tell Douglas it's of critical importance that he holds off for a few minutes. I'll come back into the operating room in a few minutes to explain everything, but first I have to speak to Mike."

"I'll take care of it," Madison said, hurrying toward the exit.

With a puzzled grimace, Mike said, "I'm listening."

In a calm voice, Jack took the next five minutes to explain the basics of his plan. Mike asked no questions. In fact, he didn't utter a single word until Jack was finished. Finally, he looked at Jack, his face flushed with a mixture of anxiety and disbelief.

"Are you serious?" was all he could manage.

"I said my plan was unconventional."

"'Unconventional'? Jack, *unconventional* means straying slightly from the normal path. I'm not a doctor but what you're suggesting sounds like pure insanity," Mike said, looking at him as if he had grown a second head right in front of him. He covered his mouth and then tapped his upper lip with his fingertips. "Do you understand what you're asking me to agree to? You're not exactly pitching me on some wing-and-a-prayer business deal. We're talking about Tess's life here."

"If I didn't truly believe this would work, I wouldn't be proposing it." Jack blew out a breath and said as calmly as he was able, "I know I'm asking you to take a blind leap of faith, Mike, but I know what I'm doing."

"But Sinclair is planning on beginning—"

"I couldn't care less about what Sinclair's planning," Jack said, his voice gaining in intensity with each word.

Jack looked over at the door and saw Madison coming toward them. She motioned to him to continue their conversation in one of the small family rooms that adjoined the larger waiting area. After they both had taken a seat on the couch, Jack answered all of Mike's questions. He felt Mike was able to process the information. Sittting in silence, fiddling with his watchband, he appeared anxious but not on verge of becoming unglued.

"Even though you're my best friend," Mike began in a measured voice, "if I were making this decision using only logic, I'd tell you that you were insane and to go shit in your hat. But since that doesn't appear to be the case, go ahead and do whatever you think will help Tess. I'll sign the consent."

"Tess is already asleep but they hadn't started the C-section. I called Dr. Willwade. She's been fully briefed and is standing by if we need her."

For a few moments, Jack tapped his chin with his fingertips. "Please let Dr. Willwade know that Mike's agreed and that we will require her services as soon as possible."

"I'll let her know. She told me if we should decide to go ahead, she'd like to come down and speak with Mike. And in the meantime, I think you and I should go speak with Dr. Douglas. He was somewhat less than pleased about us putting his C-section on hold."

79

After looking at the clock for the third time, Lyman Douglas walked over and picked up Tess's clipboard. After a few seconds, he tossed it back on the table and folded his arms in front of his chest.

"Until I hear differently, we should at least go ahead with our pre-op safety check."

The circulating nurse again confirmed Tess's identity by checking her identification band. When she had finished, Douglas went through each and every critical piece of information related to the C-section.

"Has the neonatologist on call been advised we're almost ready to begin?"

"She's in the suite," his scrub nurse answered.

"If we don't hear from Dr. Shaw in the next sixty seconds, page her."

Just then, Madison poked her head into the operating

room and motioned to Douglas. He put Tess's chart down and joined her and Jack outside in the hall next to the scrub sink.

"Lyman, this is Jack Wyatt. Jack's a visiting professor from Ohio State. He's been working very closely with us on the GNS cases."

Douglas shook his hand, and with a slow smile said, "Yes, I believe I've heard Hollis Sinclair mention your name a time or two. If you don't mind me saying so, Madison, you look like a lady with something on her mind."

"Before you scrub, we'd like to speak to you. It's rather important."

"Of course."

"It might be better if we spoke in the patient consultation room." From the look on his face, Jack got the feeling Douglas sensed he was about to hear something completely out of the ordinary.

Douglas blew a breath out between pursed lips. "Let me tell my team I'll be a few minutes."

Fifteen minutes later, Douglas walked back into the operating room with Madison at his side. Standing next to them was Dr. Amy Willwade, the chief of head and neck surgery at Southeastern State. Everybody in the room stopped what they were doing, their attention locked on Drs. Douglas and Willwade.

"We have a change in plan," Douglas announced. "The C-section is canceled. Dr. Willwade will explain how we'll be proceeding." He raised a hand above the murmur. "I understand this is a little unorthodox but I assure you everything's been carefully thought out. I'm sorry but we don't have the time to answer a lot of questions."

Douglas took a few steps back. He caught Willwade's eye, who raised her hand and crossed her fingers.

Willwade said, "My instrument trays are being pulled now and should be ready in five minutes. I'm going to scrub. The consent for the new operation we'll be performing is signed and on the chart. I'll explain the rest when I get back in the room."

The circulating nurse, who was anything but a rookie, asked in a hesitant voice, "Is there anything we should do while you're scrubbing?"

Without breaking stride or turning around, Willwade said, "Yes. Put a roll behind Mrs. Ryan's shoulders, prep her neck and say a prayer."

80

Not long after Tess's C-section was on put on hold, Hollis Sinclair received an urgent phone call from one of his moles in the ICU. Before he'd stormed out of his house, he'd called Helen and left her a message that he needed to meet with her urgently. By the time he'd reached the hospital, he had left two more.

It normally took him twenty-five minutes to make the drive to Southeastern State University. On this particular morning, he made it in fifteen. He parked in the overflow doctors' lot behind the hospital. He slammed his door shut and quick-walked toward the entrance. This was one morning he had no interest in courting the press. To his dismay, fifty yards short of the entrance, he was descended upon by a drove of reporters. Over the cacophony of their questions, he raised his hand in a dismissive manner and kept walking.

"I have no comment on anything at this time."

Finally, one reporter broke through the crowd. Walking backward, he practically blocked Sinclair's path to the hospital. He shoved a microphone a few inches from his face.

"There are unconfirmed reports there's been a breakthrough. Are you sure you have no comment, Doctor?"

"I have no knowledge of any breakthrough other than the one I've already discussed with you linking GNS to a virus." His denial did nothing to quell the barrage of questions.

A reporter in the middle of the gaggle made her voice heard above the rest. "We have received an unconfirmed report that an operation is underway that could possibly cure GNS. Are you saying there's no chance this could be true?" Sinclair stopped. A dozen more microphones were thrust in his face.

"It doesn't make a difference if it's true or not. You can't cure a devastating viral infection like GNS with surgery; you need an antiviral drug." He picked up his pace. "Now, if you'll excuse me, I have patients to attend to."

In a headlong charge of sorts, Sinclair managed to reach the hospital without answering any more questions. With his blood practically bubbling out of his veins, he stormed toward the back elevators. The moment he arrived, he slapped the Up button repeatedly. Waiting for the doors to open, he swore out loud that before the sun went down, he'd have Jack Wyatt's and Madison Shaw's collective asses in his briefcase.

81

Hollis Sinclair was not the only doctor at Southeastern State with a network of sympathetic informers. When Jack saw Helen Morales walk into the waiting room, he nudged Madison. They both stood up. Fifteen minutes earlier, she had phoned Madison, informing her she'd like to meet with them as soon as possible.

With a blend of circumspection and worry etched on her face, Helen walked straight over.

"Perhaps we should speak in one of the consultation rooms. I suspect it will afford the privacy we're going to need." Jack and Madison came to their feet and followed Helen into the largest of the three family consultation rooms. "Please sit," she told them. She did not, electing instead to pace as she spoke. "I'm sure you two can imagine my surprise to learn that Tess Ryan's C-section had been canceled and that she was being operated on by Amy

Willwade, who, the last time I checked, was a neck surgeon." She turned back around, folded her arms. "I know both of you are highly skilled and thoughtful physicians, so I'm going to assume there's a logical explanation for why Tess Ryan is having her thyroid gland urgently removed. I was also informed that Mike's pulled the plug on Vitracide therapy too." She paused for a few seconds, and then, after a few measured shakes of her head, she continued, "It seems you two have had a rather busy morning. I've had at least ten phone calls already, most of them from frantic board members and administrators wanting to know what the devil's going on around here." Her focus on each of them intensified. "I've been informed . . . no, make that *warned*, that Hollis Sinclair's in a volcanic uproar. He's already awakened every living soul of authority connected with Southeastern State University, the State Health Department and the Surgeon General's Office. If he had the president's cell phone number, I'm sure he would have called him as well." She paused for a few seconds and then walked over to the coffeemaker but didn't reach for a cup. Jack was accustomed to prickly political situations, but at the moment he felt like an intern on his first day trying to stay out of trouble.

"Something unexpected happened this morning," Madison explained. "I was making rounds when Jack called to fill me in. We had to move quickly. The bottom line is we think we've figured out what's causing GNS and how to cure it."

Helen took a seat and in a calm voice said, "I'm all ears, but could you be a little more explicit than that?"

Jack's eyes shifted to Madison. From her expression, it was obvious she wanted him to take the lead.

"One of our GNS patients, Sherry Rosenfelt, has an identical twin sister who is also pregnant. We did some checking and she received the same flu vaccine at the same time Sherry did. So, for all intents and purposes, they're genetically identical in every way."

"Except that she's fine and Sherry has GNS," Madison said. "So there has to be some critical difference between the two of them that gave Lisa immunity to the disease."

With her lips pressed together, Helen shook her head slowly. "I still don't see how all of this leads to Tess having her thyroid gland removed."

"We believe it's the chimera cells," Jack explained, "which are in part responsible for GNS. When Lisa was a teenager she was diagnosed with severe Graves' hyperthyroidism. She was given radioactive iodine, which destroyed all of her thyroid tissue. We've recently come across some convincing evidence that GNS may be an autoimmune disease like rheumatoid arthritis or lupus."

"I haven't heard anything about that. How did you happen to come across that information?"

"I asked another pathologist to have a look at the slides from Sherry's brain biopsy," Jack explained, with the full knowledge his judgment would be called into question. "His opinion was that GNS was likely to be a new, never-before-seen autoimmune disease. He also asked a colleague who's an expert in the area to look at the slides and he agreed."

Her eyes squinting, Helen asked, "Would it be safe to assume that this pathologist is not affiliated with Southeastern State?" When neither of them responded, she added, "I thought so. For now, I'll reserve whatever comments I might have regarding the wisdom of that decision for another time," she said. "So, what's your theory, Jack? What's really causing GNS?"

"If GNS is a new autoimmune disease, then we have to assume the patient's antibodies are the problem. We believe the chimera cells of the GNS patients are interacting with their normal antibodies. This interaction somehow makes these antibodies defective."

"In what way? How are they defective?"

"They mistakenly recognize normal brain tissue as foreign and react by attacking it. We believe this . . . this faulty interaction is the cause of GNS."

"The antibodies only form in the presence of chimera cells," Madison said. "So, if we can eliminate the chimera cells . . . well, we eliminate these destructive antibodies, which should result in a cure."

"But my understanding is that chimera cells are found in several different areas of the body, not just the thyroid gland. What about these other cells that aren't in the thyroid?"

"Based on our tests, and for reasons we don't totally understand, women with GNS have almost all of their chimera cells in their thyroid gland."

Helen's eyebrows lifted. "So you're saying no thyroid gland—no GNS." They both nodded at the same time. "Theoretically, what you're saying might make some sense, but that's still a pretty thin limb you two have climbed out on."

"It's the only limb we have," Madison said.

"And I assume Mike Ryan has been fully briefed and has given . . ."

"He understood everything and gave his consent for the thyroidectomy," Jack assured her.

"Since Tess is already in surgery, I guess there's not much I can do to unring this bell," she said coming to her feet. "I better get going. I have a lot of phone calls to make. I can't decide if the first one should be to the surgeon general to inform or Hollis Sinclair, to try and calm him down." Gazing upward, she added, "The rumors are already flying. We have to figure out some way to keep a lid on this thing. If any of this becomes public knowledge before we know if the surgery's been successful . . . well, it could cause a national frenzy."

"Do you think Hollis will talk to the press?" Madison inquired.

Helen shook her head. "He'd have to be crazy. That would be a serious breach of professional ethics with significant consequences. I don't think he'd risk it." She paused and after an audible sigh that faded to an edgy smile, she added, "I'm going to set up a meeting with him right away. I'd prefer to find him before he finds me."

82

"I don't care what Jack Wyatt and Madison Shaw think," Sinclair told Helen with defiance. "What occurred this morning was nothing short of a travesty of professional conduct on both their parts. For reasons I can only equate to gross medical malfeasance, we're unnecessarily delaying the care of thousands of critically ill women by withholding Vitracide."

"We're not telling other hospitals what to do. They're free to go ahead with antiviral therapy."

"Without my lead and the support of Southeastern State? That's never going to happen." He threw his hands up in the air and leaned forward over the edge of Helen's desk. "And, to make matters worse, we're subjecting these patients to a dangerous form of never-before-tried therapy that makes Vitracide look like a mild laxative. I'm going to speak to every board member, and when I do, my official position will be that changing Southeastern State's recommended treatment plan without even discussing it with them was unconscionable and a flagrant breach of medical ethics."

Helen held up a calming hand. "I've spoken to every board member and given them my opinion. Because of the new circumstances, they have instructed me to proceed as I see fit."

"Even if that means—"

"I'm the dean of this medical school, Hollis, and I believe there's sufficient scientific merit in Jack Wyatt's theory to justify waiting a little longer before initiating Vitracide therapy."

"I advocate the use of an FDA-approved drug and I'm called a medical heretic. Wyatt and his girlfriend propose an experimental operation with no scientific basis and you tell me it makes sense to you. Pardon me for being a little grumpy regarding your sense of fairness and request for my support."

"I'm sorry you feel that way, but my decision's final. We're going to give Tess Ryan a reasonable amount of time to show signs of recovery before beginning your program of Vitracide."

"What's a reasonable amount of time?"

"A few days. And, as I'm sure you know, Mike Ryan has given his complete consent and favors waiting as well."

"If Mr. Ryan wants to consent to a misguided private medical experiment and turn his wife into a guinea pig, that's his choice. But in my opinion this is a page right out of Dr. Josef Mengele's diary."

"Your concern for the safety of Tess Ryan is duly noted."

Sinclair's face tightened with rage. "Every day brings more deaths from this disease. Supposing, while we're waiting to see if this ridiculous treatment plan works, other patients deteriorate and we lose the one opportunity to cure them and their babies. How will you be judged then?"

"I'm not saying we should be inflexible. If there's good reason to proceed with Vitracide sooner, that's exactly what we'll do. In the meantime, let's hope Tess Ryan improves."

With a defiant snicker, he said, "You're wasting your time. That's never going to happen. She's a dead woman."

"Hollis, as your dean, I'm again asking for your support on this."

"That's not going to happen. I'm not going to dismiss the oath I took just so that I can be politically correct. Any further delay in beginning Vitracide puts our patients in grave peril." He pushed back in his chair. "I'm sure you're aware there's a strong feeling amongst many of the medical staff that Dr. Wyatt's presence at Southeastern State has been extremely disruptive. Just because his best pal's an important donor doesn't mean inviting him here was a wise or appropriate thing to do. He should have been thanked politely for his services and then asked to leave days ago."

"It was my decision to invite Jack Wyatt to Southeastern State. If you or anybody else on this faculty has a problem with that, then I recommend you submit a formal complaint to the board and we can handle it as prescribed by due process."

Making no effort to conceal his smirk, Sinclair started for the door. "I don't care what the board members told you informally. I'm going to insist on an emergency meeting. Let them look me in the eye and tell me they're willing to let thousands of women die needlessly." Without waiting for a response, he marched out of her office.

Feeling a tight lump forming at the top of her stomach, Helen pressed her palms to her eyes. She opened her desk drawer, pulled out one of her chewable antacid pills and popped it in her mouth. After a minute or so, she reached for the phone. Anticipating Sinclair's next move, she dialed the president of the university.

83

The hospital coffee shop was only about half-filled. When Jack walked in, he was a few minutes early for his meeting with Special Agent Westenson. He spotted a table toward the rear of the shop and sat down. A minute or so later, he saw Westenson and Barbier walk through the door.

"We apprehended the suspect this morning," Westenson said. "I wanted to come over and thank you in person for your help."

"I appreciate that, Mr. Westenson, but other than to inform you about the call, I really didn't do very much."

"It was your call that led us to him," Barbier said. "We knew he was in South Florida, but we didn't know exactly where. He had acquired a significant number of forged documents, which would have made locating him a nightmare. We knew why he was here so we figured he'd attempt to draw you or Dr. Sinclair out."

"No offense intended, but what was your plan if he decided just to wait outside the hospital and shoot me?"

"That probably wouldn't have worked. You see, Dr. Wyatt, you've been under pretty tight surveillance for the past several days."

"He was very convincing on the phone. If you hadn't warned me, I probably would have met him at his hotel. If you can share the information with me, I'd be interested in knowing who he turned out to be."

"I can't tell you very much. Suffice it to say he's a highly trained scientist. Unfortunately, he's also criminally psychotic. For reasons yet to be determined he became wildly delusional about GNS to a point that he believed he had masterminded every detail of the outbreak. From what we can decipher from his notes and computer files, he believed he was working for Russia as a bioterrorist."

"The first time we spoke, you didn't give me too many details. Why do you think he was after me?"

"We didn't at first, but we did have strong reason to believe he intended to kill Dr. Sinclair. I met with Dr. Sinclair the same day you and I spoke. I made the same request of him that I made of you."

"And?"

"He told me the entire FBI was out of their collective minds for pursuing a bioterrorism possibility. A few days ago, we discovered Vosky had managed to penetrate hospital security and get into the crisis center. He was in the room when your team met to discuss the state of your research on the flu vaccine. It wasn't too hard to figure out why he became focused on you as the person who would destroy his plans to continue to spread GNS."

After Barbier and Westenson left, Jack returned to the ICU. In all honesty, he had never given much thought to his conversation with Westenson at the restaurant. As soon as he reported the call to Westenson, he dismissed the entire matter from his mind. Jack was pleased the man was in custody, but unfortunately, his incarceration would do nothing to stem the rising death toll from GNS.

84

NUMBER OF CASES: 8,004
NUMBER OF DEATHS: 41

Helen Morales's first order of business after returning from lunch was to place a call to the surgeon general. For the better part of an hour, she briefed Brickell on the medical and political state of things at Southeastern State and their probable impact on the rest of the country.

When she was finished, she called Jack and Madison and asked them to join her in Tess's room.

"How's she doing?" Helen asked

"About the same," Madison answered. "No signs at

all of improvement as yet, I'm afraid. But's it's only been twenty-four hours."

She turned to Jack. "How's Mike holding up?"

"Poorly."

Helen pressed her palms together. "Needless to say, Hollis Sinclair is still pretty angry."

"What a surprise," Madison said.

"He's made sure all the hospital board members know that he will be the one directing the national program of Vitracide treatment and that Southeastern State University School of Medicine would be recognized as the key player in the cure of GNS. He's certainly intimated that he will be closely involved in deciding where and when the drug will be distributed."

"Is there a specific reason that Jack and I haven't been asked to attend any of these meetings that seem to be taking place every two hours?"

"There are several," Helen answered flatly without further explanation. As far as Jack was concerned, none was needed. "Let me fill you in on where we are now. At least through Christmas, we'll be making no changes in the treatment plan. If Tess fails to show any signs of recovery, we will officially endorse a program of Vitracide therapy under the direction of Dr. Sinclair."

"I'm not sure another few days is enough time to start seeing improvement," Jack said.

"Unfortunately, that's all the time we've got," Helen stated again. "A little while ago, I called the surgeon general. She's on board with the plan. She's going to speak with the president later, but she thinks he'll be comfortable waiting as well."

"Did she have a sense of what the rest of the medical community in the country is thinking?" Jack asked.

"There's still controversy, but there's no question that most hospitals and physicians are feeling the pressure to start Vitracide. As much as I hate to say it, Hollis has done a yeoman's job of rallying support for his parvovirus theory." She looked down at her watch. "I've got to get going. Please call me immediately if there are any changes in Tess's condition."

Jack shuffled his feet and then rubbed his temple. He still believed the key to curing GNS was removing the thyroid. But he had dealt with enough neurologic diseases in his career to realize the recovery time for many of them took weeks and sometimes even months. Originally, he'd hoped for at least a week following surgery to see if Tess would show signs of recovery. At the moment, it didn't seem like Helen thought that was going to happen.

Jack reminded himself to cling to a positive outlook, but he couldn't deny the obvious—the clock was ticking, and before long Dr. Hollis Sinclair would get his way.

85

NUMBER OF CASES: 7,456
NUMBER OF DEATHS: 52

The first thing Jack did when he got out of bed was to call the ICU. The nurse caring for Tess reported to him that there had been no change in her condition through the night. He thanked her and told her he'd be in later.

"No change in her condition," he whispered. It was a term that most experienced physicians had heard countless times. Sometimes it was reassuring and portended improvement. But, in the case of Tess Ryan, Jack suspected that wasn't the case. It had only been forty-eight hours since her surgery. Jack knew that wasn't enough time to declare either victory or defeat.

After a long shower, he got dressed. He brewed a cup of coffee, walked over to the desk and sat down. Before going to the hospital, he decided to review some of the latest articles he had already read on autoimmune diseases. While they were all of interest, there was nothing specific he could identify that would further help him in speeding Tess's recovery. He closed the top of his laptop, gathered his things and left for the hospital.

When he was crossing the lobby, he saw Mike standing at the elevator. He caught up to him before the doors opened.

"I called before coming over to the hospital," Mike said. "Her nurse told me she had an uneventful night . . . whatever that means. Do you think she's any better?"

"I haven't seen her yet but it sounds like she's the same."

"I was kind of hoping we'd see some signs of improvement."

"It still may be a little early to make any judgments."

The doors opened and they stepped inside the elevator. They rode up in silence but as soon as they got off, Mike said, "I'm willing to give this two more days, Jack. If we don't see . . . at least some signs that Tess is getting better, I'm going to reschedule the C-section."

Jack didn't say anything. He simply nodded. It was obvious both he and Mike knew his statement was definitive and didn't call for a response.

86

Helen Morales sat behind her desk reviewing the agenda for the emergency meeting of the hospital board that was scheduled to take place in a few hours. When Hollis Sinclair had told her he would make sure such a meeting took place, she hadn't doubted it for a second. She was still looking over the agenda when the beep of her intercom startled her.

"Dr. Morales. President Carmichael would like to speak with you."

"Put her through, and please hold any other calls."

"She's not on the phone . . . she's here in the office," Ali said in a voice just loud enough for Helen to hear.

"I'll be right out."

Donna Anne Carmichael had been the president of Southeastern State University for the past sixteen years. Formally educated and having earned her doctorate in ancient languages, she was a consummate academician, masterful at defining crucial initiatives and rallying people to the cause. Her fund-raising efforts and accomplishments were a model for all university presidents to aspire to.

Helen greeted Carmichael warmly and escorted her to the couch.

"I hope you don't mind me dropping in without calling first, but I thought it might be a good idea if we spoke before today's meeting. To begin, I want you to know I have supreme confidence in your judgment."

"Thank you."

"As president, the only higher-ups whom I'm constantly massaging are the university trustees. I'm not generally bombarded with phone calls from the hospital board members," she explained. "But it's understandable that this whole GNS thing has left them . . . well, in a prickly mood. Some of them have been persuaded by Hollis Sinclair that Dr. Wyatt's presence here at Southeastern State has been quite counterproductive."

"Jack Wyatt is an outstanding physician with a laudable national reputation. I feel fortunate he agreed to serve as a guest professor. His input has been very helpful. Hollis Sinclair's a talented physician but he's been behaving badly for the past week or so. The bottom line is I have no regrets about inviting Jack Wyatt here."

"I'm sure you're aware that there are a number of highly respected doctors on Southeastern State's medical staff who believe his chimerism–flu vaccine theory is a Hail Mary at best."

"I guess that remains to be seen."

"Has Tess shown any signs of improvement?"

"It's only been a little more than two days since we removed Tess's thyroid, Madame President."

"I'll take that as a no. What's your long-term plan?"

"I'm not sure I have a long-term plan. For now, we're going to continue to wait for signs of recovery."

"Any idea how long?" Carmichael asked.

"I think that's up to her husband. As far as the other families are concerned, we can offer them other treatment options."

"Dr. Sinclair strongly opposes that idea, and I believe both the trustees of the University and the hospital board members agree with him. And to be honest with you, I'm not sure I don't as well. We don't want to come across as desperate and experimenting with people's lives. Dr. Sinclair insists as long as we're observing Tess Ryan, it would be a grave error in judgment to proceed with Vitracide."

"Are you asking me for a specific date when we should abandon Jack Wyatt's treatment plan?" Helen asked.

"Yes, I am. On a national level, Dr. Sinclair's been by far the most verbal proponent of Vitracide. I think our colleagues across the country are watching us here at Southeastern State waiting to follow our lead." By her tone and demeanor, Donna struck Helen as a woman who was sensing she was running out of room to maneuver.

"If we don't see any improvement in Tess's condition in the next three days, I'll support abandoning Dr. Wyatt's treatment plan and recommend moving ahead immediately with Vitracide."

"Shall we say the morning of the twenty-sixth?"

"Of course."

"One final thought: If and when we do begin Vitracide therapy, perhaps that would be an appropriate time for Dr. Wyatt to . . . to resume his responsibilities at Ohio State." Helen shook her head and splayed her fingers out on the armrests of her chair.

Carmichael started to get up and Helen followed. "I'll ask you again. This time just between us girls: Any regrets about inviting Jack Wyatt here?"

Helen sighed. "I'm not sure. Ask me again in forty-eight hours."

87

DECEMBER TWENTY-THIRD

NUMBER OF CASES: 9,123
NUMBER OF DEATHS: 52

Lying wide-awake in bed, Jack stared overhead at an antique-style ceiling fan. It was six A.M. To say the least, it had been a restless night's sleep. He had been at Tess's bedside until midnight before he finally left the hospital and returned to his hotel.

Tess had shown no real signs of improvement. Watching the fan making the slowest revolutions it was programmed for, Jack tried to convince himself to the contrary. But in his heart he knew her coma was just as deep as the day Dr. Willwade had removed her thyroid gland.

He threw back the covers and sat on the side of his

bed for a minute or two staring aimlessly across the room. Finally, he picked up his phone from the nightstand and dialed the ICU.

"How's she doing?" he asked the nurse caring for Tess.

"Dr. Fuller's here. I'll put him on."

"Hi, Jack. Tess had a stable night. I see no sign there's been any change in her mental status. Her vital signs are holding but she's still in a coma."

"I was hoping for a little better news than that."

"Let's see how she does today," he suggested. "By the way, I'm concerned she may be getting blood clots in her legs. I'd like to start her on some heparin. It won't dissolve any of the clots that are already there but it will prevent the formation of any new ones."

"I think that's a good suggestion, John. I should be there in the next hour or so. Have you seen Mike?"

"He finally left a few minutes ago. He said he'd be back in a few hours."

"I should be there in about forty-five minutes."

"I'll see you when you get here. I assume you've heard."

"Heard what?"

"The hospital officially informed everybody that the Vitracide program will begin the day after Christmas. They've already started scheduling the first group of C-sections."

Through sliding glass doors leading to the balcony, Jack watched the last few minutes of the dawn. His mind wandered in several directions but he kept coming back to the same thing: Two days earlier he was convinced that removing Tess's thyroid gland would cure her, but during the last twenty-four hours, his conviction had eroded.

He got out of bed and walked over to the coffeemaker. Reaching for a cup, he thought about his conversation with Fuller. He was just about to hit the Brew button when it suddenly struck him. He closed his eyes and threw back his head. It wasn't a revelation or realization born of careful thought. It was like a crack of thunder followed by somebody shaking him to wake up and see the obvious.

"Shit," he muttered, as he grabbed for his phone to call Madison.

"I think I screwed up," he told her.

"What are you talking about?"

"Tess isn't going to get better. I missed something. I'm certain of it."

"What makes you think that?" she asked.

"I just got off the phone with Dr. Fuller a few minutes ago. It was something he said. He wanted to let me know he was putting Tess on a blood thinner. He mentioned he was going to use heparin. He reminded that it would take care of new clots but not the old ones."

"And that comment made you realize you had overlooked some critical piece of information? Excuse me for saying this, Jack, but you're starting to sound like somebody who's ready to stick his head in an oven."

"What's your point?"

"My point is you're panicking. It's only been a couple of days since Tess's surgery. You need to give this more time."

"I'm not saying we should have seen a complete recovery. I'm saying we should have seen at least some subtle signs of improvement by now."

After a quiet few moments, Madison said, "I'm not trying to be harsh or unfeeling, but do you think it's just possible your relationship with Tess and Mike is clouding your objectivity, and that you're becoming a little desperate? Jack, we've done everything we can. Helen told us it's over the morning of the twenty-sixth. She's not going to change her mind. If Tess doesn't start to improve pretty soon . . . well, I guess we're both going to have to get on board with what the hospital officially recommends."

"I'm not going to worry about politics and deadlines right now, he said."

"What are you going to do then?" she asked.

"One of our assumptions has to be wrong. I have to make another phone call. Then I'm going to get back on the computer. I have a suspicion . . . no, call it an inkling, of where I went wrong."

88

An hour later, Jack had again reviewed most of the scientific articles he had accumulated on autoimmune diseases. He continued to be plagued by a vague recollection of one of the articles, but the more he prodded his memory to recall which one, the further he found himself from remembering. As he approached the end of his review, his confidence that he would find the article was waning.

It was at that moment, when he brought up the next article, that he knew he'd found what he was after. The article was written by a group from the University of Texas in Galveston discussing novel new therapies for patients with autoimmune diseases. The author mentioned a group at the Rockefeller University in New York that was conducting exciting new research on treating the neurologic symptoms of autoimmune diseases. The article then went on to mention the work was under the leadership of Dr. Jessica Tau.

Raising his eyes from the screen, Jack drummed the desktop. He brought up Rockefeller University's website. Moving to the faculty tab, he was able to locate Dr. Jessica Tau. Her bio was impressive. Not only did she hold an M.D. and a Ph.D. in immunology, but she had also been awarded several NIH grants. It was still early, but he dialed her office number anyway, assuming he'd be prompted to her voice mail.

To his great surprise a woman answered on the second ring.

"This is Dr. Tau."

Jack stood up. "Dr. Tau. My name is Jack Wyatt. I'm a neurologist at Southeastern State working on the GNS cases. I apologize for the early hour, but I was hoping you might have a few minutes to speak with me."

"It seems everybody's arriving at work early these days, Dr. Wyatt. I'd be delighted to speak with you. By the way, I'm quite familiar with your extensive work and contributions in the area of difficult neurologic diagnoses."

"Thank you. I recently became aware of the innovative work you're doing on the neurologic symptoms of some of the autoimmune diseases. I was wondering if you had published any of your findings as yet?"

"Actually, we received notification a few days ago from the *New England Journal of Medicine* that they intend to publish our first manuscript in the fall."

"Congratulations."

"I would be happy to e-mail you a copy of the manuscript if you'd like to review it."

"I'd greatly appreciate that."

"If you'll give me your e-mail address, I'll send it right now."

Jack proceeded to ask Tau a number of questions regarding her work. She was more than cooperative, answering all of them in extreme detail.

"I look forward to reading your manuscript. In the event I have further questions, would you mind if I call you back after I have a look at it?"

"Of course not. I'll give you my cell number."

Jack provided Dr. Tau his e-mail address and entered her number into his electronic phone book.

"Thank you again, Dr. Tau. I look forward to speaking with you again."

He walked over to his nightstand to grab his legal pad and pen. By the time he returned to his computer, Tau's manuscript had arrived.

For the next hour Jack drank coffee, read and then reread every word of it. It was an incredible piece of scientific work, a true research marvel. Finally, he lifted his eyes from the screen. His mind was doing backflips. When he finally snapped back to the here and now, he reached for his phone and located Lisa's number.

"Good morning. This is Dr. Wyatt. I apologize for the early hour, but I have something rather important to ask you." He nodded a few times as Lisa assured him he had not awakened her. "You mentioned that Sherry had her tonsils out but you didn't."

"That's right. I think we were about six at the time."

"Have they ever given you any trouble?"

"I've had strep throat a few times over the years. It always got better right away with antibiotics. I asked my internist about having them taken out, but she said it wasn't necessary."

"Do you recall when you last had strep throat?"

"Let me think a moment," she answered. "It was right before I got pregnant. I took antibiotics for a week and I was fine." Before the words were out of her mouth, Jack felt his stomach drop.

"Thank you, Lisa. I apologize again for calling you so early." He found Marc's number and dialed it. The phone rang several times before kicking over to voice mail.

"C'mon, Marc," Jack said out loud as he ended the call and then hit the Redial button. "Pick up your damn phone." While the phone rang, Jack paced the carpet. He assumed he was one ring away from getting his voice mail again when Marc answered.

"Good morning, Dr. Wyatt."

"I need some information from the National Data Record as soon as possible. It's urgent."

"Sure. Just tell me what you need."

Jack paused to gather his thoughts. He then took the next few minutes to tell Marc in very specific terms the patient information he was interested in, and that he'd meet him in the ICU within the hour. Jack set his phone down on the nightstand and started getting dressed. His hands were shaking and he could feel drops of perspiration creeping down his brow. Although it was a rare experience for him, Jack Wyatt recognized an overwhelming adrenaline rush when he felt one.

89

"You look like hell," Jack said to Marc when he walked into the ICU.

"I didn't exactly make it home last night. We had another GNS death at about three. We did an urgent C-section. The baby's pretty sick but holding his own in the newborn ICU."

"I'm glad the baby survived," he said. "Has there been any change in Tess's condition?"

"No, not really."

"I know it's only been an hour or so, but did you have any time to look at those patients on the National Data Record we talked about?"

"I did," he answered, pulling out four pages of patient printouts from his pocket. "And, as it turns out, I was able to locate four women in Florida who were suspected of having GNS, but they turned out to have something else. Two were from Miami, one was from Tampa and one was from Pensacola." Marc continued to refer to the printouts as he spoke. "The two from Miami were hospitalized at Suncoast Medical Center. They both presented with mild confusion, spasms of their legs and a sore throat. Neither had a dancing eye syndrome, fever or a rash. But to be on the safe side, the physicians at Suncoast admitted them with the diagnosis of possible GNS. Both were in the hospital for a couple of days, got better and were sent home."

"What was their discharge diagnosis?"

"Viral syndrome."

"Did their records mention if they had the flu vaccine?"

"They both got it."

"What about their past medical history?"

"Nothing of interest. They were both very healthy."

"Was there any mention if they had their tonsils out?" Jack asked.

"Their tonsils out? Is that important?" Jack returned Marc's inquiry with an icy stare. "Sorry," he said, leafing through the pages. "According to their past surgical history, neither of them had any prior surgery."

"What were the final diagnoses on the other two women who turned out not to have GNS?"

"They had pretty similar symptoms and hospital courses. They both had received the flu vaccine and neither of them, apart from C-sections, had undergone any other surgery."

"Did any of the four women have a strep screen done?"

"Let me check," Marc said with a degree of hesitation

while he again shuffled through the printouts. At the same time, Madison walked up. "It looks like two of them did, and they were both positive."

"You didn't call me," she said to Jack.

"I've been a little busy. I need to talk to you two," he said, before turning to Madison and adding, "and then you and I need to meet with Helen Morales immediately."

Jack watched as Madison rolled her head from side to side as she massaged her neck.

"Sure, we can talk in the conference room."

She made a grand gesture toward the other side of the ICU and the three of them walked off.

90

Madison had no trouble arranging the meeting with Helen that Jack had requested. They were already seated in her office in front of her desk when she came in and sat down.

As Helen's eyes fixed on him with guarded anticipation, Jack cleared his throat and slid forward in his chair.

"I no longer believe that removing Tess's thyroid by itself will cure her," he said.

Helen's face went slack. "I hope you're kidding, because after all we've been through . . . I mean, are you now telling me you want to abandon your plan and give Hollis the go-ahead to start Vitracide?"

"Absolutely not," Jack said with complete certainty. "We're convinced we can still cure Tess and every other woman with GNS. We still believe GNS is a new autoimmune disease. In order to cure Tess or any other women with GNS we have to eliminate the abnormal antibodies that are attacking their brain tissue."

"I believe you've already explained that to me. That was our justification for removing Tess's thyroid."

"Removing the thyroid will prevent the formation of any new toxic antibodies but what I overlooked was that the operation won't eliminate the abnormal antibodies that are already present. Based on cutting-edge research I've just become aware of, the existing antibodies will continue to attack the brain tissue for at least six weeks. I don't believe any of the women will be able to survive that long." Jack moved back in his chair and placed his hands on his thighs. "If we don't eliminate the antibodies that already exist, we won't cure GNS."

"Is there a way to do that?" Helen asked.

"I believe there is. There's a group at Rockefeller University who have recently discovered that certain strains of streptococcus bacteria produce an enzyme that destroys these abnormal antibodies. They're calling the preparation Streptogenase V. The result has been a complete reversal of the neurologic symptoms."

"Theoretically, every woman with GNS should recover if she receives Streptogenase V," Madison added.

Helen guarded her silence, tapping her leather blotter with a pencil. "I've had people try to sell me encyclopedias door-to-door who offered a more persuasive argument than that." Her expression suddenly changed, and with ping-ponging eyes, she asked, "Do you two realize when the average person hears the word *streptococcus* they don't think of a sore throat? They think of the deadly flesh-eating bacteria or toxic shock syndrome, which instantly makes their blood run cold. It would be like telling people we want to cure GNS by giving their loved ones arsenic or the Black Plague." She stopped for a few moments. And then, in a calmer voice inquired, "Do you have anything else to support this theory besides this experimental information?"

"Sherry Rosenfelt had her tonsils out but Lisa didn't. I spoke with Lisa this morning. She told me right before she got pregnant she was treated for a strep throat." Jack then spent some time informing Helen of the other four women Marc had located in Florida who were thought to have GNS but turned out not to. He made a point to emphasize that they had all received the flu shots and that at least two had positive strep tests.

"Are you trying to tell me that if a woman still has her tonsils in, she can't get GNS?" Helen asked.

"Not exactly. We're saying that a certain strep infection contracted just at the right time offers a high-grade protection or even a cure against GNS. Marc's combing through the Data Record right now trying to find more women with the same clinical history."

"This research being done at Rockefeller University. How many women have taken part in it?"

Jack tugged at his collar. "Unfortunately, all of their studies to this point have been done on animals."

"I beg your pardon."

"But Dr. Tau did mention that they have received permission from the FDA to begin clinical trials in humans."

"Assuming I should agree to this, how do you plan to administer this Strep . . ."

"Streptogenase V," Madison said in a meek voice.

"Streptogenase V," Helen repeated. "You can't inject a preparation like that directly into the bloodstream. It would be too dangerous."

"Actually, Dr. Tau and her group have determined that's the only way it works."

"You're telling me this . . . this bacterial concoction, or whatever in God's name you want to call it, is nowhere close to being FDA approved. That means the only way we could justify administering it would be as the only conceivable treatment to save a life."

"I've been involved in a few cases where we did that," Jack said.

"I have also. But I think you'd agree, not on this level."

"I'm not sure this country's ever faced an epidemic like GNS before," Madison said.

After a deep sigh, Helen stood up. "So tell me exactly what you're proposing."

"We already have Mike's full approval, so we'd like to acquire the strep preparation from New York and administer it to Tess as soon as possible. Dr. Tau has agreed to provide us with enough as long as you'll sign off on it."

"I must be out of my mind. I should be calling psychiatry to come down here and drop a net over the three of us." Helen leaned forward, placed her palms squarely on her desk and locked eyes with both of them. "I sure hope you two know what the hell you're doing. "

"I'm not sure I can offer you that guarantee," Jack said.

"How long after administering this drug will we know if it's been successful?"

"We can't predict exactly but according to Dr. Tau, the effects of the Streptogenase V occur fairly quickly."

"In mice, you mean," Helen said with a slow shake of her head. "I'm going to have a lot of people to answer to on this thing. As soon as the word gets out, they'll be coming after us with pitchforks and lanterns. And it's not too hard to figure out who'll be leading the mob." She raised her eyes. "How soon can you get this stuff from New York?"

"I was planning on flying up to New York tomorrow on Mike's plane. We can give Tess the first dose as soon as I get back."

Helen started for the door. "I hope you two understand this is it. The board and the medical staff are at the end of their respective ropes. Once they hear about this strep treatment, I can assure you we have played our last card. If there's nothing more, I have some phone calls to make."

Jack and Madison came to their feet. A number of worries leapt to Jack's mind but he said nothing. Madison gestured toward the door and he followed her out of the office.

91

NUMBER OF CASES: 9,676
NUMBER OF DEATHS: 56

The last thing Jack did before leaving for the airport was stop in the ICU and check on Tess. She had had an uneventful morning and fortunately hadn't deteriorated. Regrettably, she hadn't shown any signs of improvement either.

The flight to New York took a little over two hours. Jack had the opportunity to spend quite a bit of time with Dr. Tau going over every aspect of her work. She was careful to advise Jack of all the possible complications Tess might encounter from receiving the specially formulated strep preparation. It was Dr. Tau's advice to administer two doses five hours apart.

Thirty minutes after his plane touched down in West Palm Beach, Jack walked into Tess's room. It was three P.M. Mike, Madison and Marc were there waiting for him. Mike had already signed a litany of documents, which Southeastern State's legal department had prepared outlining in great detail his agreement to treat his wife with an experimental drug. The nurse manager and the attending physician were also present. A few minutes before Jack had arrived, Marc had wheeled the crash cart into the room. The cart contained all the necessary medications and equipment to deal with a cardiac arrest.

Mike pointed at the portable incubator Jack was holding. "I assume that's it."

Jack shook his head. "Have you changed your mind about going ahead with this?"

"I've made my decision, Jack."

Jack removed one of the single glass containers from the incubator. He was normally steady-handed but on this occasion his hand was quivering like a feather in a gusty wind. After cleaning the top with an alcohol swab, he carefully drew up three CCs of the sky blue fluid into a syringe. After checking the amount twice more, he walked over to Tess's bed. Selecting one of the rubber ports on the IV line, Jack slid the needle in the sterile tubing. His thumb found the back of the plunger, but instead of pushing the fluid into Tess's bloodstream, his thumb froze in place. He raised his eyes to Mike.

"Go ahead," he told Jack with an encouraging smile. "You're just a couple of seconds away from saving Tess's life."

With his mouth as dry as a handful of gravel, Jack gently eased the plunger down, sending the Streptogenase V coursing through Tess's veins.

92

It was eleven P.M. Three hours earlier, Jack had given Tess her second injection of the Streptogenase V. Jack was used to working long hours, but the amount of time he'd been out of the hospital over the past few days could be calculated with an egg timer. Adding to his fatigue and stress, he was dealing with Mike's unchecked anxiety and unpredictable mood swings. If it were possible to do so, Helen made matters worse by phoning Jack and Madison to remind them that unless Tess showed true signs of recovery by the morning of the twenty-sixth, Hollis Sinclair's Vitracide program would begin. It was a reminder neither of them needed nor wanted to hear.

An hour after Jack had given Tess the second injection, he convinced Mike to go home and get a few hours of rest. At the moment, he was alone in the room with Tess. True to Dr. Tau's warnings, Tess developed a high fever after the second dose. Jack was just about to do another neurologic examination when Mike came through the door.

"I wasn't expecting you back for another couple of hours."

"I couldn't sleep. It hasn't exactly been the Christmas Eve I was hoping for," Mike answered in a deadpan voice as he made his way over to the bed. "Has there been any change?"

A short breath slipped from Jack's lungs as he shook his head and answered, "Not yet, I'm afraid."

With defeat spreading across his face, Mike placed his hand on Tess's and then curled his pinky around hers.

"Did Madison come back in to check on the baby?"

"Right after you left. She said she's still in mild distress but holding her own."

"How much more of this can the two of them take?" he muttered. "Sinclair left me a message. He wants to reschedule the C-section for the day after Christmas and start Vitracide six hours later. He's certainly no amateur when it comes to cranking up the pressure. He didn't mention a single word about what's going on."

"What are you going to do?"

"I don't know. That's a day and a half away. I guess we can talk about it later."

Jack had the feeling Mike had already made up his mind but couldn't find the words to tell him.

"Maybe you should consider speaking with Madison again before making a final decision."

When Mike didn't answer, Jack shifted his gaze to him.

His posture was statue-like. His lips were widely parted and his eyes were fixed on Tess. Suddenly, he sucked in a couple of fragmented breaths. Jack reached for the hand control and turned the dimmer on the overhead lights all the way up. Jack's own breath snagged, leaving him feeling as if he had been robbed of his air by a powerful blow to his abdomen.

Tess's eyes no longer appeared inert and hollow. To the contrary, they were without glaze and focused on Mike. Her complexion, which for weeks had been chalk-like was now a muted shade of red. And for the first time, there was true animation to her face.

Jack took a few steps back, reached for a chair and slid it next to the bed. "Go ahead," he told Mike, lightly placing his hand on his shoulder.

Covering his mouth with his hand, Mike sat down and leaned forward over the bed. He waited a few seconds and then placed his hand on top of Tess's. For a minute or so, he said nothing. Then, barely noticeably at first, Tess slipped her hand out from under Mike's. It wasn't a reflex or a random movement; it had purpose to it.

Mike spoke to Tess in just above a whisper. She didn't respond in words but her changing expressions spoke volumes. He talked to her as if he had no concern she understood every word he uttered. He brought her up to date on everything from her charity work to how much her family and friends loved and missed her. Looking through wet eyes, he told her their baby was fine and how much he needed her to get better.

Suddenly, Mike's face blanched in disbelief. When Jack

looked back at Tess, he understood why. She had moved her hand on top of Mike's, and the unforgettable smile that made her Tess Ryan was upon her face.

Choking back his own tears, Jack lowered his head and whispered into his best friend's ear, "I wouldn't have said this five minutes ago, but I bet this turns out to be the best Christmas of your life."

93

Renatta Brickell was half-asleep when she glanced over at the digital clock on her nightstand. She had always been an early riser, but five thirty was a little extreme even for her. She pushed herself up against the leather headboard and then looked over at her husband who slept soundly. It had become an unshakable tradition for them to sleep late on Christmas morning. Once they were up, they shared a breakfast of strawberry pancakes heaped high with whipped cream and then opened their gifts. Over the years, the day had become one they both looked forward to with great anticipation. But this year, with the GNS crisis looming over the country like a stubborn ocean fog, it seemed like just another day to Renatta. Although they hadn't discussed it specifically, she suspected her husband felt the same way.

She was considering getting out of bed when her

phone rang. Her staff knew she didn't mind being called early, but she doubted even they would call her at such an hour on Christmas morning. She reached for her cell phone and checked the caller ID. A little surprised, she took the call.

"Good morning, Helen," she said, bracing herself for bad news regarding Tess Ryan or one of the other GNS patients at Southeastern State.

"I apologize for disturbing you so early."

"Actually, I was awake. Under the circumstances, it just doesn't seem like Christmas morning."

"My information's still rather preliminary," Helen began in a cautious voice, "but I have reason to believe we've made a major breakthrough." Renatta threw back her comforter and shifted her legs over the side of the bed. "A few hours ago, Tess Ryan began showing signs of improvement. It began with her opening her eyes and displaying purposeful movement. Since then, she's become even more alert. I'm here at the hospital now. In the last hour, she's uttered a few words and has been responding to simple commands."

"How can we be sure this is all related to the streptococcus therapy?" Renatta asked. "Perhaps we're just seeing the beginning of spontaneous recovery."

"I don't think so. None of our other patients are showing any signs of improvement. We've also been calling as many of the other hospitals as we can. None of them have seen even the slightest hint of recovery in any of their patients."

"It's only been a few hours," Renatta said. "It would

be nice to keep things quiet for a while to see if she continues to improve. This is wonderful news but it may be a little premature to declare GNS has been cured and begin a national celebration."

"I understand."

Shaking the last bit of sleep from her mind, she stood up, "Is there any possibility this has already leaked out to the media?"

"I've no way of knowing for sure, but our staff has been advised in no uncertain terms that family and patient confidentiality is of paramount importance, and that they would be putting their jobs at risk if they spoke to anybody."

"I appreciate you calling. Could you phone me again in a few hours to let me know what's happening?"

"Of course."

Brickell glanced out of her window. It wasn't very often she turned to divine intervention but on this occasion, she made an exception and said a short prayer. She slipped on her robe, crept out of the bedroom and then climbed the circular staircase to her third-floor library. She knew the intelligent thing to do before calling President Kellar would be to wait for Helen Morales's next call. That way it would be a little later in the morning and she'd have more information to share with him. For the moment, she was a tad short on answers—a situation she knew from personal experience the president found irritating. The more she thought about the strategy, the more convinced she became that a short period of watchful waiting was the prudent way to go before phoning Kellar.

Sitting at her desk, she had a sudden craving for her morning coffee. With her mind still racing, she turned off the highly polished brass desk lamp and left the library. She was halfway down the spiral stairway when she stopped. She'd never been one to rely heavily on intuition, but just this once she was going to make an exception. She could feel it in every cell of her being—the enigma that was GNS had been solved and one of the worst outbreaks in modern history was about to come to an end.

Renatta reached the bottom of the staircase where her eye was caught by the phone sitting on her hall table. A few seconds passed and a slight smile crept to her face.

"The hell with good sense and optimal timing," she muttered. And then, without an instant's hesitation, she walked over to the table, picked up the phone and tapped in the number to the White House.

94

DECEMBER TWENTY-EIGHTH
East Room of the White House

For the first time since she had accepted President Stephen Kellar's invitation to serve as the surgeon general of the United States, Renatta Brickell felt no apprehension stepping up to the lectern. To the contrary, she was bursting with anticipation at the prospect of addressing the press corps. Even with the president in attendance, standing a few feet from her, she felt completely confident.

"Good morning, ladies and gentlemen. My statement this morning is one of profound national importance." She waited for the murmur to die down before going on. "I understand the rumors regarding GNS have reached enormous proportions. My hope is to dispel all of them today." She paused long enough to allow her comments to be well seeded in the minds of the reporters. "Several days ago, a patient with GNS underwent a bold treatment to cure her disease. It involved both a surgical procedure and an innovative new therapy. I am extremely happy to report that she is now well on her way to making a full recovery. She is alert and responding to questions, and almost all of her symptoms have disappeared." Renatta stopped just for a few seconds and raised her eyes, expecting a barrage of questions. Instead, the room was overtaken with a ghostly silence. She went on, "It is the opinion of the Presidential Task Force on GNS that this disease is being caused by the interaction of three factors, and that all three must be present for a woman to contract the illness. The first is an unusual genetic profile termed chimerism; the second is the altered hormonal state of pregnancy; and the third is the administration of a specific type of flu vaccine. The combination of these factors creates an illness that is quite similar to lupus or rheumatoid arthritis where abnormal antibodies attack the brain. Several days ago, researchers at Southeastern State were able to formulate a multifaceted treatment plan that reverses that process."

The end of her remarks met with a flurry of hands. She recognized Edmond Carlisle from the Associated Press.

"What about the babies? Will you be recommending termination for those under twenty-six weeks?"

"No. We believe once the mothers are cured, the babies will follow suit."

Renatta next gestured at Larry Jensen, representing Reuters.

"Since the beginning there have been rumors that GNS might be the result of a terrorist act. Are you saying that possibility no longer exists?"

"After doing an exhaustive investigation, it is the firm belief of the FBI that GNS is categorically not an act of biological warfare."

Jensen then asked, "Can we assume the same is true for some type of environmental toxin?"

"Based on the research done at Southeastern State, we are comfortable we have identified the cause of GNS, and it's not in any way related to an environmental toxin, be it an e-waste product or nanotoxin."

"Do you anticipate having enough of this special strep injection?"

"We prefer to think of it as a vaccine. We presently have twelve separate facilities manufacturing the product. We do not anticipate having a shortage."

"In that case, when do you expect to complete treatment on a national level?"

"Obviously from a logistical standpoint, we're looking at a monumental project. Our latest projection is to have every woman treated by the end of the second week in January."

"Have you determined what's wrong with the flu vaccine?"

"We don't believe there's anything wrong with the vaccine. The process to manufacture vaccines changes all the time. Our theory is that there's a complex interaction between these two particular vaccines and the chimera cells that makes certain pregnant women susceptible to GNS."

"Any idea what that interaction is?"

"At this time, no. But our scientists are already at work trying to answer that question."

Renatta again scanned the room. She pointed toward the back at Alice Quay of the *Cleveland Plain Dealer*.

"Assuming this outbreak of GNS is now cured, what's to prevent another outbreak in the future?"

"The only way to prevent another outbreak is to develop a test capable of predicting if a particular vaccine will trigger the body to produce toxic proteins. The development of such a test will of course be of the highest priority."

"Is there any way of knowing if there's been any long-term injury to the babies?"

"The simple answer to your question is no. However, our perinatologists continue to advise us that the babies appear to be holding their own. Obviously, we expect to have a lot more information as the women recover and begin to deliver."

For the next thirty minutes, Renatta answered questions. What followed when she finally brought the press briefing to a conclusion was unprecedented. With her first step back from the lectern, every reporter in the room came to their feet and participated in a jubilant display of applause and cheering. Renatta watched for a few seconds and then returned to the podium. With her signature smile, she raised her hands high over her head in a gesture of absolute triumph.

95

When Hollis Sinclair heard the light knock on his office door he looked up from his computer. His administrative assistant, Maya, was staring at him with anxiety in her eyes.

"Dean Morales is here," she said softly.

He took note of the time while at the same moment a sour look wrinkled his face. The last thing he wanted to do was see Helen Morales. He had been dreading the meeting since he had learned about it yesterday.

"She's fifteen minutes early," he said.

"Shall I ask her to wait?"

He shook his head a couple of times in annoyance before turning off his monitor.

"No, show her in."

Maya withdrew, returning a few moments later to escort Helen into the office.

"Good morning," Helen said, taking a seat in a high-backed chair in front of his desk.

"If you've come to share the GNS survival statistics with me, I've seen them," he said. "It's a little early in the day for gloating, isn't it?"

"That's not the purpose of my visit, Hollis. I wanted to let you know that your name has been removed from the list of those under consideration for the chief of neurology appointment."

He leaned forward and curled his fingers around the edge of his desk.

"If you're waiting for me to act surprised, you'll be up way past your bedtime. I've been expecting some sort of juvenile retaliation like this for days." He tossed his pen down on his desk and said, "I'll stay on as acting chief for a few months while you recruit somebody because unlike some others around here, I have manners. I've already had several offers far better than the position I presently hold."

"I'm afraid it's not that simple, Hollis."

"I beg your pardon."

"There are those who are concerned you engaged in unprofessional behavior during the GNS crisis."

With protruding eyes, he asked, "Really. Who thinks that?"

"I do," Helen said unequivocally.

"The notion's absurd and you know it. This is nothing but a witch hunt."

"How many families did you ask to undergo a brain biopsy?"

"What's that got to do with anything?"

Helen renewed her question. "How many?"

"Five or six, I guess. I felt the more information we had the better."

"Did you promise any of them preferential treatment if they cooperated?"

"What do you mean by that?"

"It's a simple question. Did you tell them they would be amongst the first treated with Vitracide if they agreed to the brain biopsy?"

"I don't recall specifically, but supposing I did— what's the difference? The country was in a crisis. I did what I felt I had to do. The families were desperate for answers. The times called for bold action, not your Pollyanna approach to things. And as I recall, there were a number of physicians and board members who wholeheartedly supported me."

Helen couldn't help rolling her eyes.

"I might have been able to overlook your gross insubordination toward me and maybe even the way you quietly leaked some key facts to the press against my instructions, but unethical behavior in the care of our patients is not something I'm prepared to ignore. In case you've forgotten, we're not in the business of promising families preferential access to medications."

"If that's the extent of what concerns you, I think you should rethink things and—"

She held up her hand. "I'm not finished. The manufacturer of Vitracide contacted the FDA. They claimed that even though the drug was never administered, you used undue pressure to control its national distribution."

"Let them try to prove it. My position is that I've done nothing unethical or inappropriate," he responded with an uncaring shrug. "Any other news or advice you have for me, Dr. Morales?"

"As a matter of fact, there is. You'll have to appear in front of the Professional Conduct Committee to answer allegations of improper and unethical behavior. You will be afforded full due process as prescribed by the medical staff bylaws. You will have ample opportunity to present your side of things."

"I remind you, Dr. Morales, that I am a tenured professor at this university."

"Tenure is an honor. It doesn't imply blind exoneration for unscrupulous conduct."

"I'm not without influence in this state," he was close to shouting now. "If you force me, I'll fight you all the way to the governor's mansion."

"You're not a gubernatorial appointee, Hollis. The one who hired you was me."

"I'll tell you what really galls me about you. When was the last time you laid hands on a patient? I'm guessing . . . what, fifteen years ago? But that doesn't stop you from having the unmitigated audacity to sit in judgment of those of us with the courage to face dying patients every day." He picked up a report from his desk and began reading it. "You're a disgrace to our profession. If you have any further communication for me, take it up with my attorney."

"Why, Hollis," she responded with a knowing grin as she came to her feet, "you may sling all the accusations at me you like, but if you're spoiling for some ugly fight, you can forget it."

"I know exactly what you're doing," he said with a snicker. Helen noticed a sheen of sweat on his forehead that hadn't been there when she walked into his office. "You're trying to force me to resign."

"That's a decision only you can make. But it's an option I would urge you to consider carefully. You understand if Southeastern State decides to terminate your academic appointment, we would be unable to support any application you might make to another medical school." Helen started for the door. "As I said, if I were in your position, I'd seriously examine all of my options."

96

When Jack walked into Tess's room, she was sitting in a chair talking to Mike.

"What do you think of this girl?" Mike asked in a voice drenched in pride. "She's acting as if nothing ever happened to her."

"She's certainly as beautiful as ever," he answered, walking over to Tess and kissing her on the forehead. "How are you feeling, shorty?"

"Like I've overslept everything on my agenda for a month. Your best buddy over here keeps telling me I have you to thank for saving my life."

"He's always been prone to exaggeration. How's your headache?"

"Better. I'd say it's now similar to a three-martini hangover."

"I'm pretty sure it will be gone in a few more days."

Mike said, "We've been talking for over an hour. It's unbelievable. Her memory's perfect."

"Really? Did she remember last year when you forgot your anniversary and called me in a panic to—"

"Easy, buddy," Mike said with a short laugh. "That's privileged doctor-patient stuff."

Tess tapped on the armrest of the chair next to her. He sat down.

"When are you going to tell me all the details of what happened to me?"

He pointed at her abdomen. "How about when baby Katie goes off to college?"

She shook her head. "You're as bad as Mike."

"Sinclair stopped in for the first time yesterday," Mike said with a disapproving smirk. "At best, I'd call it a drive-by visit. He acted like nothing happened."

"Tess is fine. No need to dwell on the past."

"I hope you're kidding because as far as I'm concerned that son of a bitch should be—"

"Let it go, Mike." He turned his glance and attention back to Tess. "Did Madison do an ultrasound this afternoon?"

"Uh-huh. She said everything looked great." With a coy smile she added, "Mike's been telling me you have a little thing for her. She's really cute, Jack."

"It's too bad he's afraid to ask her out," Mike said. "Even his mother called him a coward."

"My mother? You've been talking to my mother about Madison?"

"Of course. Let's see. How did she put it again? Oh yeah. She called you the *Hindenburg* of relationships."

Jack rubbed his hands together and said, "Okay. I think I've heard about enough of this. If you don't mind, let's talk about something else."

"Mike tells me you're going back to Columbus tonight, and that he's flying back with you."

"As much as I like hanging out with you guys, I'm afraid I have to get back. Do you mind if I take a quick look at you before we leave?"

Jack completed his exam in about ten minutes. There wasn't the slightest hint of any permanent neurologic injury.

"When can I go back to work?" she asked.

He shook his head at her. "Take a few weeks off. You've earned it."

They talked for another half hour about a host of different things. Jack promised Tess he'd be back to check on her in a week. He couldn't help noticing that Mike kept stealing peeks at his watch and stalling.

"You about ready?" Jack asked him.

"This isn't a scheduled airline. We can go anytime. If you want to hang around awhile longer, we can. I think Madison said she might stop in again."

"Nice try. I'm fine to go now."

Tess motioned him to lean over. She reached up and hugged him around the neck. He could feel her tear-soaked face against his cheek.

"Thank you for everything," she whispered in his ear.

"I'm the luckiest woman in the world to have two guardian angels like you and Mike in my life. I love you."

Speechless for the moment, an affectionate smile came to his face. "I'll be back in about a week to check up on you." He looked over at Mike. "Ready?"

Mike was a nonstop chatterbox all the way to the airport. He was unmistakably back to his old self. Jack smiled the whole time thinking how nice it was to have his best friend back.

97

Jack didn't arrive home until eleven o'clock. The flight back to Columbus was uneventful but he'd said an emotional good-bye to Mike at the airport. After dropping his luggage in the entranceway, he strolled into the kitchen, opened the refrigerator and reached for a beer.

It was unseasonably warm and he decided to go out on the balcony. From the tenth floor, he had a great view of the Ohio State University campus and the Short North. He realized his involvement with GNS was far from over. To the contrary, it was just beginning. In the weeks and months to come, there would be scientific papers to write, lectures and seminars to attend and dozens of meetings with state and federal medical agencies.

He thought his mind would still be racing with the events of the past few weeks, but it wasn't. He stared out beyond the lights of the city. His view seemed infinite.

The scattered clouds were made silvery by the vibrant light of the moon. He took a slow sip of the beer, and for the first time in a long while, it seemed he was able to take a breath without feeling it catch.

Three hundred and fifty miles away from where Jack stood, Connie Recino sat beside her daughter in the intensive care unit at Illinois Memorial. It had been four days since her surgery and just over twenty-four hours since she had received the strep preparation.

Catching herself in a yawn, Connie quickly smothered it with a cupped hand. She gazed back at Maggie. Even though she was heavy-lidded from complete exhaustion, Connie suddenly became wide eyed when she saw her daughter's lips moving as if she were trying to speak. She craned her neck forward and set her gaze squarely upon Maggie's face. It took her only a few seconds to be sure—Maggie was trying to speak. Connie reached over to the bed control and raised the intensity of the overhead lights. It took only a few more seconds more for her to realize her daughter was mouthing the word *mother* over and over again.

Choking back a sea of tears, and speaking to Maggie as if she were three years old, she whispered, "Welcome back, angel. I love you."

Two days later, Maggie was sitting in a chair watching television and brushing her hair. When her husband walked into the room three months earlier than she expected, she dropped the brush. A few seconds after it hit the floor and long before she could have pushed herself out of the chair, he was kneeling at her side, gently pulling her head to his chest.

98

THREE MONTHS LATER

The elevator came to a smooth stop at the eighth floor. With a box of peanut brittle tucked under his arm, Jack made his way down the central corridor of Southeastern State's obstetrical unit.

To say the least, it had been a tumultuous three months. In addition to his clinical responsibilities at the medical school, he had made four trips to Florida to visit Tess. He had also attended more meetings and debriefings on GNS than he would have imagined possible.

Jack had just walked past the nursing station when he saw a man approaching. Jack didn't need to study his face. His distinctive limp and paunchy silhouette instantly revealed his identity.

"When did you get into town, Doc?" Bud Kazminski asked.

"I just arrived." Jack extended his hand. With a reserved grin, he asked, "I assume you're not here visiting a friend?"

"Sherry delivered this morning—a healthy eight-pound boy." Kaz's grin was uncontrollable.

Jack shook his hand again. "That's great news, but I thought she wasn't due for another couple of weeks."

"So did we, but Sherry's never one to do anything in a conventional style or on schedule."

"Is she still feeling okay?"

"Thanks to you, she is."

Jack said, "I saw your latest story on GNS in the Sunday paper. I thought you told me you weren't going to write any more articles."

"My editor had other ideas," he answered. "You know, I once did a story on a guy who had been rescued from a mountain top after being struck by lightning. A total stranger carried him down on his back two miles to a hospital. I interviewed the victim. Do you know what was the most interesting thing he told me?"

Jack shrugged. "I have no idea."

"The guy was forever plagued by his inability to sufficiently thank the man who had saved him. I could never quite figure it out myself until about three months ago." Kazminski took a few steps forward and placed his hands on Jack's shoulders. "Thank you, Dr. Wyatt."

"I . . . I really don't know what to say."

"You don't have to say anything," Kazminski assured him. "Are you here to see the Ryans' baby?"

"I am."

"I assume you heard about Sinclair."

Jack shook his head. "Only that he had resigned several weeks ago."

"The hospital gossip has it that he hasn't been able to find another position anywhere in the country." Kaz shrugged but said nothing further on the topic. "I won't hold you up any longer, Doc. By the way, I'm sure Sherry would love for you to see the baby. If you have time, stop in and see what your good work has accomplished."

"Of course," Jack promised. "If you don't mind me asking, any progress with Lisa?"

"I'd say there's been a noticeable thaw over the last couple of months. We had dinner together the other night for the first time in a very long time."

"That's great to hear," Jack said with a broad smile.

Jack started back down the hall. He snuck a look back over his shoulder. Kaz was still watching him. Smiling broadly, Jack tossed him a final wave followed by a celebratory fist pound.

99

Jack knocked twice and then pushed open the door to Tess's room. She was sitting in a recliner cradling Katie Michelle Ryan to her chest. With a gleam in his eye and a prideful grin, Mike hovered over the two women in his life, looking as proud as Jack had ever seen him.

"Hi, Jack," Tess said. "Where have you been? We expected you a couple of hours ago."

He walked over and placed the peanut brittle on her nightstand. "I brought you a month's supply of your favorite junk food." He leaned down and kissed her on the cheek. "That's some beautiful baby, shorty. You did well."

Mike pointed to himself and then gave Jack a bear hug. "Don't I get any of the credit?"

"Congrats to you too, Papa."

"I hope you're planning on staying for at least a few

days this time," Tess said. "We really haven't had a chance to visit with you."

"We'll see. How are you feeling? Have you had any more of those headaches or—"

"I'm fine, Jack. I'm the most grateful patient you'll ever have, but it's time to stop worrying about me. Every time you and Mike look at me, you make me feel like you're staring at somebody on borrowed time."

"Okay, I'll ease up," Jack said.

"Have you been in touch with Madison?" she asked with a nonchalant inflexion in her voice, tucking a pink blanket snugly around little Katie.

With a forgiving frown, he shook his head. "Why is that the first thing you two always ask me?"

"Because you never give us a straight answer," she explained. "It's a shame. You guys make such a cute couple."

"I think you've already mentioned that to me about a million times. It's too bad your illness didn't erase that part of your brain that's obsessed with fixing me up. Madison and I are colleagues—and that's where it ends."

"Please, Jack. Everybody knows you have a huge crush on her."

"Really? Who's everybody?"

"Well, your mother for one."

"My mother was cut from the same cloth you two were and doesn't—"

"I'm willing to bet Madison doesn't even know you're in Florida," she said.

Jack looked over at Mike and gave him the kind of knowing smile only the two of them could understand.

"Don't look at me for help. I'm on her side," Mike said holding his hands up in surrender.

Just at that moment, the door opened and Madison walked in. Jack absently cleared his throat.

"Hi," he said, with a wave of his hand.

"How did your meeting with the president go? I heard he awarded you some kind of hero's citation," she said, walking over to Tess. "And how's that gorgeous baby?"

"She's perfect."

"We've completed all of our tests. Katie couldn't be any healthier. You guys can take her home in the morning."

"We were hoping you'd say that," Mike said as he reached into his back pocket. "Chicago's in town tonight to play the Heat. I have two courtside seats I can't use. I thought you might like them . . . as a small token of our appreciation."

"I'd love to go," Madison said, accepting the tickets from Mike. "I went to Northwestern for undergrad. I'm a huge Bulls fan." She studied the tickets. "Boy, these really are great seats."

Mike turned to Jack. "You don't have any plans tonight, do you, buddy?"

With wary eyes and caution in his voice, he answered, "Actually, I was planning on spending the evening right here with my dearest friends in the world."

"Don't take this the wrong way," Mike said, putting his hand on Jack's shoulder. "But I think Tess and I would rather be alone tonight." He looked over at Tess. "Isn't that right, baby?"

"Alone—definitely alone. We can spend a lot of time with you tomorrow, Jack."

They all looked at him at once.

"It looks like you're free after all," Madison said. "So, what do you say? Would you like to go to the game with me?"

"Uh . . . yeah, sure, why not?"

"Great. Mike told me you're staying with them. I'll pick you up at around five thirty. I know a terrific Indian restaurant that's a couple of blocks from the arena."

"Sounds great." Jack cleared his throat again and added, "I'd like to show you that GNS article I've been working on for the *New England Journal of Medicine*."

"And I'd love to go over it with you in detail . . . but not tonight."

"Well, I . . . I didn't necessarily mean—"

Mike play-pinched Jack's cheek. "Enjoy the game, buddy."

With a grin he had no hope of containing, Jack looked at Madison. It was at that moment that all the awkwardness and anxiety that always consumed him in her presence vanished as quickly as skywriting on a windy summer's day.

M14G0610